TIMELESS PIROUETTE

TIME ✦ FLIES
BOOK TWO

Jill Wallace

TSOTSI
PUBLICATIONS

TIMELESS PIROUETTE

by Jill Wallace

Copyright © 2024 by Jill Wallace

Paperback ISBN: 979-8-9912915-0-7

First edition

Published by Tsotsi Publications

www.jillwallace.com

About the Series
Time Flies

These books are best read in sequence:
Timeless Beginnings
Timeless Pirouette

Lucky Van Niekerk—psychic, self-proclaimed hermit, FBI consultant, and ex-Air Baobab air hostess—is frankly pissed with the Universe. After reliving a past life with her soulmate in the crew rest of a 747, call sign Zulu Sierra 216, and shortly after, connecting with him in this lifetime, she lost him again. A trick of Fate, she's sure, and she's not happy about it.

After all, she's no chicken, and she needs to find him *now*.

The Universe strikes a bargain with her: Help others interpret the dreams they had in the same crew rest, lead them to happier lives, and maybe Lucky will find her missing Roy.

Reluctantly Lucky posts an SOS on a rogue site for the late '70s and '80s cabin crew of Air Baobab, to see if anyone else had a dream about a soulmate that still haunts them.

Four virtual strangers respond: Brie, Chantelle, Moxie and BJ. As young women, they'd had the fortitude to experience a mammoth leap backward in time to past lives with men they loved and lost too soon. However, the power of those dreams, and the passion their soulmates in past centuries evoked, made life *after* the dream less than satisfying. They always felt they were missing something.

The motley crew arrive within the week from all corners of the globe. Their sole—or is it soul?—purpose is to attempt to make sense of their lives and the losses spawned during their haunting dreams. Lucky believes their collective mission is to free themselves from the ties that bind them to the past, so they can all live their best lives in the present.

But there's no telling how each of these volatile women will react when reliving their dramatic past existences.

One psychic. Five women. Five past lives to decipher. Six days to help them all. One telepathic Australian shepherd, one murderous bastard and, just to make it interesting—well, you'll see.

This is Brie's story ...

This book II is dedicated to:
DEBBIE SHANNON

Deb, whenever I call in a literary panic, you're there as a fellow writer, as a sharp-eyed pundit, as a developmental advisor, as a brilliant sounding board, as a sandwich board for my work, and best of all, as a true friend from the days when WAR SERENADE was a screenplay.

I doubt I could do this writing thing without you. Please, please, never make me try!

Chapter 1

Brie

Hong Kong, July 31, 1980

I couldn't believe my eyes.

I found myself in the most extraordinary place I'd ever seen.

And *I* was permitted to be here.

Me! Brie Lenz.

Imagine!

I'd never seen such a sight as the lobby of the Hong Kong Hyatt Regency. I rubbed my eyes, not caring if I smudged my mascara even though I was still in uniform.

Miraculously, when I blinked, nothing had changed.

Not the endless ceilings where crystal chandeliers sparkled nor the exquisite fixtures and furnishings.

Not the smell of unadulterated opulence.

Not the ornate vases, as tall as my armpits, filled with fresh flowers reflected a hundred times over in the brilliantly angled mirrors.

Not the elaborate patterns of the bamboo floors that took

over where the plush, intricately woven carpets bursting with color ended.

Who wudda thunk it. I was in the Far East!

It was a long way from a ramshackle caravan park in Kempton Park, South Africa.

Never in my most extravagant dreams, where I'd lived most of my life—buoyed by the thousands of books that had stimulated them—had I ever imagined such luxury.

Front and center in the luscious lobby was a small, roped-off area. Inside was an ornate couch on which sat a petite woman in a yellow creaseless silk knee-length dress, embossed with hundreds of peonies waving on stalks. Her stockinged legs were pressed together and pushed to one side. Motionless, she could have been mistaken for a life-size old photograph of a demure war bride: shy, polite but ready.

Her shiny raven hair was cut in a precise bob, and when she moved it was as if a mannequin had suddenly come to life. As her bangs shifted, artfully shaped eyebrows peeped out. Her hands were so still, it looked like her arms ended in a small bouquet on her lap.

On the low, lacquered black table in front of her were two empty cups and a coffee percolator. A discreet sign was artfully angled for all to read: "Your future is at the bottom of your cup. Let's have coffee together."

My heart did a cartwheel. A fortune teller!

But trying to act nonchalant, I strode, with the rest of the 747 cockpit and cabin crew, toward the cashier in the lobby. There were sixteen of us, and the others were decidedly less awestruck than I with our opulent surroundings.

I pulled back my shoulders, held my head high and prayed I didn't trip—which I was often apt to do—because my cool would surely have been shattered. I would hate to disappoint the many eyes that always followed airline crews strutting toward or away from, well ... anything.

I wore my uniform with great pride: a sky-blue jacket and matching pencil skirt with a slit up the back, exposing neutral hose ending in black stilettos. The Air Baobab uniform was never complete without an orange, green and blue scarf tied at the throat and, of course, white cotton gloves.

My turn. The bespectacled Chinese woman behind the glass solemnly handed me a wad of Hong Kong dollars courtesy of Air B, and I thanked her profusely. This sustenance and travel allowance would buy me much more than the food and transport for which it was allocated during our three-night stay.

I was still in awe that, besides my monthly salary, at each destination our dramatic entrance into each elegant hotel lobby ended at the discreet cashier's window, and we crew were given —in that country's currency—the equivalent of three meals a day in our five-star hotels.

At last in my luxurious room, I twirled, breathing in pure affluence. A smell still so new to me, I vowed it would never get old. I felt like a princess as I ran fingers over sheets with the thread count of well over a thousand. As I stroked the bedspread, I had a vision of four bazillion silkworms working their little tails to the bone to create the masterpiece that anywhere else would have hung on a living room wall.

Fortune had smiled upon me.

To other Air Baobab crew members, it might have been "a nice room."

To me, it was nirvana.

AN INDULGENT BATH in the oversize tub successfully washed away the odors generated by laboring to make fifty-six passengers in my section, thirty-seven of whom smoked, feel like they were in a lovely lounge, and not trapped in the tube-like cabin of a 747 for nine long hours.

I'd flown internally for two years on Jumbo 737s and Airbuses, which meant trips from Johannesburg to Cape Town, Durban, East London, Port Elizabeth and occasionally Maputo in Mozambique. Then, after the grueling 747 overseas conversion, I literally spread my wings internationally. I was dazzled by everything. Even though this was my tenth overseas trip, it was my first to Hong Kong.

My last trip was to London. I'd thought the Kensington Palace Gardens Hotel was heaven, but other crew members pooh-poohed it because the rooms were "so small." Little did they know the space was as big as the one I'd grown up in, with two, three and sometimes four adults breathing the same stale air.

I dried myself on the fluffiest towel on the planet and spied a plush cotton dressing gown, with *H* embroidered on the pocket, tempting me from its hanger in the open cupboard. Wrapping myself in its bliss, I waltzed around the room like Cinderella practicing for the ball.

But the Chinese lady with the crossed legs and the little sign tempted me so, I threw on the first outfit I pulled from my suitcase and blow-dried my hair. In no time I was bobbing on the balls of my feet in anticipation, waiting for one of four elevators.

I tripped into one of them and whooshed down thirty-four floors.

My conviction that life could get *even* better—I was living proof that miracles happened—completely negated my inbred need for privacy. Here I was, ready to have my fortune read in the midst of the Hyatt's comings and goings. Any passing crew member could see me.

But that was the thing about airline crew. There was no judgment. Everyone was free to act, feel and do as they pleased, as long as they didn't harm themselves, anyone else or publicly disgrace our airline.

I relaxed and marveled at how the woman epitomized grace.

As I unhooked the red velvet rope of her cordoned-off area, the fortune teller's smile seemed genuine, and she gestured for me to sit next to her.

She busied herself pouring dark coffee into a delicate china teacup and handed it to me.

"You wish to learn your future?" Her English had a classy British tinge. Hong Kong was a British protectorate, I recalled.

I nodded and blanched when I took the first sip of mud-like java. Seven sugars and a hefty dash of milk couldn't have helped it go down any easier. But I'd long since learned that nothing comes easy.

Especially not your future.

We smiled a lot and talked little as I tried my best to delicately glug down the thick, dark brew without gagging. Before I took a final sip, she waved a small hand and took the cup from me. She whipped it around three times, starting and ending at her heart, then upended the cup onto the petite saucer.

Leaning toward me, she enveloped my palms with her open ones, making mine look like grizzly paws.

Black eyes bored into mine so hard, I cast my lids down lest she see what I didn't want her to see. I knew my past. I was here for my future.

Too late!

She dropped my hands as if she needed to remove herself from what she'd seen.

I felt panic set in.

I swallowed. Nobody was allowed to see my past. Ever. Not even somebody in Hong Kong who never knew my name.

I wanted to run.

But then the sumo-wrestler-like security team would run after me because I hadn't paid the lady.

Please, not a scene. Anything but a scene.

I concentrated on sitting still. Any slight movement and I couldn't stop my body from fleeing.

It was the natural reaction of the guilty.

Her small-boned fingers picked up the cup, and she examined it expressionlessly. I was hoping for even a small smile. But nothing. My heart began to pound.

Why had I come? My present was more than I could dream of. What did I care about the future? What was the pull to know the unknown? My life was perfect. Why worry about tomorrow when today was all my heart could desire? But my stubborn legs wouldn't lift my bum off the seat.

She began in a whisper loud enough so only I could hear. "You have left behind much ugliness." She managed a contrived smile. "Now we will see a much brighter future. You will meet your husband soon. You will live in your own country. You will have one child. Your life will change when you are in the third quarter of your life. You will open like a cherry blossom in early spring, and you will no longer be afraid to live." She muttered some things in her own language. It was okay. I didn't need the details; I got the gist of it. I needed to get away before she conjured up any bad news.

I reached for my purse and yanked out my dollars. With a pained smile I fanned out notes and offered them. She took the number she thought appropriate, and as I rose, she put a hand on my arm. It burned through my skin. I stopped and looked into those black eyes.

"Stop wearing your beauty like a jilted bride's dirty veil. You hide in the shadows trying to look unbeautiful. Accept your beauty as a gift, not a curse. Only then will you begin to live."

CHAPTER 2

BRIE

Rosebank, Johannesburg, present day

As usual, Ryan had called to say his day was to be longer than expected, so I aimlessly googled myself smarter, looking forward to being sucked down the deep, interesting rabbit hole that whiled away time.

Big, fat, vacant chunks of time were all I had without Ryan. Without Maggie.

My airline life felt like it belonged to someone else. I seldom thought about those years. It had been a privilege to be an air hostess, but there were no regrets about leaving when I did.

Then why, after years and years, I searched for an Air Baobab social website, I'll never know. This thought simply arrived in my head, spawned by nothing at all: *Air Baobab had literally thousands and thousands of crew members who'd passed through cabin services. They have to have a way to communicate ...*

And there it was. *The Orange Tail*. Named as a nod to the color of our aircrafts' tails during Air Baobab's formative years.

There were obituaries and shares of sepia-colored photos with exotic backgrounds and young people laughing and drinking in the foreground. Crew members sharing memories of yesteryear.

I was once like that. Sociable, carefree and traveling the world.

And then The Post hit me over the head.

I read it again. "If you had a weird dream in the crew rest of a 747 that changed your life, or still haunts you, email me." The email address started with Lucky7.

Sure, a Boeing 747 registered as Zulu Sierra 216 had marked the beginning of the end of my flying career ... and that dream!

Immediately intense feelings of that evocative dream in the crew rest came flooding back. After more than thirty years, it was as vivid as ever. I'd shared the dream with Ryan soon after we met, explaining it was so much more than a dream, rather an out-of-body experience that took me back centuries. He'd laughed, like it was a little silly and a lot far-fetched, but he admitted he was thrilled with the outcome.

I soon forgot about the dream because my life became a fairy tale. But what if ... what if that dream had more significance than either of us had given it credit for?

Perhaps the dream *had* changed my life. Perhaps I'd never have met Ryan—or recognized him—if not for the dream.

How did Lucky7 know this was just what I needed when *I* didn't even know?

Oddly, I heard the English words tinged with an Asian cadence whisper in my ear: *Your life will change when you are in the third quarter of your life. You will open like a cherry blossom in early spring, and you will no longer be afraid to live.*

I caught my image reflected in the window. That woman in the third quarter of her life was shaking her head. No.

Behind her were shadowed glimpses of all the things around me. Beautiful things. Valuable paintings and photographs by renowned artists. Plush modern furniture toned down by rare antiques. Subtly placed spotlights highlighting the vaulted ceilings of my luxurious one-story suburban home. I was surrounded by *wereld se goed.* Worldly goods.

So why was the woman in my reflection so negative?

Even the bright colors of my designer blouse were caught and reflected with a small distortion. The labyrinth of shadows startled my face back into focus.

I was a walking contradiction. If it were up to me, I would wear drab clothes in wishy-washy colors. I knew calling attention to oneself led to a road full of hurt. But I dressed for Ryan because I never wanted him to stop noticing me.

Here I was, surrounded by things that didn't make me happy, but I lived in hope they made my husband so.

Where was *I* in this equation? Had I lost myself?

My reflection was still shaking her head. "What? You want me to be placid? Not to rock the boat? To be grateful for what I have? I am grateful. But I want to find myself. I want to live my life to its fullest instead of living *only* to please someone else. Is that so terrible?"

And still that reflection shook her head.

"Oh, to hell with you. For once I must do something out of the ordinary. Something just for me. Something that might very well make me more interesting." I got up and closed the curtain, eliminating the negative woman with the slow left-right headshake.

Enough with the fear of anything but the familiar.

I placed fingers on keys: *How did you know I needed to talk to someone else about this?*

Messages poured in, one popping up within a second of the other. All desperate, it seemed, and all had names that were vaguely familiar.

The reply to my question came in a group email to me and three other people: *Perhaps the universe used me to gather those who, like me, had dreams that still make me wonder. And perhaps, now is the time to explore why, in all their evocative detail, they still haunt us.*

I considered the other responders.

Chantelle. Thoughts of her on a two-day Cape Town night stop made my heart smile.

BJ. Holy shit. The Airline Queen with the foul Shakespeare mouth. I shivered.

Moxie. My stomach roiled.

It's your own fault. You didn't have to agree to bring home a Playgirl *for her.*

And Lucky7, the initiator. Surely there was only one girl in the airline called Lucky? If indeed it was the one I knew vaguely, good for her. She'd plucked up the courage to apply to the airline.

Apart from Chantelle and maybe Lucky, did I really want to get involved?

I snarled at my reflection even though she was safely behind the curtain.

Hell yes!

But my fingers hadn't waited for permission. "I'm in" was already typed and sent.

"Holy shit," I muttered, reading the messages from the four

others as they popped up on my screen. I hadn't felt this ... this ... urgency since the 1980s.

Everyone but me had agreed to meeting in a week. *A week? In Boston?*

I should talk to Ryan before I commit.

It's nearly too late. I'm already in the third quarter of my life.

I must go and find how I open myself up like a cherry blossom and stop being afraid to live.

I watched, virtually helpless as my own fingers searched for flights to the States. I booked my passage and typed: *Where shall we meet?* Then clamped my hand over my mouth.

What had I done?

My chest hurt, and my head felt light, as if I were on an aircraft with a loaded drinks trolley and the metal bird suddenly dropped 10,000 feet.

Much later, after I'd snuggled into Ryan's open arms and he'd fallen dead asleep, I wiggled onto my back and let a million happy times flash behind closed eyes. There were thousands of feelings my time in the airline evoked, but the most lingering was the sense of belonging. Belonging to that crew on that flight and for those five, seven, or ten days of night stops that followed. Each trip was a world unto itself.

I wondered if our daughter would have enjoyed a life in the airline.

A sigh of regret escaped my closed lips. Times changed, and our Maggie had gone on a different path.

The thought of leaving Ryan for nine days, with travel time, was unfathomable. I'd never left him. He was always leaving me. For work.

But I was going on an impromptu adventure of discovery.

Was I ready to deal with the consequences?

If I didn't allow myself to discover myself, how would I ever know myself?

I think I'm ready to no longer be afraid to live.

I turned back into Ryan's outstretched arms, grabbed the comforter and threw it over our heads.

To protect us.

CHAPTER 3

BRIE

Johannesburg, present day

Ryan didn't understand, and I couldn't really explain the desperate need that drove me to take this trip. I hated to leave home. To leave him. I'd long ago stopped going with Ryan on his trips ... since ... *If you don't think about it, it won't hurt.*

I loved my husband. More than that, I adored him. No other man would ever take his place in my heart, but I saw too little of him.

Ryan had told me repeatedly that he worked so hard so we'd have a "decent retirement" to enjoy the rest of our life together.

Since accepting Lucky7's invitation, I'd come to the realization that all we have is *now*. Nothing more. Nothing less. Ryan or I could be dead by the time he'd accumulated enough money to retire. What good would that do?

Sure, I could continue to wear expensive clothes into my dotage, but without Ryan, would I give a flying frolic *what* I wore? No! Everything I did, I did for him. To please him, to make myself more attractive to him.

Was I being terribly selfish? I'd never ever done anything like this. Frankly, I felt culpable for pressing "send."

Ryan loved me, of that I was certain. I never believed he'd have an affair, though I often wondered why not. He was surrounded by tall, slender dancers and actresses all day, while I waited for him, well-padded and dressed to the nines.

What would he do while I was away?

My logical mind said he'd be just fine. Perhaps he'd even miss me. Hopefully he'd discover how *much* I did for him. After all, I lived my life to spoil him.

Yet, guilt gnawed.

Why did I feel so beholden to my husband?

He didn't expect or demand anything at all from me, and I owed him nothing but my faithfulness and my love. And he had that. So why did I feel I owed him something more? And what more could that be?

But I pushed away these peculiar thoughts as I tugged off the designer tags before packing perfectly coordinated outfits in the suitcase hastily, so as not to think of how many starving children I could have fed instead of buying this blouse, that pair of shoes. More and more went in, until the elephantine suitcase with leopard rosettes was fairly bursting at the seams.

At least it'll be easy to spot on the airport carousel.

And then it was time.

"I DON'T KNOW why you have to go halfway across the world to discover something you can't define." Ryan turned his head away from the raging airport traffic to glance at me as he gripped the wheel.

"I can't put it into words, Ryan. I just feel it's something my soul needs. I dreamed that odd dream I shared with you so long ago, and I have a feeling it has deeper meaning. The electronic call for those of us who had a dream taking us back centuries in a crew rest on a specific 747 hit a chord. It's a dream that still lingers for at least five of us. That's mind-blowing. And it's an opportunity to broaden my mind. God knows it's been stagnating since Maggie left us."

Ryan shifted uncomfortably.

I barged on. "It's not like you'll miss me. You're hardly ever home before dark during the week. Sometimes I wonder if I just went away on a Tuesday afternoon, when you'd notice. Would it be Wednesday? More likely Thursday when you finally put your hand out to find me on the other side of the bed." I knew I was being bitchy, and I knew, too, it was a defense mechanism for my own guilt.

I was Ryan's constant. Not that he asked that of me, I just sort of volunteered.

I never ventured out to join anything. I had no desire to find friends. My pleasure, besides the once-a-week romp with my beloved and thoughts of our Maggie, was being whisked away by books about *other* people's adventures. Oh, and chocolate— dreamy, decadent, chocolate. And cookies. Ice cream ...

It's true when we went away together during his annual vacation, it was always like a honeymoon, even decades after we found each other. But there were those forty-eight weeks between trips.

And then there was my guilt. Some of it well-founded. Some of it a complete mystery.

We had pulled into the parking lot, and it was our turn to take the ticket spat out by the red box. Ignoring what was required of him—to take the ticket—Ryan unfastened his seat belt so he could turn to look me in the eyes. "Are you saying you want to go away to evaluate our marriage?" His ever-changing, now sage-colored eyes were a sure window to his confusion. Or was it concern? Or fear? I was almost glad to see these reactions.

The machine beeped urgently, and its ticket moved in the breeze like a thin, scolding finger.

But I focused on Ryan as intensely as he focused on me.

A line of impatient drivers hooted behind us.

A cacophony of honks became background music. Ryan seemed frozen. Lost in my eyes. It was easy for me to be lost in his emerald orbs.

Then the beeps from angry drivers became the soundtrack to a love story as he grabbed me like he hadn't for years. He held me tight—like he'd never let me go—and whispered in my ear, "I think I'm the luckiest guy in the world to have you for my wife. I need you more than you'll ever know. Being married to you is a privilege. A joy. Please, never leave me. You're my world."

And then he kissed me. I mean *really* kissed me. I swooned girlishly. How I'd missed his passion.

The love song of hoots and honks continued blissfully, and only a fist pounding loudly on Ryan's window interrupted our hunger. We pulled apart guiltily, like young lovers caught in a policeman's light beam. While I straightened my clothes, Ryan mumbled his thanks to the attendant who'd hastened over to unsnag our snafu, grabbed the ticket, and we cruised slowly into a parking spot, ignoring the middle fingers being fired at us.

When he turned to look at me after he'd switched off the car, I said, "The problem is that you are truly my entire world. Have been since the moment I laid eyes on you. Even when Maggie was born, you remained my number one. I am *your* world when it's dark outside and mostly over weekends. You have your work, where you spend most of your time. I have you. Period."

We got out of the car, and he hoisted my heavy suitcase effortlessly from the boot and said, "I had no idea that you feel I'm distant." His eyes looked misty, as if he wanted to cry. It hurt me to see those eyes I loved obscured by tears. He tried blinking them away but only succeeded in changing the hue of those expressive windows he allowed me to peep into.

Jade eyes marred by hurt drilled down into mine.

I bullied on. I didn't want this to be about him. "You're consumed with your work, Ryan. I go to that damn shop once a week to do the books for your sister's pet store. Apart from seeing a baby koala or an iguana, there's no stimulation. I wait for you to come home. It's what I do. My job is making sure our house looks good and your food looks fabulous. I look as good as I can and make sure your bed is warm ... not that you notice any of it. You come in exhausted. I know you're happy to see me, but you're worn out. I feel dull because I have nothing stimulating to share with you, and you won't share because you insist on forgetting about work when you walk in the door. I know so little of your life, and there is nothing interesting about mine. Before life just passes me by, I've got to do some living, even if it's without you. Then at least I'll have something interesting to share with you."

"Oh, my Brie," he said and dropped his still-thick eyelashes down to mask his hurt.

My tone was gentle. "I love you with all my heart, and I am not doing this to hurt you, but somewhere along the line, we've lost each other," I said. "I know you think it's your fault, and it is ... but it's also mine. I must be dishwater-dull, because my uninteresting life revolves around your comings and goings. I hope this trip will change that. And if it does, I'll be so fabulously scintillating, you'll need to wear shades."

He smiled and kissed me like he owned me. About time!

I WAS UPSET after I left Ryan to go through customs, but the duty-free offered some solace. I bought two giant slabs of Cadbury's chocolate and nipped off pieces from under my blanket throughout the flight so the guy next to me wouldn't label me a glutton. Or maybe it was because I didn't want to share. Either way. After dinner, when he left his finished food tray on the table and squeezed passed it to go to the loo, I whipped off the mini KitKat he hadn't eaten and hid it.

It was still wrapped. I didn't stoop too low.

I touched the gold locket hanging from its chain around my neck. Ryan's loving gaze popped into my head, and suddenly I felt hot and sick. *I'm jumping into the unknown, ten thousand miles away from my security blanket, to go to a place I've never been with people I barely know. Holy shit! No small wonder I'm having a panic attack.*

I took a sip of coffee and concentrated on breathing in through one nostril and out the other without touching my nose. I smiled to myself. Thank God I was easily entertained. Pretty sad, really. But all this distraction with nostrils caused the panic to subside.

Ryan left me six voicemails, though he knew I was in the air and my phone was off. That made me smile when I landed. He was trying to be attentive, but I needed time to myself. Ironic, since that was one of the reasons I was on this journey: I resented having to spend so much time on my own. And if I'm honest, I relished thinking of Ryan sampling the angst, uncertainty and loneliness of being the one left behind.

Life's complicated, isn't it?

I'd planned to spend the night at the airport hotel before we old hostesses met early the next morning. I wanted to be rested and ready. Who was I kidding? I would be more worn out tomorrow than I was today, worrying all night about making this impulsive move and the million ways it could turn into a nightmare.

When I checked into the hotel, there was a massive bouquet of flowers on the long reception desk, and I thought how inappropriately positioned they were. I had to peep around the dozens of exotic and colorful florae to find a person to check me in.

My sneezing started and wouldn't stop. I had people fussing over me when all I needed was to move away from the damn flowers.

At a safe distance, the sneezes ceased. The guy with badge saying "manager" asked, "Are you okay, Mrs. Sekula?"

I nodded.

"Sorry they're making you sneeze, but those are your flowers, ma'am." He handed me the card, still in its little three-pronged message holder, that had huddled inside the vast arrangement.

My Love, I know you're allergic, but my creative mind is

*not capacious enough to find an alternative gesture with
as much panache as flowers waiting in the foyer. I wanted
desperately to demonstrate publicly how MUCH you
mean to me. It's you and me forever. I adore you and
always will.*

Your Ryan.

I smiled and wiped my nose.

Touching my gold locket, I accepted my room key card and told the manager to enjoy the flowers.

The room was stark but functional. I cursed myself for having way too much time to think.

I told my husband once I was at this "retreat," calls would be on my time, based on when I was free. I think that freaked him out. I was usually always free and at his disposal. Not that he took advantage of that; he just took it for granted. I was free as a bird, but not calling Ryan was the right thing to do. I switched on the TV and thanked God once again for my ability to be easily entertained. After a long shower, I hauled out a family-size bag of Kisses I'd bought at the airport, lay down and picked up the new book by Lucy Lakestone, the third in a series. I knew her mystery would intrigue and her heroine Pepper would soon make me laugh.

CHAPTER 4

BRIE

Boston, present day

I set the alarm for three hours before the scheduled meeting with the other invitees at the airport Hertz counter. My goal was to look better than my best to compensate for the fifty-two pounds I'd added to my five-three frame since my airline days. But there's only so much designer clothes can hide and makeup can do. Stretch jeans with a tummy-flattening insert are just jeans when you have to lie down to pull up the fly.

I remembered Lucky vaguely as the vivacious girl who often came into the bank where I worked before the airline. We'd randomly shared a coffee when my favorite café was full and Lucky had called me over to share her banquette. She was eager to hear about my airline adventures and seemed to need reassurance about applying to Air B. I gave her what she needed, apparently. For that I was grateful.

It was she who'd insisted on us all wearing scarves around our throats as we did as Air Baobab air hostesses in the '80s, so we could find each other. There would certainly be no one else with neck scarves flapping away, not in this decade! Thank God she hadn't called for white gloves!

As for the other women who would be at this retreat? There was funny, bright, beautiful Chantelle, who had a handsome brother I'd met while she and I were on a Cape Town night stop decades ago. Brother was delicious and I'd flirted mercilessly with him, but he wasn't at all interested in me. Frankly, I'd never flirted in my life. I didn't know what possessed me that night. But there was no response whatsoever from him. I thought he might be gay. I didn't mean to think I was the be-all and end-all, but to have absolutely no response to my first attempt at flirting was, frankly, quite deflating. Besides, even if he'd flirted back, that would be that. I had no desire to have sex with anyone. But he didn't, and I had to look long and hard at my appeal or lack of it.

And then came Ryan. There was no room for mind games. We were immediately in love. It was the most peculiar thing. Ryan made me feel brand-new. The sex was spectacular and swoon-worthy. Uninhibited. The stuff HOT romance novels were made of.

There was no other man for me.

My brief encounter with Moxie still pissed me off, how many years later? I'd smuggled a banned *Playgirl* center spread through customs for her because she'd enjoyed a roll in the hay with the model prior to airport pickup. A notch in Moxie's bedpost for which I could have been kicked out of the airline. Back then such things were considered pornographic, and I might even have been sent to jail if the customs office had discovered it. And she never even thanked me.

Moxie had triggered my hatred of being used by a stranger

—something I thought I'd left behind. The bitterness was so pungent, I had to suck on the last remaining rectangle of Cadbury's chocolate I found in my bag before I climbed into the bus from the hotel to the airport.

Once the chocolate had calmed me down about Moxie, I considered BJ. She was an airline legend most '70s and '80s crew went out of their way to avoid because of her wicked tongue and biting sarcasm.

Chantelle excluded, it wasn't the company that had lured me to this shindig. That's for sure.

And, quite honestly, for someone who had long lost the easiness of socializing and certainly had no practice in making friends, what the hell was I thinking? I was ill-equipped to come on this little soiree so far away from all that grounded me.

I saw the Hertz sign under which we were to meet.

Holy shit!

My stomach knotted.

Nope.

No can do.

I did an about turn, though I'll admit it was fairly ungainly with my mammoth suitcase. I ripped off my scarf, put my head down and began to flee while, at the same time, expertly using my free hand to dig around in my bag until I found the open bag of Hershey's Kisses.

"Brie!" I heard but kept going, aware the unmistakable foot-falls belonging to the voice were catching up to me. *Shit. Too slow. I wish I were built for speed and not comfort and that my cases were lighter.*

I turned only when I felt her hand firmly on my arm.

"Chantelle!" I said and couldn't stop my mouth from split-ting in pleasure. She looked just the same, and I felt her genuine warmth. "I was about to run away," I confessed, and she pulled me in for a big hug.

Leaning away, she held on to my shoulders. "What? No! I won't let you! I don't know these others either. Don't you dare bail. Then I will have to, too, and frankly, I am so intrigued by it all, and so far from home, and so jet-lagged, I just couldn't turn around and go home. So do it for us!" Her voice cracked before she pulled me in for another hug. Well! No man, woman or child—well, except Ryan—had paid me this much attention since ... well, since I last saw Chantelle. She made me feel special.

CHAPTER 5

BRIE

Boston, present day

I t was clear Moxie didn't remember me. She rushed in to hug me when Chantelle and I returned to the Hertz counter.

She said I smelled like chocolate. It was no wonder. Chocolate was probably seeping out of my pores by that time. I blushed furiously, but that was lost on Moxie, who was onto her next squirrel—a man wearing a Hertz shirt who wandered over.

"Are you here for Lucky van Niekerk?" he asked.

We all flinched at his butchering of the Afrikaans surname.

"Well, your friend BJ ..." We all looked horrified at the implication. *Friend?* He continued unfazed, "recommends you carry on without her." And he turned on his heel. I do believe we all hoped, with a devilish fervor, the message meant she wasn't coming at all.

As Moxie hailed a cab, Chantelle proved to be just the same.

Radiant and exuding joy and confidence. And that voice! Well! It had a personality of its own.

I felt frumpy, uninteresting and bloblike in their bold presences, and I succeeded in pulling in my stomach for a whole thirty seconds.

We were under Lucky's strict instructions not to discuss where we lived and other personal details until we were all together. En route to Hull, Chantelle let it slip that, like me, she had not been to the States since she'd left the airline.

Chantelle kept up a running commentary, which tickled us pink.

"Oh, my God. Is that guy on the radio really telling us that his legal competition is a turd? ... What the hell. That billboard that we just passed shouted: 'For the best blow job in town. Super Cuts.' Sounds like an S&M joint."

"It's a discount hairdresser," explained Moxie, and we laughed so hard the driver braked and looked back to make sure we weren't convulsing.

Moxie put on a thick American accent and said, "You needed to check in your South African decorum at Oliver Tambo Airport, ladies. We 'muricans believe in freedom of speech. Have a nice day."

I smiled at the taxi driver peering at us in the rearview mirror. I didn't want him to think we were making fun of his fellow countrymen. I caught his eye. "New York City in the '80s was my favorite place in all the world. Americans were so open-minded."

"Don't worry to explain why you like it here, ma'am," the taxi driver said. "I'm from Pakistan."

"I am serious," I said to the other two, who were laughing their asses off at me. "I love Americans."

"What are all those hundreds of brown ups vans?" I asked after we'd passed five of the massive trucks.

Moxie laughed and laughed like she knew so much about America—hell, as if she'd come over on the Mayflower. "It's not 'ups.' It's U-P-S. They are a carrier, an international delivery service. Like the post office on steroids."

Chantelle smiled kindly, and I figured wherever she came from had those brown vans too and I was the only silly ass in the back seat. But strangely, I was okay with that.

The trip from the airport to Lucky's place was more fun than I'd had in years.

As we walked downwards from the cab into Lucky's driveway, I saw twenty-foot-high steel beams held up the house. A Jeep was parked between the solid weight bearers.

By the time we'd climbed up two flights of stairs to get to the front door, I was huffing and puffing like a rhino after a charge. Whew. What a schlep. Of course, it had nothing to do with my blisteringly heavy suitcase, weighed down by an unopened bag of family-size Hershey's. And let's blame the other two bags of chocolate for the weight of my cabin bag. I hoped those steel beams were strong enough to accommodate my bags and me. Otherwise, it would be a disastrously short visit.

I hung onto the railing and threw my head back. This funky, uber-modern house was *seven* stories if you counted the two stories we'd climbed and the dance-floor-looking thing that balanced above the roof in midair. I glimpsed an exterior spiral staircase to get there. It seemed to be just a floor until I spotted a glint of sunlight reflected off what must be strong, high, clear Perspex that kept the dancer from falling to her death. How odd. I wondered if you *had* to dance or you could just stand

and admire the view. I didn't say anything out loud, because Miss Know-It-All Moxie likely would have thoroughly enjoyed putting me straight. Smart-arse!

Across the road to the left, where the distance between the ocean and the lot was too short to squeeze in even a little cottage, the ocean pounded against a rock seawall. On the other side of the peninsula, maybe a quarter of a mile away, was a huge, calm bay dotted with islands. In the distance was the metropolis of Boston. Quite the contradiction.

So now you think you've justified all the afternoons spent watching travel channels, you couch expert, you! How sad that I lived and learned through TV programs and Google and not real life or interaction with others. I hoped it didn't show.

Since I'd met with these women a few hours ago, they'd seemed to rewind in years. It was as if my mind took them back to when they were girls. Wouldn't it be lovely if that same magic time-slip made me look fresh as a daisy?

The door opened with a *whoosh*! Out bounded an enormous dog, friendly enough but rather big for my taste, and on the threshold stood Lucky. Yes, she was the Lucky I remembered. Tall, lean, shoulder-length auburn hair; the bright-red lipstick was new. Those same hazel eyes didn't look *at* you but *through* you. But when she smiled, no matter what stress you were going through, you realized the world was still on its axis, you were still alive, and you couldn't help but smile back. It was surely that smile that got Lucky into the airline.

She sniffed, and I could literally see her nose twitching like ... an animal's? Or maybe a genie? Or was it a witch? Maybe I watched too much old American TV.

Inside and schlepping our bags up the landing steps, Lucky

casually threw over her shoulder that BJ had already arrived. My tummy contracted in fear.

It had been fun and perfectly harmonious so far. I assumed Lucky would fit right into the dynamic we'd created en route. But would BJ stifle us, insult us, belittle us or, perchance, all three?

The queen appeared as we were sorting out who slept where. I was pleased she seemed substantially less intimidating than legend had it. But then, she'd had thirty-odd years to chill. I'd never flown with BJ and counted my lucky stars. There always seemed to be a crew member amongst us who'd had a BJ encounter, and the feared one's sarcasm and Shakespearean insults were worthy of retelling.

The queasy feeling subsided when Lucky diplomatically told us in front of BJ that though the queen was intolerable and full of manure on arrival, she'd literally removed her crown, rolled up her sleeves, and helped Lucky get ready for the "onslaught"—that was us.

The queen—um, BJ—appeared before me and smiled.

"Oh, you're nice!" popped out of my mouth before I could curtail it.

"Don't be so easily fooled. I like animals a helluva lot more than people."

"You've always scared the shit out of me," Moxie confessed.

"I hope I can keep you in that state of quivering fear throughout our visit," Queen BJ threatened with a grin.

Suddenly Lucky's penetrating eyes were on me. I put out my hands. It was an odd thing to do but the only thing that came to me. And I enfolded her hand in mine. We exchanged genuine joy at reconnecting. Lucky's gaze on my throat disarmed me. I blushed and touched my locket, and her eyes were glued there, so I quickly covered it with my fingers.

Lucky was different but the same. No longer an insecure lanky girl, she was confident, like she'd grown into herself somehow. She introduced us to her bestie, her dog, Tula. I air-patted him and mentioned he was bigger than I was used to. What a lie. I had not had pets for years. Where did that come from? *I hope I get over this nervousness.*

"It took me two tries after you sweetly encouraged me to apply to Air Baobab," Lucky said, her cheeks brightening just before she clamped a hand over her mouth to silence it, lest anything else spill out. I guessed she'd never shared her struggle to make it into the airline with anyone but, having done so, her mouth wouldn't quit: "And you were instrumental in making me believe I was good enough to try the first time. Two years later, when my shattered ego had been somewhat restored, I locked up my pride and gave it a last shot, because being a hostie was my lifelong dream." Her red lips parted in a smile of relief, as if this confession had been jailed for too long.

And by sharing her insecurities, my own were reduced.

That was startling. Imagine me making such an impression on somebody. I had no idea.

"I'm so glad. Otherwise, I wouldn't be here." I smiled, too, realizing I meant every word.

Before she turned to Chantelle, she whispered softly, "You smell like chocolate, but it's covering your ... essence... or maybe that *is* your essence." She wiggled her nose, then turned so easily towards Chantelle in greeting, I wondered if I'd imagined her saying that.

Moxie gleefully threw her arms around Lucky, who frankly looked a bit overwhelmed.

My senses reeled. I hadn't been amongst so many people—who was I kidding—*any* people like this since I'd left the airline. Everyone seemed to be talking at once, and I might have been moved to give a demonstration of the exits, à la airline protocol. My cheeks burned when I thought of it later, but I consoled myself that, if nothing else, it proved me worthy of being there.

I didn't know Moxie other than being taken advantage of by her, but boy, was she a bossy little thing! Somehow, she'd organized that Chantelle and I were to share Lucky's double bed while she and BJ bunked across the passage in singles.

Sheesh. I hoped I could get my live-and-let-live self of the '80s back quickly. Otherwise, I was going to be a nervous wreck and exhausted from being bossed around.

Go with the flow, Brie. You can do this.

We settled upstairs in Lucky's very airy pad with marvelous views from every sliding glass door and oversize window as Moxie took it upon herself to pour the drinks. Foxy Moxie was constantly on the move. Mostly in circles.

She'd seemed nervous all the way from the airport that Lucky was a teetotaler, but our hostess was well supplied as far as I could see. I was overcome with relief when I saw she had a spread of South African delights—biscuits and chocolates and even Jelly Tots. I would have preferred a sampling of American delectables for a change, but sweet-toothaholics can't be choosers.

What hit me like a slap in the face as I sat in my overpriced clothes was I'd bet big money I'd been the only one who'd agonized about what to wear. No one else here had been remotely neurotic about their color palette and overall presentation. And if what you wore defined you, then I was a self-important, ostentatious snob. These girls around me didn't wear clothes. Clothes adorned them.

At first, I thought I'd feel like a fly on the wall without much to contribute, but our common thread was the airline, and the stories woven there made up the fabric of who we still were. We all had stories or had heard stories that were bubbling over to be shared with those who understood them. Passenger tales. Cockpit egos. Airline legends. Larger-than-life characters who controlled our roster and thus controlled our lives. I'd slipped back into my sky-blue uniform quite comfortably, thank you very much. On the outside looking in for just a second, I was truly surprised how quickly that had happened. Once a sociable air hostess, I'd become almost agoraphobic and isolated, but I'd regained my skills just by being amidst these women.

The only blip on my radar was when Moxie tried to force booze on me, but once I confirmed coffee was my jam, she left me alone. I didn't need booze to feel high. The company was exhilarating, and I was a willing part of the whole.

That's not fair. You are also part of a whole that is Ryan, Maggie and you. You're a lucky girl to have that. But true, you've isolated yourself by your own volition. And you need people who interest you to be truly interesting to others.

Holy shit! That thought rocked me and forced me to listen more. When immersed in such clever banter, I spent more time thinking of cunning responses than paying attention to what was being said.

Relax, Brie.

Someone once said to be truly interesting, all you had to do was listen.

And then it happened. I became *part* of the conversation.

Whew! To be engaged *and* engaging came back like riding a bicycle. Ha! Who was I kidding? Bicycles were never part of my upbringing.

CHAPTER 6

BRIE

Hull, present day

W*hat are you doing without me, my love?* It felt odd *not* to be considering Ryan every minute of the day. I missed him desperately but concentrated on the fire-engine-red fabric of Lucky's living room furniture. The deep vermillion was speckled with splashes of bright aqua, and each of the colors seemed richer for the union.

Hmmm. Could that be Ryan and me? I certainly hoped I added the splashes of aqua to his vivid red to make him richer.

I leaned back against the couch cushions and took in the large vases of tall reeds that drew the eye up and toward the dramatic two-story-high cathedral ceilings. The very treetops swayed beyond the unadorned windows on the left, and in front of me I could see over rooftops towards the Bay of Boston. Now this was a treehouse haven. You felt you were flying most of the time. The perfect house for an air hostess.

My fingers on my left hand searched for and found my

locket. I felt guilty that it must have been at least a couple of hours since I'd last touched my talisman.

Oh, to be so occupied that there was little time for regrets.

I shook myself back to the present and looked at these women who'd become girls again. They were all quirky and fun. Nobody took themselves too seriously. That helped me loosen up.

Lucky called it; BJ looked remarkably like the gracious Katharine Hepburn, but when said lookalike burped loudly after slugging down a Diet Coke, Katharine Hepburn left the room. As expected, BJ's Shakespearian insults reared their ugly heads but were aimed mostly at Moxie, who took them well, or they targeted inanimate objects, so I stopped ducking every time BJ opened her mouth.

BJ unfurled a funny-looking wooden thing to miraculously become a guitar. Now and then she strummed it and changed chords; even a non-musical soul like mine could discern that BJ had rhythm and knew what she was doing with the strings. Lucky was excited to hear Chantelle sing, but there was so much catching up and airline chatter, I couldn't see us having much time for a singsong. Besides, we'd not addressed the elephant in the room yet. The reason we were gathered.

I would normally have been embarrassed that I nearly tripped in my quest to deliver drinks to the others. I was a hair away from shattering delicately blown glasses on the fabulous bamboo floor, but I yelled "Turbulence" and the moment passed with me laughing at myself because Chantelle recalled I had been falling over my own feet since we'd flown together so long ago. She said during our Cape Town night stop, the steward had told her as they watched me stumble over thin air for the fifth time, "Man, that chick's a real trip."

"I've been tripping as long as I can remember. Not an ideal impairment for an air hostess, with arms or trays laden with beverages and food, but I got by. The airline did give me a valid excuse though. I'd yell 'turbulence' and few passengers contradicted me. And if they said, 'I don't feel it,' I'd say, 'Well, you're lucky you're sitting down.'" The girls seemed to like that one.

Lucky said something like, "With your face, you get away with anything." She meant to be kind, but I felt my face flame. I didn't need my looks to get me into trouble again.

Now that we were gathered and the "information ban" had been lifted, it was declared that both Chantelle and I had been married a long time; BJ might soon be into husband number four; Moxie had one marriage down and another potentially coming up; and Lucky was not a lesbian.

Moxie was adorable-looking. She didn't seem to have an ounce of fat on her body, and I would bet her boobs were still naturally perky. But she was distinctly odd and ever-moving like the Energizer bunny.

To my chagrin, Moxie announced to her new roommate she would be sleeping in the nude. I spotted Chantelle's pj's when she opened her Betty Boop-encrusted suitcase. Whew! Dodged a bullet.

Then there was Tula. He was an interesting dog with weird-colored eyes, and he struck me as a fluffy person more than a hound. He was alert and part of the conversation. When someone spoke, Tula's eyes were on them, analyzing and summing them up. I found myself almost watching Tula when I said something, to see if he approved. Silly.

Chantelle had a weird little quirk. She flapped her hands from the back of her head to the front, palms out, to fluff her hair. I wondered at first if it was a jazz move or something. This idiosyncrasy happened often, and I bet she was totally unaware of it. She never did it on our Cape Town trip, so it wasn't part of her DNA. I wondered what had happened since to bring it on.

BJ and Tula were having a thing, sharing the same love seat. BJ looked quite dreamy. She couldn't be rotten to the core because animals quickly separate good humans from bad.

It was odd. Nobody was getting plastered. Surprising, because there was a ton of drinking going on. Happy, yes, but not fall-down drunk.

Oh, and I nearly peed my pants because Lucky had this "invisible" loo she had to unveil before we could use it, and I was the first to get nature's call. She touched the wall, and it revealed itself painfully slowly. For a girl who'd spent the rest of her life after her fifteenth birthday vowing never to pee in front of anyone ever again, there I was, poised to piss like a police horse in front of four virtual strangers, their eyes glued to a self-open/self-close door. When Lucky forced the designer door closed, I did some desperate tinkling! Frankly, it was more a long and thunderous *tonk* likely heard all the way to Miami.

But nobody made a big deal of it, which emboldened me. I could mess up, be ungainly, be silly, trip up a storm, make a noise like the Stanislavia Falls and nobody judged me.

By all accounts, this was my serendipitous, later-in-life chance for a six-day trip with my airline people who never judged. They were fast becoming my friends and were all so quirky that my own quirks went unnoticed.

Different—that was Lucky; then there was interesting, burping BJ; ever-moving Moxie; and pure-light-with-an-odd-tic Chantelle. A home filled with still-hot hosties and I was honored to be in their midst.

I felt uninhibited. Accepted. Free. It was how most people must feel around a big family, I imagined.

I wasn't going to bring it up, but Moxie seemed desperate to upstage BJ's story of her Spanish lover with one of her own about her one-night stand with *Playgirl*'s Mister July. The very one I'd been smarting over for decades! She'd asked me, a complete stranger, to smuggle in his centerfold through South African customs because she couldn't get back to New York before he was lining bird cages on the Upper East Side. She'd never thanked me. Lucky made sure Moxie crawled on her knees from the chair to the couch to thank me for putting my airline career at risk for her *banned Playgirl* Playmate. It was quite funny really, and I'd forgiven her hours before. I realized with a start that my insecurities recognized Moxy's. Who knew we were kindred spirits? I think we both loved feeling included.

And the other woman who'd given me stomach cramps, BJ, the queen—terror of the airline—would have scared the younger me stiff. Now I couldn't stop staring at her. She was the epitome of enigmatic. Her supercilious air was just a cover. She was oddly warm and hugely interesting, and I longed to learn from her.

Moxie and Chantelle seemed to be in competition to see who could drink the most. Both had designs on my portions and poured without asking.

Once dinner was over, Lucky finally appeared willing to discuss the reason for our presence.

"All I know is, my life changed when I slept in the only middle bunk on 747 Zulu Sierra 216," Lucky said, "and I know you all were affected; otherwise, you wouldn't be here."

While the dates and destinations of our life-altering dreams were all different, the one constant was we were in the crew rest in a specific jumbo jet, ZS216. We all found our true loves in the same place, the bottom middle bunk.

We pondered the reason why the bunk transformed into a gateway to another realm. Was it a spell? Was it a vortex? BJ quietly announced she knew exactly why. She'd been there when the portal opened. We pounded her for details, but she said she'd only tell us when it was her turn to share her dream. Fair enough. The "how" it happened was not nearly as important as the "why."

We all agreed that the men who appeared in our dreams were our soulmates, leaving a lasting impact on our hearts and a profound sense of loneliness when we woke up. The dreams remained just as vivid today as they were decades ago. Surely a testament to their significance?

I saw Lucky and BJ sneaking an intended "private look." I had no idea what that was all about, but I reckoned it would come out sooner than later. No secrets in this den of iniquity.

Lucky filled us in on how she thought we could best explore these strange phenomena. Each of us would get a chance to share our 747 "visions." After recounting our dreams in great detail, Lucky would mysteriously transport us beyond the dream's end to see what actually happened after the dream in hopes we could heal and start living our best lives.

Our hostess felt strongly that once this was achieved, if we'd already reunited with those soulmates, we'd form stronger connections with them, thanks to our newfound compassion and understanding. Or, with fresh perspective and free from fear, if we'd not yet encountered our soulmates or had lost them, like Lucky, we could confidently and fearlessly pursue our lifelong loves in *this* life.

Our aim was to resume where we left off, regardless of the

time gap or the pain of our parting, and look forward to a more enlightened future.

A fly on the wall would have laughed her arse off. It all sounded so far-fetched.

But then the fly wouldn't have been in the crew rest or tormented by the dream for years on end. So, not so surprising that we all bought it.

I could see, like me, these girls knew that the 747 experience was more vivid than a dream, and coming together in Lucky's treetop refuge was a clear indication that we were searching for something. Perhaps we were truly here to find that something.

"Oh, my God," said Chantelle. "Imagine if we're able to find our bliss. Each of us."

My stomach did a loop-de-loop. Imagine indeed. Nothing would make me happier.

But like it always did, guilt infused my anticipation. It was as bitter as bile.

How easy it would be to spill your guts to these empathetic, open women ...

No. No. Absolutely NO! Nobody must ever know. It's mine and God's to share. Holy shit! How often has Lucky caught me touching my locket? That's not why I'm here. Concentrate on the dream, Brie. Just the dream.

Tears filled my eyes. I blinked and tried the nostril breathing trick to assuage my worst nightmare with some instant meditation. All it did was force snot onto my upper lip. I quickly used a serviette to wipe away my failed self-hypnosis and forced myself to think of other things.

Look at these girls ... ha, listen to me ... girls. Menopausal women, more like it. But, like Lucky said, we are more self-assured, confident, still sexy and young at heart with worlds of wisdom under our belts. So, what the hell, I'm just going with the feeling. I hope I can hold on to it when I'm alone in my house. Waiting for Ryan. Don't think of Ryan; revel in the moment. Hold on to this glorious feeling of intoxicating camaraderie.

When we drew straws to see the order of who would share their crew rest dreams, mine was longest, so I would go first. Moxie begged me to switch with her, but I hung on to that straw like it was an umbilical cord—the kind of thingy they use in space for oxygen when they're outside the mothership on space walks.

I'd wondered all these years if my dream was real. Because I'd feel differently about myself, about Ryan, if it was. I would love him even more. But how was that possible?

You need to feel differently about yourself to make your marriage better. It was bad when voices in your head scolded you. And it was worse when the voices were spot-on.

"Those voices in your head are your instincts, Brie—your inner truth. Listen to them." Lucky's voice whipped me out of my reverie. I looked at her. Had I said that out loud? No. Definitely not! And with that spooky realization, I jumped so high, I saw Chantelle lift a smidgeon along with the couch as I landed.

Lucky said, "Don't worry, you weren't talking aloud. But I heard you." She smiled.

In that instant, I gave myself to her, and she said, "Okay, it's all yours, Brie. Tell us your story."

I took a deep breath. I was as ready as ready could be.

Riiiiiiiiiiiiiiiiiiiiiiiiing.

We all jumped. Even Lucky. It was an intrusion of the worst kind.

I was surprised when Lucky took the call. I thought we were

all focusing on what we were doing. She disappeared downstairs, followed by Tula.

We all looked surprised except BJ, and we looked to her for an explanation.

"Our hostess does something very cool for a living. She's an FBI and law enforcement psychic who helps them find victims and identify culprits. A major case came up that she has to work, but her gift is such she can work from here. I don't know the details, but she took a call last night and kind of let on, so I am sure she wouldn't mind my sharing what I know with you."

We were all visibly jarred. I sat back on the seat, and Chantelle and I looked at each other.

"Holy shit," was all I could muster.

Moxie was blowing her cheeks out so hard, her lips flapped.

We waited and waited. BJ tiptoed to the top of the stairs and listened.

She beckoned to us, and we quickly formed a circle at the top of the stairwell. She whispered, "Sounds like she's wrapping up. Let's let the FBI know she's got guests." BJ mouthed what we should say and counted down from three. "We're miiiiiiiiiiii-iiissing you," we chorused, and Lucky and Tula's heads appeared, looking upwards. She was still on the call, so we settled back in our comfy chairs to wait for her.

Next we heard a yell from below, "Clear the skies for us to fly in, girls. I have your wings." Then woman and dog bounded up the stairs, grinning.

Lucky grabbed a half-full glass of Bloody Mary before she sat down—I think it was mine somebody had not quite finished.

BJ said, "I told the girls what you do for a living. I hope you don't mind."

Lucky shook her head. "No secrets in this house. Besides, this is a tough case, and I might be on the phone more often than I'd like. I apologize, but you just can't plan when you'll be needed in my line of work."

Chantelle asked, "Can you share the case with us?"

Lucky looked pensive, then she looked at each of us. "I wouldn't normally share, but since you're in on it—I hope we solve it before you leave. You may as well know. That's if you'd like. It's pretty gory."

We all spoke at once.

The sum of the parts was, "Hell, yes, tell!"

"This is a cold case; Janice went missing twelve years ago. Andy and Jim, two of my favorite FBI agents, were involved initially, and when Janice's dad died, his probate attorney convinced the police chief in Springfield, which is about a hundred and twenty miles west of here, that she should reopen Janice's case. Her dad went to his grave believing his daughter was still alive, and he'd left a sizable inheritance. Of course, if she was alive, she'd receive the money, or if she was dead, a cat shelter in Watkins Glen, up in New York ..."

"Hey, I volunteer at that no-kill shelter! I live in Watkins Glen," BJ said.

Lucky grinned. "I don't believe in coincidences but opportunities. Hmmm. I wonder what significance this may hold for you, BJ?" she asked rhetorically, then continued. "Andy and Jim came up from DC to reopen the case. I helped them find Janice, who was entombed by the murderer, braiding tall water reeds over her body in a desolate marshy lake. This monster created a coffin made of stems so her body could never be found. My instincts took the boys—as I call the special agents—to Kansas City and a Catholic church there to find a working member. I was relieved to hear them describe Donald Cox from a photograph on the wall. It was exactly as I'd described him during my process."

"You must have been holding your breath," BJ said.

"I was." Lucky breathed out, visibly shaken. "I see these vivid scenarios, but until they're proven, they're just my visions. A fortune is spent on following my instincts, so the pressure is high. I've come to understand that I'm fallible and try not to beat myself up too much if I'm off base. Thank goodness it doesn't happen often enough to ruin my career." She crossed her fingers. "At least so far."

I admired her modesty. I guessed it was essential in her business. Psychic pride must come with a bitch of a fall.

"So, the call just now from the boys—Andy and Jim—was to tell me they'd arrived at his current port o' call in Kansas City, but Cox is in the wind. It's suspected someone leaked he was a person of interest or he overhead a conversation, but he's gone without a trace. He is a tall, lean, humorless piece of shit. About fortyish now, with dark eyes and hair; who knows, he might be gray after twelve years. Look, I find generous mouths hugely attractive on men, but this man's lips are particularly puffy and deep red, like he chews on them. They're the color of fresh meat."

I shivered. Chantelle rubbed her arms. "You're giving me goosebumps."

Moxie turned and turned like a dervish, chanting, "Lucky's gonna catch you, Donald Cox," and BJ looked pensive.

Then a hush fell. I bet the silence meant others were digesting our delicious involvement with this case, just like I was. Holy shit! This wasn't a CBS or Lifetime episode. This was real life!

"The boys have their minions working to find out if there were any strange deaths or missing women in the places Cox has lived courtesy of the Catholic Church over the years."

"So, we really get to help you solve a mystery?" I asked, excited as a kid in the Lego Store. I couldn't help myself. "At least in theory?" I finished, in an attempt to offer some adult wisdom.

Lucky smiled. "All hands on deck!"

CHAPTER 7

BRIE

After we'd sufficiently digested all this murder and mayhem, Lucky encouraged me to begin again. Her voice was soothing.

"Brie, it's you who is important at this moment. We, your friends, are gathered together to share. Please remember, no matter how silly anything you say might sound to you, it might well be important, so don't hold back. Each one of us is in a similar position. This is your safe place. And don't stress if your recall doesn't come out in order. With five heads, we'll put the pieces together, won't we girls?"

I looked at all of them, and they were all looking at me and nodding.

Lucky continued. "Sharing every nuance will just help us help you to work things out, to make sense of oddities. We only want what's best for you. You're brave to go first. Just remember, we will not judge you in any way." Lucky looked at—rather, in her case, *through*—one girl at a time, waiting for a nod of commitment before she looked to the next. Satisfied, she continued. "Brie, tell us everything that comes to mind. The more we know, the more we can help you."

Silence ensued, and very soon I closed my eyes.

It was if I was listening to myself speak without actually speaking, as I was immersed in a world that was familiar. I could smell that distinct plane smell mingled with my first bottle of Jovan Musk. As I licked sticky lips, I tasted strawberry-flavored lip gloss. I looked down at my allocated section of empty seats that would soon be filled with noisy, demanding people and I, classy Brie Lenz, would welcome them on board.

A violent shudder went through me. As the superstitious would say, I had just walked over someone's grave.

I knew who lay beneath that sealed-off burial place. Her name was Janet. And she was well and truly dead.

I'D BEEN in the airline for two and three-quarter years. Eight months on international. I was working the back right of 747 Zulu Sierra 216. We'd refueled in Sal (Ilha do Sol in the Cape Verde islands) on our way to Madrid, and the cleaning crew was on strike so we had to clean the toilets and the cabin. Although I bitched outwardly, cleaning the loos was a small price to pay for the glamour, the fun, the honor of being an international air hostess.

It was the middle of the night. The digestive systems of the pax (as we called passengers) were muddled from being forced to wake up and then have sandwiches and orange juice thrust at them as soon as we took off. It also meant the toilets were the hot spot for a few thousand miles after clearing the cabin, and all that loo cleaning had to start again.

I pulled the trolley into the back galley to stow it and head to the crew rest. The senior hostie working as galley slave waved an empty coffeepot at me and sang, "The loos are all yours! This long leg from Sal to Madrid is the worst. I'm so glad I'm in here, happily stacking and brewing. Being out there at this hour, and particularly after Sal, is so Hilda ... no, it's worse than that. It's downright Grizelda!"

I smiled at her. "Rarely do I envy you stacking breakfasts in the oven. But on these legs in the dead of night? You better believe I'm a shade of green."

"Hilda" was horrible, and "Grizelda" was even worse. I loved having our own airline language so the passengers wouldn't understand us if we needed to expel frustrations about rude, pawing or badly behaved pax.

A secret language made me feel even more included. I still marveled at the feeling of being a real part of something whole. On board, we cabin crew were usually a solid team.

"The captain who recruited me through the bars of my teller's station at the bank didn't tell me cleaning toilets was such a big part of the job," I shared with her.

"Ahhh, one of those. Did he try to get in your pants before, during or after you got your wings?"

"He was only being kind." I mentioned his name.

"He's one of the good ones. There are but a tiny handful of pilots without ulterior motives. You lucked out," she said.

I moved toward the line of toilets and waited until a door opened, then jumped the queue, shrugging off dirty looks from pax who'd been waiting for ages to do their ablutions. Once inside the tiny capsule, I slipped two sick bags over my hand and pushed it through the pile of who knows how many layers of poop. My encased fist finally hit the steel flap meant to open automatically when flushed. But shit happens after the two hundredth and third number two. Apparently, the sophisticated engineering required to get this big, fat, loaded steel bird into the air stopped at the aeronautics. The toilets had no clue they, too, were meant to be state of the art and designed for endurance and heavy loads.

When I heard the women giggle, it grounded me, and I glanced around our circle created in the twenty-first century, but the magic immersion into the past was still present. These hosties around me were on my flight, dressed in sky blue and smelling the smells and feeling the feels as they, too, held their breath in the clogged loo.

After the fist-forced, mighty flush, I let out the breath I was holding, and only when the girls around me did the same did I acknowledge we were in Lucky's living room and not on that 747.

Lucky and Tula watched me intently, but it wasn't unnerving, which surprised me. I felt protected somehow.

I glanced at Chantelle. Her eyes were closed, and a slow tear rolled down her flawless cheek. Moxie was still. Surely that was an oxymoron? The girl never stopped twirling. I felt for her.

Evocative memories could make today's busy, twirling tracks stop as time stood still.

BJ's face looked unlined and serene as she looked towards the sky.

I wondered if, like me, they were getting whiffs of the Air Baobab-supplied, pungently sweet rose-scented toner meant for passengers to "freshen up" in the loo. The cloying smell could mask any foul odor, and crew used the stuff liberally to clean the basins and mirrors in the tiny space.

I wanted to observe the girls in their own air hostess incarnations on a full flight, but Lucky pulled us all back.

"Brie, move on to your dream. Take as long as you need to. We want to understand it all." She smiled.

I felt safe and important, and I happily included them in my memories.

"By the time I pulled open the curtain that hid our little napping sanctuary, all the bunks but the floor middle bunk were taken. Sleep would be nigh impossible with the drone of the engines vibrating through the steel floor, no matter which way you lay. If the mattress slipped, the cold steel of the fuselage woke you up with a start. I shimmied out of my skirt underneath my apron, removed my shoes and, with that thin blanket and miserable little pillow in hand, I lay down without any idea of what was coming ..."

CHAPTER 8

BRIE AS POLINA

Moscow, October 20, 1876

W *hoa! Where am I? Who am I?*

I stare at the image in the enormous mirror spanning the length of a long wall. A steel bar is mounted two-thirds of the way down and runs the length of the mirror.

I peek at the slight girl on the other side of the bar. I smile. She peeks back, smiling.

I jump as realization slaps me. She is me, but reed-thin!

Yes, me. Me who so fears the check hostesses will notice the milk tart on my hips and ground me and I'll have to work in the departure hall, is standing erect, rib cage in, shoulders down, chin up. My dark hair is pulled up in a tight bun. I am about nineteen.

My eyes travel downwards over the tightly laced corset to the soft, pink, gathered tulle, past pink tights and satin ribbons laced above my ankles. I wear pink satin shoes with square toes instead of cabin shoes. It's all new to me and yet all so familiar. I am a ballet dancer ... and this is no bar.

It is a barre.

I turn to the side. Sure enough, the ballerina does the same. I allow myself a moment of unbridled joy. I'm skinny and poised, and I bet I don't trip over things. Boy, it feels so good!

Someone speaks French.

I don't know what surprises me more. That someone talks to me in French or that I understand them. I know the voice and realize this heavy-framed woman, Madame, terrifies me.

She speaks in Russian. My subconscious understands exactly what she says, and I have no time to contemplate because she ends with: "Shoo! Shoo! You're using up your fifteen minutes." Then she pokes me with her long stick. It hurts. I'm *au fait* with this instrument of discipline because my muscles harden in anticipation of where the stick might connect—rib cage, spleen, pelvis, kidneys, derriere, taut legs or extended arms ... there is no place on my body that's unacquainted with this stick.

Suddenly everything becomes familiar, and I flee to my ballet bag ... but it moves before I can reach it.

A white rat pops its head out. Instead of fear or disgust, a surge of joy fills me.

"Coupé!" I smile, and I swear the little thing smiles back. I am skinny. I am a dancer. I have a pet rat. Lock, stock and barrel. Or should I say *passé, jeté* and *développé.*

My first day as a student of Madame's comes back to me.

I see myself as a three-year-old, and I stand with a dozen little girls my age. Madame speaks in a booming voice that commands attention: "You are the gifted. You are the chosen. You are the crème de la crème. You are the future ballerinas of our great Mother Russia. Ballet is a recently evolved art form, and you and you and you are its ambassadors." She looks right at me, and the importance of her tone—because the words are lost on me—make me important.

She continues, "It is Russia who leads the world in this art, and it is you, the ballet's vessel, who interprets the works of our classical composers through your body with precision and expression."

All of us young things have little understanding of Madame's long words and provocative speech, but the same sermon is repeated so often, we soon swoon with the headiness of it. The responsibility of those weighted words are ours to bear, and we struggle, but we carry them as part of our dancer-destiny.

During each speech, she pulls out her long, thin stick, and I shiver. Not because of the stick—my mother uses a bigger one at home—but because when it prods you, you've been singled out and disgraced for being less than perfect.

Madame's homily goes on. "But to get there, you must learn French ballet terms until they roll off our tongue and you can recite them backward. You must know quavers and semi-quavers and clap your hands in time, getting your body ready to be perfectly on time with each beat. You must practice. Practice. Practice. You must stretch your limbs beyond endurance. You must point your toes until they ache and cramp. You must soak your feet in vodka to make your toes hard enough so you can stand en pointe so long, your audience will not breathe, lest they break your magical spell. But beware. You must never, ever drink this vodka because you will be banished from this studio and ballet forever. Nor do you take this vodka off-premises for your parents. It is purely to strengthen the flesh on your fresh toes for pointe shoes.

"You must use your core and make it the center of your balance. When you hold your extended leg and your arms in first position, think only of your core, as strong as a hundred-year-old tree. Not a hair on your head must move, and God forbid you wobble or lose your balance, because then the privileges you and your family enjoy because you are a dancer will be stripped away. Thus, you will use your tree trunk core and your roots that grow through your feet to ground you as your unyielding anchor as you stretch your legs, farther and farther, almost disconnecting them from the bone claws holding your hips in place ... and *still* you will hold your position. And hold it. Even though you think you can't. You can. You must. You will." Each of Madame's words hammer into me as I stand still as an old oak and feeling each blow.

"And all the while you must feel the music. Always dance for someone you love even if they're not in the room or in the audience. Deliver the message your choreographer gives you using all of your heart and interpret that message with your soul, your face, your body, all while you perform it in time to the music." I stiffen, waiting for the crescendo of her speech.

"Become the music." Her words break over me, dousing me with their meaning all the way into my soul. I resolve to think of my papa when I deliver the choreo-something's message.

I will dance for my papa. He is the only someone I love.

"Even with the best technique, if you are without real feeling for story and music, you will only ever be a ballet dancer. Never a ballerina."

Then she barks "Barre!" and waves her stick menacingly as we tiny chosen, clad in all our soft-pink glory, rush to stand in a line at the barre and hold on to the steel rail, our chins lifted impossibly high off long necks, shoulders back, stomachs sucked into rib cages, bums tight and feet joined at the heels with toes pointing east and west.

I have been under Madame's balletic tutelage for nearly sixteen years now, and still her stick terrifies me. It does not hurt.

Worse. Much worse.

It demoralizes me.

Six days a week we are forced to push our young bodies into impossible positions while Madame's long thin stick taps, slaps and pokes us with varying degrees of pain and the highest degree of shame.

This is the only world I know.

I snatch up my bag with Coupé safely inside, throw on my old, inherited, woolen shield that will mostly protect me from the cold, and I'm ready to dash off when I hear Madame's voice close by. I steel myself and turn to face her.

"Polina. I have warned you. I need full commitment to every movement. E-v-e-r-y s-i-n-g-l-e nuance, turn of the head, turnout of foot, extension of leg or arm must have a beginning, middle and end. Like a story. Push yourself, Polina. Or I shall find another budding ballet dancer to take your place. This is your second warning. There will not be a third." She could have gone on and on, listing the consequences of a third strike— sending me back in dreaded disgrace to my mother's hovel— having my ballet privileges revoked ...

But that she *doesn't* say these things scares me most of all.

For a moment I consider how the ballet money I earn is

squandered by my mother's new husband and how by now, we should have a comfortable apartment close to the studio. Yet, he spends all my ballet money on vodka and, I suspect, other women. But when I turn twenty in less than four months, that money will be my own. For now, I get to keep enough to rent a tiny room in a large house close to the studio. It's nothing but a box, and the family who live there pretend the room I rent is *not* attached to the rest of the house, but it is a warm place to lay my head.

I put on my father's old war boots, which cover my pink ballet slippers.

I am so grateful for Coupé, my only friend, as I dash past the other girls gathered in cliques.

It's always been this way. I am the only student who comes from a poor family. The rest have parents in government offices; a couple of them have royal lineages; some are daughters of retired ballerinas.

They've been trying to get rid of me for more than a decade so one of their own can take my place. I'm hanging on with all my might … but barely.

Coupé, the bag and I take the back steps from the studio two at a time.

While the other ballerinas go out the front door of the famous studio to meet and greet the waiting balletomanes during the break, I sneak unseen out back to practice. Ballet has become everyone's favorite thing. Balletomanes are the rabid fans who hover close to studios simply to catch a glimpse of a ballet dancer.

I've always been but a hair away from losing my coveted place at the barre, so every waking moment I spend stretching, marking, flexing and pointing. Only the best dancers are allowed in Madame's famed studio, and the old tyrant has no qualms about culling her students as new, more talented dancers are discovered at lesser studios. And they are. All the time. A dancer is only as good as her last dance.

"Practice" is my middle name.

CHAPTER 9

POLINA

Moscow, 1876

Perfecting my technique is theoretically impossible in my papa's coat, and to most I must look like I suffer from Saint Vitus' dance because there is much movement but little grace and my tutu is well hidden. His hefty soldier's boots seriously impair my best turnout. One foot is always colder than the other because of the hole in one sole, but this is all that remains of the only person who found me worthy. Worthy of having a career in ballet. Worthy of his love.

I love to feel my papa close, even though his body lies shattered and cold in a military cemetery, with only a wooden cross to mark his sacrifice. I've whittled "You will always keep me warm, Papa" on the cross, and it distinguishes his place of rest from the thousands of other unmarked crosses.

I can strengthen my core and practice balance and deportment out here in the open with no judging eyes, and all the while, Coupé can do her business and stretch her little legs.

I can also mark the complex steps in my mind so I can do

them automatically while trying to *feel* something, which Madame claims is more important than technique. Of all the demanding balletic requirements, *feeling* is surely the hardest?

It has become hard to summon my dead papa's face to help me do so.

MY COUPÉ HAS A SIXTH SENSE. She knows our love is forbidden. Were Coupé discovered, we'd hear the piercing screams of the entitled. They who'd never met a rat or a mouse of *any* color in their homes or along the fancy cobbled streets on which they live.

The fortunate part is, I don't count in the eyes of my fellow students. I am not worth observing, thus my secret friendship is safely cloaked in invisibility by hiding in plain sight.

"Coupé, go, do your business and no mischief. I have but eleven minutes to practice my *adage*." I lovingly place my white rat down, and while she acclimates herself, I am three bars and eight steps into the music playing in my head. I concentrate on the repetition of the steps so I can clear the path for perfection to make an appearance whilst under Madame's watchful eye. Or at least, for once, spare me the humiliation of her cane.

Every so often an irregular "clink" disrupts my focus. Metal on muffled metal. Annoyed, I follow the sound and see little Coupé on her way to investigate a tin cup set on the pavement. She ducks, fortunately, before she's pelted with a coin.

I try to concentrate: "*Chassé, pas de chat, tendu ...*" but I imagine Coupé being harmed and leave my makeshift barre to search for her.

"You're a tame little fellow," says a timber-rich voice holding a smile. I glance up from the tin cup and around the corner, to where a bearded man sits on the pavement. His body is turned sideways, and he holds Coupé in both hands, an inch from his face.

The little minx has a look of bliss in her pink eyes.

He must feel me watching because he twists to face me, still smiling.

I first check out his smiling mouth and see straight teeth between the hairy upper and lower lips. The condition of those teeth alludes to someone who cares what he looks like, although the bushy beard contradicts that notion. And there he sits. One leg gone. Missing. His pant leg neatly folded and pinned so a hand's length of flat trousers hangs from one hip.

I trudge to him through the snow in Papa's boots and put my hands out to retrieve Coupé. "I'm so sorry ..." I begin, but when he stares up at me, his green eyes arrest me with their intensity.

So powerful is his gaze, I feel my body reel away from it and yet ... and yet, I can't break eye contact.

But more importantly, I don't want to.

A force like a horizontal lightning bolt emits from the man's eyes. His life force seeks out my heart, finds it, and earths itself there. Then the glow of familiarity and deep love, planted by that bolt, seeps from my heart into my soul.

I force my mouth open to gulp in some icy air and restore my good sense. He is, after all, a beggar and I, a ballet dancer.

There must be a mistake.

I sense my face, conditioned to express *feelings*, shows him my dilemma. But when he puts my Coupé down and turns his torso away from me, my sensation is one of barren loss.

I have a desperate urge to pull his head around with both

my hands so his green eyes will hold mine again. Then, perhaps, the sense of belonging will return.

Although his back is to me, the invisible cord between us refuses to stop its magic sizzling, nor will it allow me to move away.

Not that I want to.

I have the feeling I've known him for as long as time itself.

I pick up Coupé and hold her to me, then try to finish my apology, though my voice shakes. "Coupé doesn't usually trust strangers. I'm sorry she disturbed you," I say loudly, to his back.

"Disturbed?" He turns back and smiles again, this time avoiding my eyes. "She's delightful," he says, leaning as far as he can from his sitting position to scratch my pet behind her ears again and make her swoon.

We watch her bliss when he says, "You are the first girl I've ever seen with a white rat as a pet."

Avoiding my face, he deliberately looks from my bulky coat to the gigantic boots. "Or perhaps you're a soldier whose voice has not yet broken, back from a skirmish at the front." His lips twitch, teasing me, then spreading into a smile. His perfect teeth demand my attention.

He points with an index finger peeking through his worn glove, right at his heart. "I am Mikhail."

I let Coupé snuggle into my neck and feel myself aligning my feet into a balletic fifth position, placing my left arm in first position and my right hand over my heart, fingers slightly apart and curled, as if I am holding a delicate rose by its petals.

I wonder, fleetingly, why I want so much to impress this beggar with my balletic interpretation of love. "I am Polina." I feel desperately silly when I remember the beautiful movements I've created just for him are lost under Papa's coat.

But that has not deterred him. He stares up at me from the ground, then closes his eyes like a camera's aperture capturing a moment.

Ballet photographers are always evident, and their instruments intrigue me, but his emerald eyes fascinate me more, and I teeter as if on a tightrope, waiting for him to open his eyes.

He lifts them slowly, as if he's dreading something, like someone might no longer be there ... but she is. He smiles the biggest smile I've ever seen. His eyes twinkle from green to gray to sage and back to emerald, and my heart lurches, pumping hot blood through my veins at a radical speed.

To cover this odd effect the depth of his eyes and his dazzling, albeit furry, smile have on me, I say possessively, "This is my spot," then frown at my own rudeness. I blame it on this odd reaction he has ignited in my usually trained, disciplined body.

"Well, may I share it?" he asks simply.

His sincerity makes me smile. "Of course. You're here and I'm"—I move quickly back to the stone wall—"over here."

A safe distance away and yet I still feel the cord that connects us, and I have the urge to never stop smiling ... and suddenly I realize smiling is something I seldom do.

CHAPTER 10

POLINA

Moscow, 1876

"They're like a pack of wolves," I whisper to Coupé, who's nestled safely in my ballet bag, balancing on a spool of pink thread, three pairs of clean tights and two sets of rabbit skin toe caps.

I aspire to master Coupé's balancing skills.

In the studio, in the hall and in the changing room, the twittering she-wolves distance themselves from the one they overlook, surmising I will never make it into Madame's favor, let alone into the corps de ballet of prolific choreographer Vaclav Julius Reisinger.

"They're separating their strong species from what they believe is my weak one so their conscience won't prickle when they leave me to die on my own in the dirty snow." I glance into my bag to see what Coupé thinks of my animal metaphor. Since she is my only friend, I'm convinced we communicate superbly. I hear her say, "Don't be so dramatic, Polina."

"But Vaclav Julius Resinger? Coupé, you must understand.

He was a mere leading soloist and then he *mastered the romantic repertoire*! Imagine! Vaclav rose to fame, and now he directs the Moscow company of the Bolshoi Theater, and now he is coming here. Here! And you think that does not warrant some dramatics?"

I could see she felt bad, for her little whiskers twitched uncomfortably. Coupé was my confidante. My papa gave her to me in a little cage before he went off to what was to be his last military assignment. He said, "This little mite will give you all the answers you need while I am gone. Ask her anything, and she'll steer you right."

I missed my papa every day, but I have him close by, in warmth and in spirit. And I have Coupé in all her cute glory.

I have no other allies.

My tiny room gives me a glimpse into the middle classes even though I may not interact with the family. I am always surprised how quiet the rest of the big house is. Like it's pleased with itself and its genteel inhabitants.

I come from a noisy part of town with tiny dwellings too small to be called houses. Every day I count my blessings that I have escaped. I no longer live under my mother's roof, even though I pay for it. I do not have to watch my mother use vodka to find oblivion from the fury of her new husband, and I no longer have to duck from the vicious blows she believes are her duty to deliver to me when I tell her so.

It was only when Coupé was threatened with a blow that I left the only home I'd known.

I didn't know where to go or what to do, only that I could not put my best friend in danger.

As usual, my papa was right. Coupé steered me to the house with the notice for a room to rent. Though we are sometimes lonely during the long Moscow nights, we are never cold.

Coupé has all the answers, and she's also a superb listener. Life has taught me those two qualities seldom go hand in hand.

I told her about Russian composer Pyotr Ilyich Tchaikovsky, who had composed a ballet fashioned from Russian and German folktales—the story of Odette, a princess turned into a swan by an evil sorcerer's curse.

"It's titled *Swan Lake,* and a brilliant stage designer named Karl Valts has agreed to create a sensational set with moving parts never before seen on a stage. Reisinger—the Great Vaclav—is on the hunt for the crème de la crème to perform this new ballet. Oh, Coupé, can you imagine? Every ballet school in all of Russia is priming and primping ballet dancers to impress him."

Madame's school had a history of producing exquisite dancers. That's why my papa had taken my hand and we'd had an exciting trip in a buggy pulled by a horse, when open auditions were being held at Madame's studio. All the other little girls were my age.

I was too young to be afraid, and my papa was standing against the wall with the other parents, so I never felt alone. I realized now how courageous my papa was to take me there. The chances of my having talent that could be discovered were slim. There was absolutely no chance it could have been inherited, and, God knew, there was no finesse to be found in our squalor.

Papa simply wanted more for me. He dressed carefully in his army uniform. He had no medals to adorn the dull green, but he brushed his hair three times. Though he looked smart, he must have felt completely out of place amongst the expensive brocade and velvet garments worn by the many mothers reeking of money and breeding. I smiled. Perchance Papa stood out because he was the only man in the room.

Madame was terribly scary, but when her voice rose, I just looked for and found the eyes of my beloved papa, and all was well in my world. It was when I was accepted into the program and he had no option but to leave me at Madame's school that I found my loneliness.

One had to show immense promise at an infantile age to be enrolled. I've seen many fall from pedestals year after year as they hit the street, ballet bags in hand, with no alternatives. Such is the intense hard work and dedication this art demands.

"Acceptably talented" is not acceptable at all.

Madame's mantra recently became "Dance like you're auditioning for Odette, not one of the swans." I doubt, based on the number of times I endure the brunt of Madame's stick, that I will have the honor of being a swan or even a swan stand-in, let alone Odette, but I won't let the she-wolves count me out before I have my fair shot.

The day following the electrically charged meeting with the one-legged beggar, I seem to need fresh air—cold as it is—more than I need to find a gap in the tight ballet circle into which I am never welcomed.

I can't get his arresting green eyes with their multiple shades or his hypnotic smile out of my head. Silly!

Indeed, just yesterday taking Coupé downstairs to do her personal business was a chore. Today it's become a much-anticipated event.

With Coupé safely in my bag, we fly past the wolves.

"Don't feel bad for us, Coupé. To them I say: 'To Siberia with you all!' Come, let you and me get inspiration from the one-legged man with the striking green eyes as we learn the new *adage*."

How, I wonder, could I feel more excitement *outside* the ballet studio than *inside*? It is but one day since I'd first locked my basic blue eyes with his exceptional, multi-shades of green. It feels like three glorious centuries ago.

I peep around the corner to see if he's still there. How silly that my heart thuds so. My chest hurts until my eyes find him. I'm ridiculously pleased he's positioned himself so he can watch for generous penny-throwers and thank them, as well as keep an eye on the back entrance of the studio.

His handsome face lights up when he sees us. My heart skips a beat.

I tear my eyes away. Remembering poor Coupé's needs, I gently lay her down. When I glance up, those magnetic green eyes are waiting. The same tug almost makes my heart ache as we stare. Reluctantly I pull away from his gaze, only to stop so I may imagine under the bushy beard is a pair of exceptional manly lips that border his perfect teeth that peep out from under the bush.

As I catch my breath, I'm drawn inexplicably closer to him, and the atmosphere changes.

Though my mind has not yet consented, my knees bend in a *plié*, and I lean on my haunches so my eyes are on his level. My unladylike position will be unnoticed thanks to Papa's coat.

I shiver as that same bolt of electric lightning hits us both at the same time. Even if I wanted to, the cord between us wouldn't let me move away. In fact, it's pulling me towards him ... and ... wait! I'm pulling him towards me. Our strength is equal.

It's all so out of our control, but somehow, when our faces

are a foot apart, the cord allows good sense and decorum to prevail, and we stop but continue to stare into each other's eyes.

I know the only way to break the cord is to look away. I don't want to. My heart aches and begs me not to.

But if I give in and let the cord pull me right in ... what then?

I close my eyes tight because they want, more than anything, to immerse my whole being into the depths of his magnificent orbs.

But break the spell I must. I turn my head away and run, as best my papa's boots allow in thick snow, and at last, lean my palm against the wall. Good. It's cold and sturdy. Sensible.

Exactly what I need to calm my raging heat and spineless frame.

With my back to the magic force emitting from Mikhail, I feign a position at my imaginary barre, and I feel something I've never felt before yesterday. Before Mikhail.

The need to impress.

But my wonky knees are much more in need of a crutch than one-legged Mikhail might be at this moment. And what kind of an impression will I give in an army coat and boots? Still, I find myself doing my best, in case he should be watching.

Though Coupé bounds over to him the next time we take a break, I hang back, tentatively. I don't know what the cord binding us is made of.

And I fear what I don't understand.

But I clutch my imaginary barre and then turn on my toes as if the choreography calls for it, so I can watch him. I'm eager to learn about him by observation only. I dare not get too close.

Because anything could happen.

With his back to me, I can safely assess his body language—

something I am good at, since the body and its movements are my purpose—and I am thrilled to see how reverently he treats the passersby, whether they drop a coin or not. Dogs on or off leashes come close for a loving pat; even feral cats find the courage to rub themselves against him. And my beloved Coupé is entirely besotted with him.

Animals always know.

I see the reaction of each person he's addressing, and there are many smiles from men and much coyness from women and giggles from children before or after they toss their coins.

His genuine kindness endears him to me, though we've not spoken since "the cord" between us established itself.

At the end of the day, when ballet is done and my young body burns from overuse, Coupé and I trudge down the back steps once more but, as the memory of Mikhail's eyes pops into my head, so does a niggle of hope that he will still be there. It turns slow steps into skips.

And he is.

It's dark, the night having overtaken gray skies hours ago. The beggar's cup is put away because the masses have receded to their warm homes and lavish dinners, gatherings around fiery hearths to later dress in finery and dance in great ballrooms.

But here he is.

My heart lurches.

And he's speaking to me!

"You dance all day, and yet you're still radiant. While I sit all day and feel exhausted. How do *you* fare, Coupé?" He turns his eyes—those eyes that in the light of the streetlamp have taken on a mystical glint—to my rat. Ridiculously, I feel jealous.

I laugh at my ludicrous reaction to a man I've only seen a few times and sitting down at that. He smiles back, those perfect white teeth defying the darkness as he stares at me. I feel myself clomping towards him while wishing I was *en pointe* and graceful so I could thrill him.

He indicates a wad of newspaper he has set beside him, patting it in invitation.

Shockingly, I don't hesitate. I sit and cross my legs, feeling like one of the great sages or saints of India who, thousands of years before, had invented the art of yoga. They whom Madame encourages us to imitate so that we might find our "peace" or some such foolishness before a performance.

In this position, I find myself open and inviting. Quite the opposite of peace.

Coupé jumps into my lap.

"Is this a rendezvous?" I hear myself asking.

Though I feel my cheeks turn crimson, I really want to know.

"I wish I was more prepared and more ... whole. I would have strewn flowers I'd stolen from a hothouse in your path, then I would take your arm and we'd walk with Coupé to the soup shop over the road."

"The soup shop?" I giggle, having expected his fanciful proposition to be considerably more lavish, but I'm impressed he has the courage to be frank.

He laughs. "A man must promise only what he can deliver. Except the 'walking' part. That was fanciful." His face twitches in an attempt to smile, but I see pain.

I look into his eyes at that moment, and the cord zaps me so I physically feel my shoulders and head jerk towards him, and his eyes tell me he feels the same.

Our eyes are four inches apart ... as are our lips. I feel my lips part as the rest of my tautly wound body relaxes as if opening up to him like an exotic flower.

Vulnerable. Beautiful. Delicate.

Pluck me.

His breath is warm, intoxicating as his eyes bore into my own. Together we travel through my mind, down to my heart, to my belly, down again to the root of my womanhood.

The flower opens wide, wider, widest, and I catch my breath and feel warmth flow from my secret place.

I close my eyes because I can't take any more of this blissful sensation without exploding into a million fragments of satisfaction and release.

Mikhail takes my hand reverently, like I matter, and I keep my eyes closed, acutely aware that his sensuous mouth has moved away. But knowing his eyes are still on me, I reel from the journey our sublime connection took us on, conscious that I have given myself to him freely, lustfully, completely. And he has devoured all of me.

We are jointly, deeply and fundamentally cognizant that we are one. That we remain a maddening foot apart is inconsequential.

In the light of day, it might seem impossible, but this is no time to be sensible.

"Shall we give in to this divine flow, Polina? Shall we let our minds join, even if our bodies cannot?"

I feel a rush of disappointment. "Why can't our bodies join?" I clamp a hand over my loose mouth, shocked by the thick longing in my voice.

His voice is husky and sad, thick with regret and disappointment. "Because you are a ballerina, Polina. And I, a one-legged beggar."

CHAPTER 11

BRIE

Hull, present day

"Oh my Gaaaaaaaaaaaaaaaaaaawd, Brie!" Chantelle's voice went up four keys and scared me right back to the present amongst these strangers who I knew instantly were dear friends.

"Holy shit, Chantelle. Don't pull me out of that divine dream with such a screech. I was loving every second!" I was cross she'd interrupted my bliss. I looked at Lucky, only half joking. "Did you spike my coffee?"

"Nope," she said calmly.

"I slipped into that dream as if you'd clicked your fingers like a hypnotist." I tried to read Lucky. No luck. She was an open-closed book!

Lucky smiled mysteriously and was saved from answering by Chantelle's excitement. "Brie, I swear you were talking funny. Like somebody would talk—well, centuries ago. It's uncanny. You even have the trace of a Russian accent. Well! You sound like those Russian bad gals on TV but softer. The way you described things ... it did, but it didn't, sound like you."

I think I blushed.

Lucky said calmly, "There is nothing odd or mysterious about it. Your dream has always been there, Brie, whether you've consciously visited it again and again, like I have my own dream, or not. It's deep inside your psyche. You're *allowing* it to come out again. But it's all about *you* being comfortable with what you're doing. Only you can make that call."

"There is so much to analyze about your dream, it's probably best we do it bit by bit. Right, Lucky?" BJ said without even raising a cynical eyebrow.

Lucky nodded.

Chantelle fluffed out her hair again and did that little quiver thing as she gazed at me. Moxie, the ever-moving elf, sat stock-still, mouth open.

Lucky said, "BJ's right. There is so *much* going on here. You've been transported back in time and you're in a trance; by stopping now and then, we can *all* help you remember the details. Then, when we examine the whole picture, we'll know which pieces of the jigsaw puzzle fit, where and why."

"All I know is it's all so beautiful and so amazing. The tiny details. The feelings you're feeling that *we're* feeling." Moxie looked in more of a Zen state than I felt.

I was suddenly infused with fear. "But what if I can't get back?" I looked beseechingly at Lucky.

"Get back here or there?" Moxie looked stricken that she might be denied more story.

"You're just telling us your dream in all its detail. You're not going anywhere." I swear I heard Lucky add under her breath, "Yet."

Okay, so for now, all I had to do was tell my new old friends about my dream.

BJ looked ... well, I'd go as far as to say she looked a bit dreamy. Pretty much like me.

But Lucky was cucumber-calm. "How do you feel, Brie?" she asked.

"Pissed to be back here in the twenty-first century." Then I laughed to soften the blow. I didn't want them to see just how disappointed I really was to be back in this life.

Movement tugged my eyes over to Moxie. She was turning around and around anticlockwise, arms out, like a lost Tasmanian devil, eyes open. She seemed to be *un*winding herself. That one was strange. Seriously.

I glanced at BJ, who cocked her eyebrow at me and smiled like the Mona Lisa as she said, "Thank you, Brie ... for Polina and Mikhail. All because of that sizzling cord you two were sharing, I just unwittingly, exquisitely and prematurely executed all my Kegel exercises for the next two months. But then Chantelle felt the need to *screech* us back to the present. How rude!" BJ shot Chantelle a dirty look.

"Screeching?" Chantelle looked mortified.

"Okay, this is about Brie," Lucky, the moderator in the room, chided, then smiled kindly at me and wisely said, "It's healthy to check in with us now and then to see how this dream is affecting you in the moment."

I felt myself beaming so hard, my bulging cheeks almost closed my eyes. "I am loving every feeling, every touch. I am loving Mikhail. I swear I feel I dreamed this dream only last night. Oddly, afterwards, after what happened, I didn't think about the dream. There was too much else to think about."

"Which we'll get to. One step at a time. Do you know Polina, or *are* you Polina?" Lucky asked.

There was no hesitation. I think my heart spoke before my voice. "I am Polina."

Lucky nodded as if she had all the confirmation she needed.

"Of *course,* you are!" said BJ with great authority.

And then I had a vision of the little white rat in my dream. "I'd clean forgotten about Coupé, yet now, sitting here, I miss her. I loved her so much. Not so strange then that later I ..."

Lucky put up her hand. "Wait, Brie. We want to know everything, but I want you to only consider your feelings right now. No charging ahead because you'll lose something and ..."

"NO!"

We all jumped. Moxie again stood still as a pillar. Wide-eyed, she said in a low, firm voice: "You must not lose a thing."

They were all looking at me. Eight hours ago, that would have made me slither down into my shell and never peep out. But shy Brie had long since left the building, so I took the floor because I was, after all, a ballet dancer and I loved attention.

I touched the muscles in my arms, flexed my feet and winced, twirled my wrists and they hurt. My stomach felt like I'd done ninety sit-ups, but I didn't even know what that felt like. Exercise and I had long been long parted.

"I feel the pain in my muscles from exerting my body hours and hours a day as an old ballet dancer. How is that possible when I only walked to baggage claim and up your stairs?"

"Well, let's not kid ourselves. There's the matter of your suitcase that's as heavy as a hippo. My muscles were sore just watching you lug it," Moxie started, but Lucky cut her off.

"This whole exercise is meant for you to feel everything you possibly can while living that life."

What? What was she saying? I looked around. Only BJ was unfazed. The rest of us were—by the looks on the others' faces—freaking out!

"Tell them what it was," BJ urged. "I think they're ready."

Lucky smiled slightly and bowed her head towards BJ. Those two were definitely on the same page. Silent co-conspirators.

"So what *was* it?" Moxie demanded. She'd somehow landed at Lucky's feet and looked up at her like a puppy who thought she'd heard "walkies!" I swear I even saw the little scamp's tail wag.

One beat. Then another. The silence hung heavy with expectation. "I believe—no! I'm convinced—we all traveled back to past lives in that crew rest. That those weren't dreams at all, rather lives we lived centuries before with those soulmates," Lucky said.

There was an audible exhalation in the orange-hued living room as the sun threatened to dip over the horizon, but no one said a word. It seemed a verbal endorsement of what we'd all been feeling, even if we didn't know how to articulate it.

Lucky continued: "Lives where we never accomplished what we were meant to, by order of the divine code. Lives that haunt us because they are unfinished. Lives in which we met our soulmates but, because of choices we made or didn't make, were left half-lived and unfulfilled."

Lucky looked around, and I followed her gaze. BJ was nodding slightly, agreeing with Lucky's philosophy.

Chantelle looked completely stupefied, like a great mystery that had puzzled her since birth had been solved.

Moxie had moved to the chair and was lying with her legs

hanging over the armrest, one arm hanging off, staring straight up at the ceiling. A sight to behold.

I, on the other hand, was thrilled with this information. Though I could barely remember anything about the dream when I thought about it over the years, here I was, living a past life in Technicolor with all the feels. And I knew Mikhail as well as I knew myself. I was, in fact, relieved he was real. The electrical cord between us had centuries of voltage driving it.

"Is it possible that we have the same soulmate in many lives?" I asked.

Moxie and Chantelle glared at me like I was adding to their sensory overload.

"I have no doubt that's possible," Lucky said and looked to BJ for her opinion.

"I think it's probable. I would reckon the times we haven't found our 'person' are the times we were here briefly to serve *another's* purpose," BJ said flatly. Certainly.

"What the hell are you two talking about, and did you break the rules and convene and collaborate before today?" Moxie was up, bouncing from foot to foot like an eager prosecutor who moonlighted as a soccer coach.

"Nope," said BJ simply, after a long Diet Coke glug followed by a burp. She was a study of contradictions.

"No, Moxie. Those were the rules. No contact prior to this gathering. I sensed BJ was on the same page as me somewhere in the time we spent together last night." Lucky looked at BJ, and they both nodded and smiled. "But we never discussed it."

"And what page is that exactly?" Moxie asked suspiciously.

I thought Lucky was going to start with, "Well, Mr. Prosecutor ..." But instead, she said calmly, in her low register, the one that meant business, "Moxie, nobody knows exactly what this complex universe is all about, but one thing's for sure, to me, anyway. We are not just born to look forward to dying. There would be no point. We're here to live and learn and make the best of any circumstance we're dished out. I also believe that we come back with our people. I would bet all of us were in one or many lives together. Sucks that we had to wait to regroup until now, but that was our destiny, and I am damn sure we'll make the most of this reunion forever in this life.

"My quest for all of us, here and now, is to find out why we dreamed what we dreamed in that crew rest, which was clearly a portal to our past lives, and what we have to get right *this* time in order to live our best lives. Once we have recalled our dreams in detail, like Brie's doing, and we've dissected them collectively, we have a better shot at finding our true north.

"Past lives are very powerful, and if we've brought them to this life, they're prodding us to learn something from them by shining a light on phobias we don't understand and reservations that have no place in this life.

"Once we know what caused these states of unease, we can deal with them now and close a wound for good." Lucky finished and looked directly at Moxie. "Does that kinda sorta make sense to you?"

Moxie sat quietly again. It was most disconcerting. She had multiple reactions. There was the manic turning soul, the coquettish flirt, the clever little pup and the quiet adult. Then she nodded. "I am prepared to go with the theory and see where it takes us," said Moxie the grownup.

Lucky spoke to all of us. "Those crew rest dreams or past lives have held all of us back in one way or another. Now's the time to understand the details and see how they affected us then and now—physically, emotionally, sexually, spiritually, even medically—then we can choose to learn from them, keep them, or let them go. All we brought with us from that life is ours to keep or discard, as best it serves us in our present."

"Gobbledygook!" Chantelle sang.

There was disquieting silence.

She looked at me and said: "So whatever you feel, even if it seems like gobbledygook, is important, right, Lucky?"

As Lucky nodded, I saw signs of the tension caused by her perceived negative outburst being expelled from the lungs of the others. Chantelle—the wariest of us all—was in.

We collectively sat with this revelation, examining our own complexities. A companiable and necessary silence and relief to know we were all prepared to take this journey together.

The first to speak was Moxie. "Shame," she said. "Those other dancers are such bitches to Pol—to you, Brie, and Madame is so freaking scary!"

"I want Mikhail. Right here. Right now. One leg. No legs. I don't care," declared BJ.

There was a chorus of "me too," including my own.

Levity was restored. I sighed. So relieved.

"So, just to be sure, Brie. Are you okay with continuing with Polina's journey, no matter where it takes you?" Lucky asked.

"YES!" I shouted. I'd never shouted in my life—well, before I arrived in Boston. "Let's go all the way."

The innuendo caused an eruption of giggles, but BJ said very quietly, "Be careful what you wish for."

And I shivered.

Yet I couldn't wait to become Polina, ballet dancer, once more.

CHAPTER 12

POLINA

Moscow 1876

We sit at a small table. The shop owner is anxious to close up, but we shut him out of our awareness, choosing instead to enjoy the warmth of the little tearoom and embracing the normalcy of two people getting to know each other across a table. Or so others will think. We have known each other, Mikhail and I, since before time was invented.

Looking at me, nobody would know I had my first orgasm sitting on a newspaper without anyone or anything physically touching me.

Mikhail knew.

"You're as pure as the driven snow." He smiles at me.

My face splits with pleasure, though I find the grace to blush a little as I scold, "And yet, you had your way with me on our first rendezvous."

His eyes deepen. Green turns to emerald. "No, Polina. It is

you who had *your* way with me." His voice is husky again, and I feel another hot rush to my secret places.

Though we are both ravenous, our soup turns cold in untouched bowls.

I'm heady, intoxicated, and yet there is no vodka on our small table.

"You are a man. Have you done ... this... before?" My cheeks are on fire again because I can't seem to keep my thoughts to myself. "Has this happened to you before?"

He shakes his head. "This?" he asks with hand over his heart. I nod. "Never," he says.

I believe him with all my heart.

"And you?" he asks.

I swallow and look away. His question, so innocent and yet so very personal, demands I take a moment to compose myself. Unable to formulate the right words, I shake my head.

He reaches out to touch my hand and wraps his big one around it. I stare at the dusting of fair hair on the outside of his hand and relish the callouses on the inside.

The lust he has awakened in me considers other places that big hand might gently, reverently, touch.

He tries again. "Surely as a ballet dancer you receive much attention from smitten beaus, balletomanes and fans? To not would be impossible to believe. If I were a patron or a prince or enjoyed the status to afford me the privilege of courting a lady of your beauty and kindness ..."

I squeeze his hand, suddenly needing to tell him more.

"I have no interest in potential suitors, though there are many art-hungry beaus. Ballet is my focus. To take attention away from my art would mean the end of my career. The end of my world. No man, no matter how dashing or rich, has ever been worth risking all I could lose."

"And yet, here you are, having soup with a beggar." He smiles again.

"You weren't always a beggar," I say, tightening my grip on his hand. "I see you. I know you. I feel you. You don't beg. You interact. Begging is surely the means for you to be part of the society you were once integral to?"

"You're immensely perceptive."

"You make me so." I allow myself to gaze into those mesmerizing eyes, but he shifts in his seat.

I feel driven to let him know how much I think of him.

"You are worthy of so much more than you aspire to. Life has dealt you a cruel blow, Mikhail. Please consider I would never treat you as less of a man because of your station. I battle being known as the poor ballet dancer amongst rich ones every day. What does wealth have to do with the heart? Or talent? Or kindness? Nothing. Nothing at all. I won't let you believe for one more minute that you are less than anyone else. You are more. It is *I* who sought *your* attention. You are worthy of anything at all you aspire to own, cherish or love."

My sincere speech is interrupted by a little white pointed face with a pink nose and twitching whiskers popping out of my top pocket.

"Your friend might enjoy some soup," he says softly and delicately lifts Coupé in one big hand and moves his bowl to his lap where my sweet pet can have her fill. I keep an eye on the shopkeeper, who's busying himself at the counter.

In the nick of time, Mikhail returns the bowl to the table and slides Coupé into his inside jacket pocket before the shop-keeper approaches our table.

He is forlorn. "I am exceedingly sorry to disturb your meal, but my restaurant should have closed two hours ago. My wife will be wondering if I was robbed or murdered." He grins sheepishly at the exaggeration.

Mikhail stands up, steadying himself with hands on the table. "Forgive us, please. We are newly reacquainted and have many lifeti— years to catch up on. We did not mean to inconvenience you. Please extend our apologies to your wife."

We rise. He places more coins than are necessary on the table, grabs his crutch and holds the door open for me, though he struggles to do so. He follows me outside. The pavement is slick, and he slips awkwardly.

My heart flips, and I leap to aid him, prepared to break his fall no matter the consequences to my dancer's body. But he has done this before, and he rights himself, then looks at me with surprise. "You were going to cushion my blow, weren't you?"

I feel the warmth of his wordless gratitude, and he hands me his left crutch and slips his left hand into my right one.

I have never held hands with a boy or a man before—other than my papa—and I have not felt, for so very long, safer or more cherished.

It's a slow fumble, but we don't care; we're together. He walks me to my room because he is determined it's what a gentleman would do.

He cannot come inside the house. The owner has forbidden visitors.

Neither of us wish to be parted. Neither of us dare to touch lips because we know nothing will ever be the same again. Neither of us can deny our ache as longing hovers, thick and churning between us.

When he leaves me, I feel desolate. Me, the most independent of all the dancers, with a faithful friend like Coupé, feels lonely. I, who have fended for myself most of my life when my papa was off fighting a war and later when he damn well died! It's I who feels half of myself without Mikhail.

Suddenly I feel dizzy with elation, and I twirl in my tiny room feeling like a beautiful princess and I realize ...

I am in love.

CHAPTER 13

POLINA

Moscow 1876

As the glorious days pass, my heart lives in my head, in my stomach, and in my root. It has not lost its way; it's so full, this heart of mine, it has quadrupled itself to fill every vital crevice of my being.

Sublime clarity reveals there are no secrets between us. Mikhail knows the wall serves merely to steady me from our latest encounter, though I pretend to practice, practice, practice so I can watch he who wins the hearts of passersby.

I acknowledge how easily he stole Coupé's heart. She who has no reason to trust. She who has known no other human's kindness than mine.

Yes, each moment spent, even twenty feet apart, seems to intensify the magnetic force between us. We no longer have to look at each other to share our sizzling connection.

During my first break on the third day, we fly down the steps, Coupé and I, and make a dramatic entrance as we thrust open the back door of the studio. Mikhail, who leans on the wall just outside the door and uses but one crutch, turns to welcome us, and my already somersaulting heart leaps from its designated spot. Forgoing its safety net, my heart flies off the high wire and through the air, then down, down, down as it beats a hundred miles a minute even after it's landed.

"You shaved," I say but force myself to start at the top to keep the best for last. I devour his wheat-colored hair, reminiscent of grain in all its seasons. His high forehead, his eyes trimmed with long dark lashes, shining emerald this morning. His high cheekbones, his strong pointed nose, and then ... and then ... what I have been denied till now, his mouth.

At last exposed, his sensuous lips are naked. And they are so much more than I'd dreamed they'd be. Those lips alone will keep me awake and restless in my small bed. Soft and plump as the tsar's cushions, they beg for me to touch them, to run my tongue over them, to suck on them ... Oh! I feel moist and warm and wanton.

"Only for you, my ballerina," he says so softly, I wonder if I conjured up words I want to hear.

And he smiles. I feel giddy. Possessed. Those luscious lips have spread to expose straight, white teeth. I want so desperately to be possessed by him. I know being possessed by me is what drives *him*.

We are roaring down a small lane on two wild horses, hands and hearts joined, the gallop too fast to sustain, and we must hurry ... but to where?

We don't care. And we don't care where or how we land, only that we land together.

And still we haven't touched lips.

The cord of energy that sprang between us from the moment we locked eyes has intensified to a nigh-deadly degree.

Anyone who comes between us—except Coupé—will likely be electrocuted.

I was smitten purely by his eyes, his kindness and his spirit days before I could make out his features hidden by a bushy beard.

'Tis no wonder that, now I can see him in all his truth, I am beyond mesmerized. Every moment I am away from him I consider how I manage to breathe without the feeling of buoyancy his beauty gifts me.

And I realize his essence is so powerful, it gives me life.

It astounds me that I can see how *I* feel reflected in those all-revealing, ever-changing eyes that are, indeed, the windows to his soul.

CHAPTER 14

POLINA

Moscow, 1876

Coupé and I no longer wait for our fifteen-minute or half-hour breaks to rush downstairs; we do so even during the occasional five-minute breathers Madame dishes out like rare dollops of caviar. It's worth the mad dash down and up again, just to see him smile.

A few words with the newly shaven handsome devil are enough to set my world on fire. Though his eyes are captivating, my own mischievous peepers wander immediately to his oh-so-generous mouth.

I am stricken that I am slow to notice the vicious scar that slashes from his chin to below his jaw. But that's his mouth's fault, for keeping my eyes glued there. The jagged pink line mars his beauty not at all.

During my half-hour midday break, I sit down next to him on a newspaper he's laid out for me on top of the snow. He's moved to outside the studio's back door at lunchtime, away from his earning spot on the pavement, to where we can't be seen.

"Tell me about *Swan Lake,*" he says. His voice is like thick, rich pelmeni dipped in honey. Warm, wholesome, rich and delicious.

His interest is genuine, his curiosity sincere.

"It's the ballet to be choreographed to Tchaikovsky's new masterpiece. A famous Czech choreographer is auditioning here in four weeks. It's expected many of Madame's dancers will make the corps."

"Explain, please. What is a corps? It sounds foreboding." He pronounces the word like he's describing a dead person and smiles, warming the frigid air around us.

My cheeks bunch with the joy he brings me. "The *corps de ballet* is a group of dancers, not principals or soloists, who create the ambience and enhance the background for the stars of the show."

"That doesn't sound very important, and yet all of you"— he points upstairs—"hope to be in the corps?"

"It is a great honor. You see, the chances of becoming a principal or a soloist are so very slim. One ballerina in perhaps a thousand ballet dancers ... maybe more."

"But what is it this *corps* does, exactly?" His interest is not only in me but rather in what matters to me.

"The dancers, though we vary in height and limb lengths, must become one to set the scene and create a believable ambience. We have to train to dance in perfect precision so the audience sees a solid background of long-necked white swans gliding, preening and flying with slow wingbeats in a perfect *V* formation. The corps is on the stage only to create the atmosphere for the lead dancers so they may show off their skills."

"Polina, surely it must be the ... soloist?" He cocks his head, seeking assurance the term is correct. I nod, and he continues, "It must be the soloist or the ballerina to which you should aspire?"

"No, no. I must not think of such things. I refuse to have lofty expectations. Staying at Madame's studio is challenging enough."

"But why force your ballet shoes to wallow in mediocrity? Why not soar like an eagle, then aspire to reach the stars?"

"Never. I must be satisfied. I am exceptionally fortunate I am doing what I do, and I must operate within my means."

My tone is harsher than I intend. Not I, nor anyone, has ever had grandiose ideas for me.

"But Polina, these are means and limitations you have set upon yourself. If you take those imagined ceilings away, you'll be free. Free to reach the stars."

"Mikhail. You must understand, if I make it into the *corps de ballet* for Swan Lake, I will be drifting amongst the stars."

"That is not so, Polina. You will be on the level of the eagle. You should aspire for the stars and then, when you become an eagle, recognize it's a step closer to the stars of your ultimate destination."

"You're silly. You don't understand how hard it is in ballet." I feel my voice quaver with uncertainty. Nobody has ever challenged me this way.

"Perhaps, but I do understand how hard it is in life. If we have small dreams, we will always be small."

"Says you," I spit. "You sit on the pavement. A cripple with one leg. Begging for coins. How can you speak so assuredly of eagles and stars and wanting more? What gives you the right, Mikhail? Tell me. Tell me that!" As I leap to my feet, I'm shocked by my own fury and the horrible words spewing from my mouth.

His face is expressionless, perhaps even lost. His eyes look up, boring into mine and seeming to burn before he drops his chin on his chest and slowly turns his head away from me.

He has dismissed me.

How can I blame him? My words, so cruel ... where did they come from? Even when my mother's tongue lashes at me or when her husband speaks to me harshly, I never show such detestable anger or unkindness. Shame burns my cheeks, and my throat scorches from the fiery words that have traveled down its passage. I gather my bag and Coupé and run upstairs.

That afternoon is torture. I keep glancing at the big clock above the pianist's head and then out of the window. I am out of step as we perform *bourrée en couru en pointe*, our hands crossed over, making a *V* in our united form.

Madame screams "Polina!" so loudly, I slip out of my miserable trance and force myself back on track. But the minute the last note of music plays for the day, I don my father's greatcoat, pull on his boots, and with Coupé hanging on for dear life, we take the stairs, three at a time.

The door opens, and frigid air bites us. I accept the slap of icy cold as part of my penance.

But Mikhail is gone.

He is *never* gone.

But it is I who pushed him away. Disgrace fires up my cheeks.

I can do nothing but wait for his return. I know not where to find him.

Dreary day turns to bitterly cold night, with clouds tumbling furiously across the skies in giant, fluffy dark balls, rendering the stars invisible.

Those damned stars.

It's right they should hide after causing such a devastating break between us. I try to convince myself their absence allows me to forget—just fleetingly—my ugliness to him.

He, who I've known for four and a half days, has become the most important soul in my world. Well, besides Coupé. Thing is, it doesn't feel like days. It feels like I've known him longer than forever.

Coupé and I go across the road to buy a hot cup of soup to warm our bones. Here we can keep an eye out for Mikhail and dream about the night we sat across from each other.

We linger in the warmth of the small cafe as long as we dare without seeming to be homeless. We return to the place he always seems to be, but it's still empty.

I feel hot shame and deep regret pour down my icy cheeks. "Oh, Coupé," I lament and quickly wipe away the tears with the rough greatcoat sleeve so they won't freeze and scar my skin.

Ballet dancers wear their scars on the inside.

CHAPTER 15

BRIE

Hull, present day

"Nooooooooooooooooooooo!" It was Chantelle again, but this time she pulled me out of my misery. She searched frantically for a tissue, a serviette ... anything to deal with her eyes and nose, which had become Hull's waterworks.

Lucky disappeared and returned with a toilet roll. "Whatever else you forget from your visit to Hull, remember always that my taste in personal products is superb. This, my girls, is *Charmin*." She handed it to Chantelle, who was gasping through hiccupping sobs.

After a massive clearing of the sinuses, Chantelle blubbered: "Oh my God, it's all your fault, Lucky. Yours and BJ's. She shouldn't have gone on. Now look. She's devastated." Chantelle had taken the role of my fairy godmother, it seemed.

"I'm here, so you don't have to talk about me in third person," I piped up. "And I am devastated too, but if you think I can stop now, you must be out of your mind, Chants!"

Moxie attacked me. "How could you be so cold? So cruel? He only wants the best for you. Can't you see?" She too looked close to tears.

Chantelle gave such a forceful nose-blow it made poor Tula whimper. I figured I should just be quiet. They would work me out between them.

"She's never known love from anyone but her dad," BJ said. "And he's been gone for years. She doesn't know how to handle these new feelings of love, desire, somebody actually caring about her. Nobody but her father has ever encouraged her. Give the girl a break."

"Thanks, BJ." I was suddenly close to tears myself.

"Okay to keep going, Brie?" Lucky asked with softness in her voice.

"Oh, please!" begged Chantelle and Moxie, dragging out the plea in unison.

"Ha! How the tides have turned." BJ threw at them, "You two viperous turncoats!"

Chantelle glanced at Moxie, who looked six feet tall in fight mode, hands on hips. Chants realized Moxie had the moves but not the words, so she continued for them both: "We were just worried for Brie." She sniffed.

"Yeah, so cutting her story off at the knees is kinder than seeing her suffer?" BJ challenged.

Chantelle smiled coyly. "Okay, you got me."

Moxie's arms dropped, and she sat down on her chair, looking contrite.

"Brie, try and pick up where you left off," Lucky encouraged me, her voice calm and unthreatening.

I closed my eyes, and this time the one-nostril meditation worked ... or I was just eager to become Polina again.

CHAPTER 16

POLINA

Moscow 1876

Coupé and I huddle in the side doorway of the studio, which was locked up while we were getting soup, so we can't even take refuge from the cold on the other side of the door. Not that I would have chosen to because we wouldn't see Mikhail. I would never choose warmth or any integral necessities over him.

Besides, with regret burning through my system, I will be warmed by the heat of my shame. Coupé crawls into my neck where the coat's oversize collar gapes and stops the bitter cold from getting in. My precious friend.

We both awake with a start. It's not yet dawn.

Mikhail gazes down on us. For once we are down and he is up. He leans on his crutch, using it as his second leg.

"Polina, why are you here? Did something happen?" His voice is pure concern.

"I waited for you all night," I chide childishly.

"Why?" he asks, genuinely perplexed.

I bite my lip. Hard. As if to punish my mouth for its cruelty. "I was unkind to you, and I hoped I'd find you to apologize before you decided to avoid me. Never seeing you again would break my heart."

He smiles, and there is not a trace of vindictiveness. "How can you apologize for something you meant?"

"But I didn't mean ..."

"What you said is true. I dare talk of eagles and stars when I sit most of the day dreaming and collecting pennies from the hard-earned wages of the generous. But that doesn't mean I can't want more for *you*. You who blossom with talent and grace and beauty. You who know the toil of dedication. You who must set your sights on the stars and nothing less or this life will pass you by. I have done nothing but spend hours feeling sorry for myself in the last months since this ..." He gestured toward the air where once a leg had lived.

"But you are ..." I begin, imploring my brain to produce the right words to make amends and illustrate his great worth to me.

But he holds up his hand. "I know what I am now. But because of you I might become more. You see, Polina, you reminded me the loss of a leg does not mean the end of expectation. Nothing should come in the way of our dreams. So ..." He waits and waits till curiosity forces me to look deep into his slate-green eyes, which are slowly turning emerald.

I feel again that magnetic pull, which seems to get stronger and stronger each time I allow myself to wallow in the bliss of his alluring orbs. My eyes well up unexpectedly. Destructive thoughts of never again being lost in the depths of his soul, by way of his eyes, have nibbled at my soul all night through.

"... So I'd like you to keep reminding me, as I will remind

you, to aim only for the stars. And then, perhaps, we will give each other the impetus to strive for what we deserve."

It happens suddenly and without warning.

My body propels itself up. I feel a moment of concern as I see poor Coupé plop out of the coat and onto the pavement, but selfishly my needs are greater at this moment, and I throw myself into Mikhail's chest, head first.

I wrap my arms tightly around his torso as I sob. Though it is but seconds, it feels like a year before he wraps his free arm around me. I hang on for dear life, and then he lets go of his wooden crutch because I hear it plop into thick snow. He holds me tightly in both his arms, and I am ecstatic to be his crutch.

Being in his embrace is entirely fulfilling. I feel my body meld into his as we stand and I use all my muscles to make sure he doesn't fall.

It is my privilege.

I feel, for the first time since my father died, like I belong.

More.

I feel like I have found my *other*.

There is a reverence cementing us together, the melding of long-lost souls. An amalgamation strong enough to heal hearts broken far too many times. And when I cry again, they are tears of pure, unadulterated joy.

CHAPTER 17

BRIE

Hull, present day

"Kiss him already!" Moxie's demand brought me back to Lucky's airy pad. I looked around at their eager faces and couldn't help but smile. Their anticipation was equal to mine.

"Bone him. Right there against the wall!" BJ insisted.

"Well, I might have, if you lot hadn't interrupted." I grinned.

"Good God, woman. I don't care if you dreamed him up. Just do it! For the sake of us all!" Chantelle stood with her hand over her heart for the last sentence.

"Do you girls mind if I ..." I threw my thumb over my shoulder.

"Oh, for God's sake, go. Go. Go! Get it on, sistah!" BJ encouraged.

CHAPTER 18

POLINA

Moscow 1876

M ikhail and I speak of so many things. Books and ballet. Disappointments and destinations. Prayers and promises.

We share like old friends—with ease and without inhibition. He is witty and clever, and he makes me laugh so hard, I tell him he should apply to entertain the tsar. He says I am the only audience he needs. We whisper like new lovers though we've not touched since I hugged him until my arms hurt and my strong ballet legs turned to jelly. The invisible connective cord sizzles so strongly, it literally stops Coupé short before she runs between us. Almost like she fears being fried by the zinging attraction of two powerful magnets.

It is Mikhail who keeps me on time for my classes. I would give up everything to stay with him on that pavement. "You must go. Dance. Dance, Polina. I will be watching in my dreams."

Imagine. Loving something ... *someone* more than I love dance.

Lately, Coupé and I find him sitting at the back of the studio, under the wide roof's overhang, his back leaning against the cold stone wall. It shields him from some of the pelting snow.

His new post keeps us well away from prying eyes. The neat stack of newspapers he's arranged allows us to sit without fear of frostbite.

Only Coupé and I use the back stairs. There is certainly not one ballet dancer, not even a janitor, who uses the plebian back entrance when the front entrance screams "Ballet Pour Danseurs" in a fanciful script of pink paint.

That the sign is in French and not Russian already gives it status. That it is only for dancers gives it exclusivity. That it is ballet—the new, prestigious art form— gives it status second to none.

No. Nobody wishes to be obscure when one can be admired coming and going from the front of the studio. We are safe from intrusion and uncomfortable inquisitions, all three of us.

"Why did you begin to use the back exit when you could have had the prestige of the front like the rest of the she-wolves?" Mikhail smiles, and my world is aflame.

"Hmmm. Perhaps I have never felt worthy of a front door. I am neither rich nor the best in my class."

"Riches come and go, but being the best in your class will define you forever. Consider, my Polina, if you were the worst in your class, you would deserve the front entrance because you would still be in that prestigious class. Now you just have to make the most of being there."

"Well, thank the heavens for the back door and my need to practice. I found you, and you want me to be worthy of the front door." I laugh.

I wonder how many rubles Mikhail gives up in a day to be with me for these stolen moments. I ask, and he says my company satiates him so completely, he has little need for food.

"Are you not compensated for the accident that took your leg and changed your life?" I worry that he struggles.

"I only lost a leg. Being unable to contribute to our society, for any reason, does not warrant reward. Besides, this empty space"—he pats the empty trouser leg—"got me to you via the pavement."

"And for that, I am deeply grateful," I say and reach out to touch his face but stop just short of doing so.

In the studio, I am shocked when I see my face in the mirror over the barre.

The mirror was merely an instrument used for correction, never self-admiration. But a week after meeting Mikhail, that same mirror shows my eyes brighter, my lips redder, my face more animated. Even my ballet feet are quick enough, pointed enough, turned out enough to avoid Madame's ruthless cane.

Mikhail's face is changed, too, from sadness hidden behind a big beard to an open, handsome face, gleaming with unadulterated delight.

We've only stood together twice. The first night when only Coupé enjoyed the soup and the last time, when I thought I'd wounded him beyond measure. Thanks be to the Madonna he'd come back to me in spite of my hurtful words.

It's not surprising we haven't tried standing together again. There are, after all, but three legs between us.

I say wistfully, "Russians feel ill at ease being demonstrative." And sadness engulfs me.

"Yes," Mikhail agrees. "Public displays of affection are taboo for the middle and upper class. So, to see a beautiful girl ..."

"And a handsome man ..." I add before he calls himself a cripple ... like I had, and for which I chastise myself hourly.

He smiles that smile that sucks air from my lungs and makes me breathless, "... locked in an embrace for many long minutes must have been more entertaining than a planned theater performance by your famous Vaclav. My cup was full without having to hold it up that early morning when we held each other with all our might."

"Perhaps they thought us street performers, a handsome man kissing a boy dressed in a big overcoat and a pair of boots. Standing up, I doubt they would have glimpsed my pink tights or ballet skirt." I smile at the image.

"Well, at least we were spared being thrown in jail for homosexuality." Mikhail laughs. "But then, I would take you any way I found you."

We make quite a pair: me, the "ballerina," as Mikhail likes to call me, bun pulled tightly back, trying unsuccessfully to contain dark tendrils intent on escape. Even when I relax with Mikhail, my back is ramrod-straight, and my neck is trained to lift two inches farther off my shoulders than other humans. As I sit cross-legged, the tulle of my ballet skirt insists on peeping out of my father's army coat. And the beggar, my Mikhail: tall, undernourished, mannered, softly spoken, with the face of a fair Greek god who's seen far too many wars and met a blade up close and a cannonball even closer.

Settled on the newspaper, I say unabashedly, "Tell me about your leg." There is no subject too delicate for us to discuss.

"Well, it was an extremely handsome leg."

He smiles, and I throw my head back and feel unbridled laughter start at my solar plexus, move through my neck and spill from my open mouth. I realize with a jolt I have never laughed so freely before in my life.

"Please," I beg through my giggles. "I need to know what became of that extremely handsome leg." And suddenly I am heartbroken that this perfect man has been robbed of the kind of life he deserves, and my laughter turns to tender tears.

He doesn't notice my wet face. He is busy pondering.

I can tell his mood by the color of his eyes now, and when they turn to leek-colored tourmalines, I know he's watching scenes beyond our realm. My question has unwittingly taken him back to destructive places and soul-destroying moments. Back to the core of his physical, mental and spiritual pain.

It's torture watching him, but at last he says, "My earliest wish when I was a small child was to be a war photographer."

"I never knew there was such a thing."

"Russia has used photography to record, influence, illustrate and interpret war zones, strategies and procedures since 1848."

I am fascinated. But then, had Mikhail been naming the parts of a wheel, I would find them equally intriguing.

I watch his gorgeous mouth move as he recounts his boyhood dreams. I could have—I will—give up the only thing I know, ballet, to watch that beautiful mouth till the end of my days.

"As a boy of thirteen, I left my home in St. Petersburg in search of my dream, much to the ire of my parents, who thought I should join the army. With scant rubles to my name and no support from my family, I volunteered to shadow a photographer. I carried his equipment until I did it well enough for him to pay me. And I learned. I saved all my money so I could one day own my own camera.

"A year later, I accompanied my mentor to shoot photographs in Siberia during the Polish Rebellion. As horrific as it was to be on those battlefields, capturing the theater of war made my job feel important. But each time my photos were published, it was a jarring reminder that war was an abhorrent waste of mankind. When my photographs appeared in the newspapers, though my coffers were filled, so were the chambers of my mind with the horrors I'd recorded.

"Before Alexander II's Turkish war broke out, I was called upon to photograph the war's preparation. I welcomed a way to immortalize potential bravery, heroes, and fallen soldiers without men being in harm's way. It was a great honor, and I was finally on my own artistic path—"

"Wait! That was only last year!" Shock courses through my veins. My mother's new husband was in the real war that followed the mock-up one Mikhail describes.

"Yes." Mikhail's eyes are downcast.

Fearful of the hurt I've conjured up, I take his hand and whisper, "What is your age now, Mikhail?"

"Twenty-four."

"And then, what happened to you?"

"I was in my element. I believed I'd found my nirvana doing what I was born to do. I was creating. I was capturing life. And the *possibility* of death but not death itself."

I wait, afraid of what's to come.

"And in the theater of a *mock* war, I was hit by a nine-pound field cannon that should never have been fired. It was a mistake."

I gasp. How cruel to be injured in a pretend war that didn't count.

I clutch his hand tighter in both of mine as he continues, "I was fortunate."

I couldn't believe my ears. Fortunate? I shook my head.

"I am alive. Here. To find you." His eyes, the most precious of all emeralds, gaze into mine, and I know beyond any shadow of doubt that it is so.

He continues, his deep voice thick with gratitude. "You see, Nikolai Pirogoff's skilled nurses and modernized medical equipment saved my life. That I lost *only* a leg was a miracle."

"What kind of miracle robs a man of his passion, his career, his art, his normal life?" Anger flares within me. If there is a God, why is he so unjust? "His *leg*?"

"The same kind of miracle that finds me a ballerina for a friend."

"Ballet dancer," I correct him automatically. It's a common mistake.

"Why not ballerina?" he asks, more concerned with my answer than his missing leg.

"The name 'ballerina' applies only to the principal or soloist. Not the corps."

"Fly high, my lovely eagle, and look to the stars," says the man who I long to become my lover.

"How can you be so fanciful for me, with eagles and stars, after your dreams were ripped from you?" My heart clenches with sadness.

"Because, my Polina—" He leans forward until his mouth is inches away from my own. "I want to watch *you* live up to your full potential."

Something in his tone stops my quick retort, and my breath hitches. He continues. "I know my potential. And I won't always sit on this pavement with a cup. And do you know why not?"

I shake my head and move my upper body toward him, leaning in, looking deep into fathomless eyes which, to my great relief, are dancing emeralds again.

"Because it's you who gives me glimpses of the passion and dedication I once had. It's *you* who has made me realize in spite of my disfigurement ..." He glances at the church clock across the square, always aware of my time. "Go, go, my ballerina. Or you will be late."

I roll my eyes at his deliberate use of the unearned title before a smile starts in my heart and spreads to my lips. I gather up Coupé and hightail it up two flights of stairs and into the studio as the pianist finishes his warm-up.

It is at that moment I realize I am regenerating Mikhail's soul, just as he is introducing me to mine.

CHAPTER 19

BRIE

Hull, present day

"You so don't sound like yourself when you're Polina," Moxie said, sheer wonder on her pretty face.

"Is that a good thing?" Why was I even insecure about the way I sounded in a dream or whatever this was?

"She's right," BJ confirmed. "You sound exotic." Coming from BJ made it all true.

"Oh, I've always wanted to be exotic," Moxie swooned.

"This is not about you, Moxie." BJ was annoyed.

"Consider, Brie, that you're not just retelling a dream, you're telling us about a real life you've lived, in what feels like real time." Lucky was dead serious.

"Deep." Chantelle's husky voice made me ponder the depths of these two existences.

"It feels like my life." I meant it. "What amazes me is that I can slip from here to there in a blink of an eye."

"You're time-slipping," BJ stated, making it all the more exotic.

There was a blanket of silence while we were all pondering this phenomenon of which we were a part, even if three out of five of us didn't have a clue how it was possible.

Perhaps part of my delirium was feeling the girls' excitement as they anticipated their *own* deep dives into lives past.

"I miss Mikhail. Can I go back now?"

"Please do." Lucky smiled, and I vaguely heard Moxie clap her hands in excitement and Chantelle's "wheeee-ful" cries of glee before I slipped back to the life I knew better than my own.

CHAPTER 20

POLINA

Moscow, late 1876

I am in the middle of an allegro when the thought of an imminent ballet break piques my spirts and warms my heart. I suspect the adrenaline rush of seeing Mikhail improves my posture, and my *battus* are faster and more precise —perfectly in time to the rapid beating of my heart when I think about him.

Since Mikhail, there's been a gigantic shift at the ballet studio.

You see, those nasty girls who once twittered unkindly and dismissed me are now monitoring me nervously. It feels good to make the wolves uncertain of their prey. Madame's stick has less and less reason to be used on me, but conversely, her esteemed and critical eye seldom moves off me when I dance. Her head is always cocked in my direction, and once or twice I've seen her nod as if she agrees with herself.

Mikhail has introduced me to my soul and then encouraged it to lead me. In conversation. In dance. In desire.

I've discovered myself because of him.

It is as if my very essence was dormant and only came alive when Mikhail's electric cord sprang from his chest and charged my soul, bringing me not only to life but to a heightened state of awareness.

In the *adage*, when we are free of the barre, I dance slowly, lyrically and with Mikhail's face before me, my feet barely touching the ground.

No matter where I move, I see his beautiful face, smiling; his artist hands now weather-roughened, applauding.

I dance—not for Madame, not to keep my career, not even for my own self-worth, but for Mikhail.

And though he is a whole flight down, sitting in the cold without a window into my world, I feel him watching me and I want, more than anything, to impress him. To make him proud.

The anticipation of the arrival of the *premier maître de ballet*, Vaclav (Wentsel) Julius Reisinger, prolific choreographer and director of the Moscow company of the esteemed Bolshoi Theater, is causing a frenzy. Even for me who has so little chance of being an understudy for a swan, let alone a swan.

"What is the worst that can happen?" Mikhail asks me when the date of the audition is announced and butterflies bash into each other in my churning belly.

My eyes fix on his so he will understand the severity of it all. "I won't be chosen for the corps in the new ballet *Swan Lake*."

"Will that mean the end of your career as a dancer?"

"No. There will be other productions. Ballet is fashionable. All of Europe wants to witness performances. But composer Tchaikovsky was commissioned to write the score for *Swan Lake,* so there are grand expectations for this ballet. It would be a privilege to be part of such an iconic performance."

"But you won't be ... evicted? Removed from your studio?"

"No."

"Then you won't lose your dreams if one man—who is entirely subjective and seeking dancers he has preconceived for his creation—decides the dancer next to you is more suited?"

"No."

"Then, my ballerina, dance as you've never danced before. You have nothing to lose."

He is right. If I do my best and fail, I have lost nothing. If I *don't* do my best and fail, my self-blame will make me lose myself.

"Tell me the story," Mikhail asks simply.

"It's a story of love, mistakes and tragedy. Prince Siegfried, in spite of his mother hosting a ball with princesses from all over Europe and Prussia, cannot find his true love and wanders away from the gaiety and banqueting to the lake for contemplation. There he sees the beautiful Odette. She tells him she's been cursed and turns into a swan each dawn. Only true love can save her and keep her in human form.

"Siegfried is smitten and professes his love for her. He promises to save her from her swanlike state. But the evil witch who put the spell on Odette has witnessed this romantic encounter and changes herself into Odile, a lookalike of Siegfried's true love, and presents herself to Siegfried once he returns to the palace ball. Siegfried, thinking she is Odette, swears his love for Odile but in doing so breaks his promise to Odette, who is destined to live her life as a swan."

Mikhail stares at me. "And then what?"

"Odette is distraught. The swan-maidens try to comfort her. Siegfried returns to the lake and makes a passionate apology, but, though Odette forgives him, his betrayal cannot be undone. Rather than remain a swan forever, Odette choses to die. Siegfried wishes to die with her, and they leap into the lake, together forever."

"That's a tragic story. Why would anyone want to dance this morbid tale? And what kind of person would want to watch it?"

"Audiences only wish to see dancers or actors being happy for a minute. Happy is tedious. It's in tragedy and heartache that a true performer can illustrate her gifts and make her audience feel. And perchance, bring them to tears. Then they stand up from their plush theater seats, thankful they are humans and not swans, and go home, some still weeping for the dead, star-crossed lovers."

"Do you think seeing a performance brought to life on a stage and then witnessing a tragic death of the most beloved characters makes the audience feel more alive?"

I smile at him and feel a rush of love for this man who listens. This man who is empathetic, understanding, interested. This man who loves me.

CHAPTER 21

BRIE

Hull, present day

"I am utterly, completely and absolutely in love with Mikhail!" This time it was BJ's voice that brought me back to ... well, this reality.

Chantelle fluffed out her hair, shivered longer than usual, and declared, "I love him. I just love him. He's so deep. So gentle. So handsome. So amusing. Mikhail is the ultimate man, Brie!"

I felt a warm glow like a hot flash. But instead of starting at my head like a normal menopausal moment, it began at my feet. I could see molten liquid flowing upwards as if no gravity existed, warming every crevice and vein and bone in my body. I was infused by unadulterated love.

"How do you feel, Brie?" Lucky asked.

I let Lucky's words tease the edge of my consciousness but dared not remove myself from this state of bliss. My entire being was bathed in gratitude and omnipotent love.

A glimmer of understanding made a wave in the flowing

gold rush. I couldn't quite grasp its meaning and feared lingering to decipher it would diminish the pleasure.

Like Scarlett O'Hara, I'd think of that tomorrow.

When the sensation quieted and only then—because it was sacrilege to stop it before its upward flow had reached my cerebellum, my crown and the roots of my hair—I opened my eyes.

I was surprised to see they stood in a circle around me, including Tula, still as salt pillars. Their unblinking eyes watched me closely, as if I might either faint or disappear.

I smiled and, at last, answered Lucky's question. "I feel warm and wonderful. Loved and cherished. Understood. Supported and rooted for." When I finished my last word, their bodies noticeably collapsed with relief, and they went back to their chairs.

"And you *are*!" BJ emphasized. "You are all that. Remember that feeling, Brie. Bring it with you into this life. Declare right now it's something you want to keep."

"I WANT TO KEEP THIS FEELING!" Boy, that was loud! When did this noisy, assertive Brie arrive? I kind of liked her.

BJ's wisdom came back to me. She'd pulled back the thick velvet curtain and revealed this ... this bequest of being something ... someone... with worth. Real value as in 24-karat gold liquid that coursed through my veins. Might it be that *even* as Brie, I was important?

I closed my eyes and said aloud: "Thank you for this feeling of being worth something. I will keep this sensation forever so that I might go back to it at any time and remind myself of my value." The words came so easily, almost as if they were premeditated.

My eyes flew open as the last syllable. I felt stupid. "What did I just say? Ha! I am agnostic. I don't believe in anything."

Lucky said, "Keep your mind open, Brie. You just found something you *can* believe in. *Yourself.* I believe in you ... we all do!"

Familiar faces nodded in consent, affirmation, affection. I was home with people I trusted, friends. No, I was home with my kin who wanted the very best for me.

Imagine.

Knowing I was not being judged but rather endorsed and supported unconditionally, I easily slipped back into Polina's blissful existence.

Chapter 22

Polina

Moscow, December 29, 1876

The day Vaclav arrives at Madame's studio to conduct the audition, girls vomit from nerves. Even steely Madame is all atwitter.

While final touches are added to transform our studio into an audition room, the door is open for me to peek in now and then at the progress: the state of the room; the arrival of esteemed adjudicators; and the catering to satiate their immediate needs. Water to quench their thirst. Vodka to warm them. Extra cushions on hard-backed chairs to make their long stay more comfortable.

A nervous pianist is set up in the corner arranging and rearranging reams of complicated music notes. He mops his brow until at last the correct music is propped up on the shiny mahogany instrument in front of him and he sits back, pleased with himself.

At a long wooden table, four occupied chairs face the empty studio.

"Vaclav," as premier maître de ballet Reisinger is called, is plump and mustached. The famous choreographer looks like he makes pies for a living and eats more than he sells, but his massive presence commands the atmosphere around him like an unsmiling Thor.

In his esteemed presence, our Mighty Madame—on his left —becomes a quiet storm.

On Vaclav's right sits famous prima ballerina Anna Sobeshchanskaya, who's been attached to the project since its inception and is cast as both Odette and the wicked Odile. She is the turbulent tornado working for Thor who has, in her fury, swept up a hot spring of sulfur. No wonder Anna looks like she has a bad smell permanently under her nose! Fancy cushions prop up her lean frame as if she were an invalid when the strength of her ballet body is legendary.

To her left sits leading man Stanislav Gillert, portraying Prince Siegfried. He is by far the least foreboding and, in relation to Vaclav's Thor, is one of the goats pulling Thor's chariot through the clouds. Harmless and obliging.

Outside the audition room, dancers are a flurry of pink: pink tights, pink corsets, knee-length, pink tulle tutus and pink pointe shoes with pink satin ribbons laced up their legs. They limber up, shoulder their legs, go down into the splits, and rush off periodically to expel dinners and breakfasts from one end or another.

I sit with my legs folded, this time to find the peace promised by Madame and the yoga masters of old so I may calmly run through the dances choreographed to Tchaikovsky's score. Each step has been drummed into our heads by Madame for this great occasion.

Every now and then I can see Mikhail nod his approval.

His smile brightens up my world all the way from downstairs.

I feel as calm, cool and collected as a Moscow midnight in May, as my body barely twitches in passive rehearsal. A gentle movement of my head, the lift of my shoulder, and the imperceptible nuance of my wrist as I dance in my mind. *Mikhail, my Mikhail, you gave me confidence. I promise to do you proud.*

The dancers are called in in threes.

The passage atmosphere is thick with fear and cold with competition. The same music plays over and over. I pity the pianist.

It is whispered all the dancers will get a chance to do the allegro and then the pack will be cut and those who make it will dance the adagio in twos, to be more scrupulously assessed.

The allegro will allow the adjudicators at the table with Vaclav—Thor—to see if they can keep up technically. The allegro is fast and dynamic, with lots of jumping and changing tempos. That will separate those who can dance in unison from those who lag behind by a millisecond, a fate worse than death for the corps. Individuality is not an asset but a distinct liability. No one will tolerate a lagging swan. The performance is all about one ballerina, not the many ballet dancers.

And then it is my turn.

I shove my head inside my ballet bag and kiss the top of Coupé's head for luck. I spiral up, concentrating on tightening my core in anticipation of its work ahead as Mikhail's beautiful smile fills my vision.

It's all I need to glide into the audition room.

I've practiced, practiced, practiced so the technical precision of the first round will not unduly challenge me. Besides, Mikhail's confidence in my ability, although he's never witnessed it, sweeps me to a place where reverence for this immense opportunity replaces restiveness.

I feel I was born on the tips of my toes with impossibly curved arches.

My back is as straight as Madame's cane, lower torso in, behind out, creating the kind of pert derriere artists paint behind closed doors.

My arms are lyrical, legs extended, neck elongated, head loose, steps quick, neat and lively, and my timing?

Perfect.

And all of it, to show my Mikhail I am worthy of being a dancer. *His* dancer.

The fast-moving *allegro* is over too soon. I still have so many things to show Mikhail.

As we exit, the other two dancers slap each other on the back in congratulations as if I am a figment of their imagination.

I head directly to Coupé. I take her out of my bag, which is risky, but the need to feel her whiskers on my cheek is overwhelming. My eyes fill with tears for no reason until Mikhail's face dominates my vision. As he smiles proudly, tears pour down my cheeks, and I cover my head with my father's coat, tentlike, and cuddle my beloved pet. As usual, all the other dancers are too wrapped up in themselves to wonder what I am doing hiding under an old coat.

"Mikhail was there in that room with me, Coupé. Did you see him?" I swear her little head nods as she sits, relaxed and happy, her front legs hanging over my fingers, whiskers expressing what her voice cannot.

When all the dancers are finished with the allegro, we sit in silence waiting for Madame to come out and call the names of those who made the cut. It's devastating that I can't hold on to Coupé for courage and luck, but it would be far too risky. But I'm able to imagine Mikhail—his full lips, his incredible fathomless eyes, his kindness, the touch of his hand, the feel of the back of his fingers gently stroking my cheek ...

And then Madame's voice: "Kira Egorova, Alina Feorova ..." My name is not there.

Panic rises in my chest like two dozen gnomes are trapped behind my rib cage, banging to get out.

Aha! She is calling names in alphabetical order, French style. The gnomes relax ever so slightly.

"Olga Ivanova ..." The gnomes again, *thump, thump, thump.*

"Polina Karpakova!"

When I hear my name, I hope my scream is on the inside. More than anything, I want to rush down those stairs and tell Mikhail.

But time will not allow.

The cuts are brutal, and those not chosen to dance the *adagio* are beyond devastated. There is more mucus and wailing from the dancers in the passage and the toilets than from wives on the quay watching their men go off to war.

Those who make the cut either preen or pacify friends packing their bags to leave the building. Likely this is the only time they'll ever use the back entrance. It pains me that while those stairs and that door take me to my bliss, others use it for disappointment and wounded pride so they might dodge the balletomanes.

I imagine my Mikhail watching the stream of rejections in

their human incarnations filing down spasmodically. I know his heart will be in his throat each time the great barricade—that is, the back door—opens.

It isn't the joy of making the cut but the thrill of telling Mikhail I did that keeps me floating on air.

Sitting with my legs in a shallow *V*, I check there is no one close by, then put Coupé down to stretch her little legs. She wiggles her way to a small knot in the wood of the wall between the passage and the studio. She peeps back at me as if to say, "Hey, come and see."

I lie down on my stomach and peer through the hole as she nestles under my neck and out of view. No one is watching. I am not important. Besides, there are girls in various positions limbering up. To keep up the pretense, and since I am already lying on my stomach, every few minutes I pull my head back and place my pointe shoe tips on the crown of my head. A common exercise to keep the spine pliable and a good reason to be lying on my stomach.

The rat's-eye view is the ideal angle from whence to watch the first two dancers' adagio.

Oh my! They are outstanding. They all resemble ballerinas.

They come and go, each as good as the last and better than expected. I feel old insecurities clamber from my satin-encased toes up, past my knees, my hips and settle in my stomach till I almost join the chunder parade in the bathroom. To distract myself from the competition, I think of the fleet of women who clean the toilets for us dancers. Only too happy are they to have a job. How spoiled we are, to firstly have inside toilets and, secondly, not to have to clean them ourselves. I feel dismally bad for those cleaning women with hordes of hurling young girls today. My stomach quietens as it always does when I become grateful.

But my heart continues to pound.

I move away from my viewing hole, pop Coupé back in my bag unobtrusively, then, to free my mind from spiraling into pessimism, I think of Mikhail, and my heartbeats change from frantic to intoxicated. He makes my heart waltz in three-four time.

I hear my name called and calmly reach into my bag, catch Coupé in my palms, kiss the top of her head, place her gently back and corkscrew up and into a standing position.

Then, pink satin toes in first position, arms in *bras bas*, shoulders back and down, chin up, I sashay into the audition hall at the same time as my competitor.

Behind the adjudicators, I see my Mikhail beaming with pride. I smile wider than my mouth knew how to before I met him and set out to impress his mirage. In position to start the adagio, but before the music plays, the hallucination that is Mikhail shows me what to do. Still smiling, I acknowledge each adjudicator with a tiny nod. No other dancer I'd observed from the peephole had done that. *Thank you, Mikhail, for giving me the courage to stand out.*

The piano begins, and so does my determination to give Mighty Thor the greatest performance he's ever witnessed. The reason, you see, is my Mikhail stands behind Vaclav's seat, and I aim to make his love for me ignite into a massive flame.

My toes must be three inches above the wooden floor because my feet are entirely unrestricted by gravity. I feel like a swirling, undulating morning mist, light and dewy and lyrical, driven by the need to show Mikhail I am worthy of his belief in me.

My arabesque extensions are greater than ever before; my newfound strength tightens my core and keeps my legs elevated a demisemiquaver beyond the piano notes. My pirouettes are lightning-quick as my head whips my body around because I don't want to lose more than a millisecond without Mikhail in my sights. I land clean because Mikhail's hands steady my body and hold me still as a statue to ensure I make a monumental impression.

In my head, the piano has accompaniments. An oboe, a flute, seven violins, a cello, a bass drum, cymbals and a penny whistle.

The music starts to ache.

I think of the travesty of Mikhail's missing leg and the loss of his aspirations. I mourn these calamities with every turn of my head, every tip of my finger, every pointe and leap as my elongated body moves to the tragic score. I convince myself this dance is magical and *if* I do it with all my heart, I'll heal Mikhail, bring back his leg and his career, if only I am good enough.

And so, I excel.

And when the adagio calls for the swans to react to Odette's pain and suffering, I realize it is not her tragic story I'm telling but my own. The impossible love between Mikhail and me.

The beggar and the ballerina.

When the music stops, the wooden floor seems to rise up to steady me, and I feel its solidity for the first time since I entered the room.

As I curtsy, the air from the downward movement rushes past my cheeks and confirms I am crying.

Crying for the impossibility of a happily-ever-after for The Ballerina and The Beggar.

I raise my head as I come up from my curtsy and hold it high.

Then, something quite, quite unexpected happens.

Three of the four adjudicators—yes, Thor himself leads the way—stand in the ultimate tribute to a performer, and they clap loudly in the silence as they smile and nod. Only at me.

It is my very first standing ovation.

I curtsy again in gratitude and seek out the eyes of each adjudicator and give a small nod of sublime thanks. I include the only one sitting, the prima ballerina. She refuses to meet my eyes.

There are two of us being auditioned in that room, but I am unaware of the other dancer. I know, beyond a shadow of a doubt, this ovation is for me and my Mikhail. Not anyone else.

Somehow, I make it out of the studio without running. Coupé is in the bag over my shoulder, but once in the passage, I grab Father's coat—no time for the boots—and rush down the stairs, perhaps a whole landing at one time, and there, of course, is Mikhail, standing on one leg and a crutch, waiting, waiting.

I can't stay—I could be called any minute—but I lean in, closer than we've been since last we stood together. I grab his upper arms and allow my soul to be swept through his gorgeous green eyes, and our quick breaths merge and dance, warming our faces ... our bodies. I long to touch his mouth with mine. No!

More.

Much more.

I wish him to fill my eager mouth with his tongue and promises of when our bodies can be one.

I want to have all of him inside me.

My body pulses at the same pace as his, and I push my hips toward his to reward myself with the feel of his excitement. I can barely get the words out between rapturous breaths ... but they have to come because words are all I can give him. All he can give me.

"I danced for you," I say at last.

CHAPTER 23

POLINA

Moscow, 1876

As I say the words, Mikhail uses his crutch to steady himself. He towers over me and bends his head to me. I love looking up at him and throw my head back to watch his beloved face on its slow, tantalizing descent towards my mouth.

His hands cradle my cheeks, and his head moves closer, closer, closer still.

My throbbing lips part as my body pulses with wanton thoughts in three-four time: *I want you. I want you.*

"Say it again, my Polina." His voice is but a whisper of longing.

My heart thumps. My insides quiver. My womanhood aches. My strong knees threaten to fail me.

Breathless, I say, "I danced for you, my Mikhail."

Achingly slowly, his beautiful head moves half an inch closer to mine.

My body tingles, and I wonder if it will explode with antic-ipation.

My core contracts, and butterflies take flight in my stomach, hitting the walls in celebration.

His eyes of striking emerald scorch mine with their inten-sity, but I'd rather be burned by them and scarred for life than never have felt their fire.

His head continues its slow passage, bringing with it the most beautiful lips in all of Russia. My stomach clenches.

And so do the muscles below.

My mouth, as if anticipating the most delicious dessert in all the world, begins to fill with saliva. I swallow, but it stays moist, hungry, as my body below my navel dances its own secret *allegro.*

Mikhail's luscious mouth is so close, I can feel his quick breaths, and I strain my neck longer than it's ever been in dance class. Please, I beg silently, let his lips reach me quickly, quickly, before I die of anticipation.

He slowly tilts my head with his hands still on my cheeks and cocks his head opposite to mine to make the delicious union of our mouths perfectly possible.

At last, his soft pillows touch my lips, tentatively at first, as if he is testing me ... tasting me. My mouth opens to receive his breath. I want to be a part of him. I want him to be a part of me.

And then his tongue touches my own briefly, and I give a little jump but cannot, will not, pull away. It feels so ... intimate. It is unexpected, but oh, how I want it.

Where has his tongue gone? But I am soon too surprised to wonder much because he's created a gentle suction between our mouths that further unites us and leaves me aching.

I lift my arms and run my fingers through his thick hair, and unbidden, my breasts push into him. I feel brazen. Wanton. I touch his tongue with my own.

An invitation so bold.

He answers with his own tender touch, and soon our tongues are dancing a passionate *adagio*. A slow, intricate exploration: a discovery, a question; an answer, an offer; a claim, all in perfect synchronicity. Our naked mouths dance to the promise of fulfilment while our bodies ache to join in.

He slowly removes his lips from mine but not his hands from my cheeks. He holds my head as if it were the most precious, priceless treasure in all the world.

He gazes at me so intently, I feel I want to cry.

Without taking my eyes off his, I lick my lips, wanting to recapture the taste of him.

As he reaches down to once more consume the swollen lips I offer, the sound of the back door whooshing open causes us both to jump. He pushes himself against the wall, and I bend down, as if I am examining a potential stone in my ballet shoe. *In the snow?* Logic has no place in guilty improvisation.

Out of the corner of my eye, I watch one of the dancers from St. Petersburg in street clothes, her ballet bag thrown haphazardly over her shoulder, and I feel for her. Her day has not gone well.

When she turns the corner, Mikhail braces himself against the wall and offers his hand to pull me back up and bends to kiss me tenderly, briefly on the lips.

"No luck for her, I see." His voice is sad, and I love him more because of it.

"But for the grace of God, there go I," I say before I squeeze his hand, grab Coupé and run back up to the studio.

I shiver with pleasure as I consider I last left this place a girl, and ten minutes later, I return, a woman.

CHAPTER 24

BRIE

Hull, present day

"Now I am the one who is jealous!" Lucky said, and I pushed my way through the haze of a century and more to join the others in the living room in Massachusetts.

I looked at Lucky, and she was all gooey. I smiled, feeling radiant. Sexy.

Boy! I hadn't felt sexy for decades. Not true. I felt sexy at the airport when my husband kissed me deeply. Passionately.

"You look like you're just about to have the Best Sex In The History Of The World!" Chantelle warbled, her voice deep and sultry.

BJ confirmed, "Lucky bitch!" and she burped. It still surprised me whenever the queen burped. I had to look around to confirm I wasn't back in the Villies where no effort whatsoever was made to hide the noises of body functions from others. Holy shit! I didn't even pass wind in front of Ryan.

Moxy did a slow pirouette. "And with all of us watching!"

"No ... no! Moxie, that was in your head. You little perve. We were just kissing."

"Just kissing, my arse," said Lucky. "That was some fore-play. Bring back The Kiss, I say. The Kiss is the sexiest thing about sex!"

Suddenly I felt passionately defensive about my dream persona or whoever I was in that other ...life? ... realm? "I was just kissing my true love outside in a Moscow alley." The absurdity of that statement tickled my funny bone, and I started to giggle.

And giggle. And giggle.

Chantelle joined in, as did Moxie. Lucky was next, and then BJ shrugged and joined in. We laughed so hard it hurt. There was a mad dash by three of us downstairs to fight over the two commodes. Chantelle beat out Lucky, who threatened to go in the sink, though I don't think she did. Even Tula disappeared through his doggy door.

When we gathered again, I announced, "Now will you girls just let me go all the way without further interruption?" I smiled at them just before I wafted blissfully back to 1877.

CHAPTER 25

POLINA

Moscow, early 1877

The choreography calls for sixty swans and fifteen swan understudies. Auditions have been held throughout Russia to find them.

The next day, Madame posts the list of dancers who will be in Swan Lake from her studio.

My eyes dart down the list as my heart thuds through my bag strapped over my body, and I know Coupé feels my every feel: Excitement. Fear. Anticipation. Dread.

Twenty-five of Madame's students are chosen as swans, three as swan understudies, and my name is not there.

Disappointment like I have never known slaps my face. Hard. I feel it redden with the blow.

If I hadn't done my absolute best, I would have expected rejection. But I had a standing ovati—

I see a third heading with one name.

It is mine.

I glance away and back again.

And another time.

Everybody is congratulating everybody else except me, but I pay no heed and simply grab my coat and bag and run down in a flurry of pink—satin shoes, tights, tulle and corset—my father's coat forgotten in my haste to tell Mikhail the news.

When I get to him, my excitement is such, I can barely breathe. He sits against the back wall, facing the small park that abuts Madame's studio. I guess he has chosen that spot because he has seen enough disappointment coming and going out of the back door for one day.

Seeing me, his face glows, and he takes off his jacket to cover my naked shoulders.

"I am not a swan ..." I begin, trying to catch my breath—something I have been taught never to lose. My body is trained to its zenith, my lungs have infinite capacity for leaps and turns and jumps, and yet here I am struggling. Mikhail takes both of my hands as I sit on my haunches facing him.

"Before you tell me, put down poor little Coupé and let her do her business," he chides.

I do, apologizing to her all the while for being so selfish.

I peep back at him, and his eyes are smiling.

"My Polina. I am not going anywhere. I am here to listen to your news and support you no matter what you heard today. And if it is bad news this time, next time it will be better news until it is the very best news it can be."

He increases the pressure of his touch, and I finally look beyond his eyes and into his soul, and only then can I find the words.

"I am not a swan," I spit out again.

His eyes turn from precious stone to faded moss. I feel his

sadness for me radiate out in waves of kindness to warm my heart.

Then I smile because it is cruel to rob him of even a second of the immense joy he deserves to share with me.

His face is a study of perplexity.

I use his hands to pull myself closer to him, over him, and I whisper, "I am one of four understudies for the prima ballerina herself!"

Pride lights up his eyes to iridescent green with a hint of blue, and he shouts so loud I am sure they can hear him in the secret rooms inside the Kremlin: "My ballerina will be Odette and Odile." His face glows as he throws back his head and howls like a wolf.

Though we are well out of sight and there is no reason for anyone to trudge to the back of Madame's building, I glance around, fearful someone will find us. But then I throw caution to the wind and throw my head back and howl with him.

He pulls his body away from me, still holding fast to my hands. "This means you are going to be a principal! A soloist!"

"No, no, no ... I am only an understudy. The principal will have to die or be ill or trampled by a horse for me to have a turn on the real stage as Odile and Odette. And there are three others with whom I must compete for that unlikely honor."

His eyes are the color of ancient sea glass. "My dove, I know you. Now you must unleash your own immense power to get exactly what you want. Never by foul means but by your sheer and undaunting determination."

I throw my head back and laugh, because only Mikhail would think the impossible and believe I have it in me to make it happen.

I can't help it. I throw my arms around his neck and allow my strong core to collapse as I fall onto him.

The heat of our close bodies makes our breaths quicken, and sitting on top of him, I feel the creamy heat of my root pulse through my corset as I straddle over his hardness. I unbutton his coat so I can feel him closer.

How is it possible I feel hotter with his coat open in this snow?

The heat inside of me, with the closeness of my Mikhail, is enough to set the world aflame.

I have the urge to move my hips around and around.

And I do.

I feel him thrust up to meet me, and I push down again harder. As his hips push me up, he grabs the back of my head and hungrily pulls my mouth to his. I answer with my hot tongue as we rock and grind rhythmically, and my nipples strain to be free to feel his chest against my tender flesh.

But his tongue reminds me, as we rub against each other, layers of cloth matter not at all, because in our minds our bodies are both naked. This body, which I can control to the last and tiniest muscle, is completely out of my domination.

And I love it.

And if Madame herself was glaring down at me in this state, I couldn't stop. I wouldn't stop. I am far, far beyond the point of no return. I feel my sex seeking out Mikhail's contained, straining hardness again and again.

A second away from that hard promise and I am lost. As my sex pushes in for a glorious moment and my body pulls it away just a fraction, I crave him far too much. So I thrust toward him again. And he is there. Strong. Waiting. Wanting.

And then my womanhood, in the deepest part of my being, she whom I have never known before, begins to tighten.

It's as if I've prepared for a pirouette with all my strength and I begin to turn on one leg. Slowly at first but then faster, faster, faster, until I can no longer spot and keep my balance, but I don't need to, because my womanhood is taut and turning all on her own ... faster, faster, tighter turns, tighter, tighter still, until my breaths are short and my need is bursting. I search for his tongue as I grind and force my sex down on him, again and again. Then the spring that my body has created is as tight as it can ever go, and it shoots open to release itself.

As my body convulses, I groan into his open mouth, and he thrusts his hips into mine and calls my full name like it's a prayer. He holds me tightly, while together our untamed bodies dance a staccato allegro.

We are one, long after our quivering bodies still.

The frenzied dance has exhausted us, but my spring quickly feels it needs to be wound up again, and my tongue begs him for more, but he gently pulls my head from away from his and gazes into my eyes. Then he turns his head and kisses me gently on each corner of my mouth.

But I am too hungry to be satisfied with "gently," and my body begs to be consumed. He smiles and pulls my head onto his shoulder, holding me still, his big hand cradling the back of my head as his other arm encircles my waist, and he rocks me tenderly.

It is then my tears begin to flow. Silently at first, but then they turn into sobs, and still he holds me tight until my tears are all spent.

Then he lifts my head and cups my face with his big, warm hands and says, "I am so very proud of you, my Polina."

Again, I weep.

This time because nobody since my father died has ever been proud of me.

CHAPTER 26

BRIE

Hull, present day

"Woweee!" Moxie's loud elation brought me back. She was like a Tibetan monk preparing for his rites again, so the "eeeeeee's" ebbed and flowed. "Best dry hump *ever!* That was far sexier than boring old in and out!"

"You nailed it, Moxie!" Lucky laughed at Moxie's graphic exclamation. "Your union, Polina-Brie, was enough to sweep away my cobwebs."

"Oh, that every girl's first time could be like that!" Chantelle crooned wistfully.

"That took me back in the best way," said BJ, who'd donned her blouse before my ... Polina's journey began and who now ripped it off again, exposing jungle boobs in leopard print as she positioned herself under the air-conditioning vent.

"That's not just a hot flash, is it?" Lucky asked with a wink.

"Hell no. It's a sex flush. Whew! Now remember that divine

encounter, Brie. You'll have the ability to drum up every single detail of that sexy union whenever you wish. Use it when you're not in the mood. Remembering that *divunch* dry hump will take you from indifference to ecstasy in no time at all." She'd brought up her fan, which she used in conjunction with the air conditioner, turning her body this way and that to be enveloped by the cool air.

"'Divunch,' now that's a word I'd long forgotten." Chantelle smiled. "No good-looking pax ever knew they were divine in our books even if they heard 'divunch'! What fun it was, having our own airline lingo."

The comments of the girls around me, as well-intentioned and sincere as they were, gave me far too much time to think. My heart sank. Like Polina, I knew nothing lasted forever. I broke the lapse into the airline years by declaring: "I hope against hope this ends happily, but I fear ..."

Lucky's voice was soothing. "Try and remember, Brie, no matter how bad yours and Mikhail's story might become—and it will, otherwise your soul would have no cause to remember this encounter—discovering that story will reveal what your subconscious has been keeping from you to protect you. But it's something you must learn in order to right the wrong or fix what's broken. It's bound to be traumatic, but we are here. This is your safe place. Come back to us when you need to, and if we see you are struggling, we'll pull you home."

Even knowing it couldn't last, I was eager to get back to Polina's life. I needed no more encouragement.

CHAPTER 27

POLINA

Moscow, 1877

Mikhail and I are both beyond excited that I will experience the Bolshoi stage. Of course, it is he who has great expectations that it will become my permanent platform.

Only we four understudies for Anna Sobeshchanskaya's Odette and Odile practice at the Bolshoi along with the prima ballerina, while all sixty swans and fifteen swan understudies practice at Madame's studio.

In spite of my love's undaunting confidence, there is little to no chance of my ever getting to dance on stage in front of a paying audience. But being an understudy for the soloist is a far greater privilege than being a swan, and it is enough validation for me, if not for my Mikhail. Thoughts of him make my mouth smile as an ode to my heart's tenderness.

There are no short breaks or lunch breaks that can afford me time with Mikhail. I am a mile or more away. How I miss him. And my beloved Coupé.

When he decided to shave for me, he came to an arrangement with the tailor close to Madame's studio. For a small fee, Mikhail can use the back entrance of the shop to wash and shave, and when the weather is bad beyond its usual inclement cold, he may sleep on a small cot in the broom closet instead of looking for a sheltered spot in an abandoned building or a wet drainpipe.

Mikhail cannot change his routine to find a new place closer to me. There is no loitering whatsoever allowed within a giant, six-block radius of the Bolshoi.

Madame's studio is on the verge of that perimeter.

The arrangement with the tailor is an unheard-of gesture toward a beggar, so Mikhail considers it a windfall. I do not want him to jeopardize this privilege. Besides, the closer to the Bolshoi, the snootier the shopkeepers and the less than little chance of duplicating his tailor's compassionate arrangement.

Nestling under his arm at the end of a long day, I say, "I am not in the least surprised the tailor agreed to give you refuge. Any fool can see and hear you are no beggar. You are a man of substance and breeding. You will be an asset to him, as you are to me."

I yearn to spill words of my love to him. But I hold back. Not because I am afraid he might not appreciate them, but I have never talked about love, not even with my father.

I don't know how to say the words because I've never heard them.

I gaze at him, and angst burns in my belly as I run my fingers over my Mikhail's handsome face. "Why do you wear such pallor, my Mikhail?" I hear the quiver of my voice and hope he doesn't. "Are you unwell?" I feel so guilty because I haven't noticed this before.

"I am better than I've been for a year because of you." He smiles tenderly and kisses me deeply, and all thoughts of my angst evaporate.

But on my way home I go via the botanical gardens, and in a greenhouse, I pluck some tavolga from a determined bush still flowering in the snow.

"What? You are no longer paid to dance and are forced to forage for food?" Mikhail's eyes are more blue than green as he beams at me. My heart lurches at seeing his joy at my return.

"Here, these are for you."

"What are they?

"Tavolga. Smell." I wave the white bushy flowers under his nose.

"Hmmm. Smells like honey."

"It has properties that will fix whatever ails you, and it's the only thing my mother ever taught me. It's good for gout and rheumatism and nausea and will reduce blood clots and more I cannot remember. Chew on it."

"Hmmm. Tastes like honey, too." He swallows and pulls me in for a honey-flavored kiss. "Ahhh, I feel like a blissful bee."

And, just to make sure I receive some of those healing properties, I kiss him again.

I pluck off a flower and offer it to Coupé. She nibbles on it as I scratch her behind the ears. "I want both the loves of my life to be well."

I catch sadness in Mikhail's eyes, but before I can air my concern, his smile erases it.

After my first grueling day at the Bolshoi, I knew there was no time to nurture my Coupé. That night, I handed over to Mikhail my prized possession. Besides my concern for her neglect, the thought of someone shooing her away like vermin breaks my heart. Though I felt like the worst friend in the world, I know Mikhail will care for her while I am dancing. It's kinder to her, but it hurts my heart. Selfishly, because I know she's company for Mikhail and he loves her as I do.

As I approach Madame's studio after a long day of dance, though the sky is dark, balletomanes and curiosity-seekers remain outside the studio in a twittering throng, in hopes of witnessing ballet greatness at close range. The coming and going of swans into Madame's studio keeps crowds ebbing and flowing and filling Mikhail's cup to overflowing.

Nobody recognizes me as a dancer when I trudge through the snow in my father's coat and boots. I have an armful of tavolga to keep my love well, but even with my overpowering fragrance, I am uninteresting to them. Just as well, because I can sneak unnoticed down the alley and to the back of Madame's building, where I wait for the two most precious to me.

As he rounds the small alley using his crutch, wending his slow way toward me, I drop my bag and run to substitute my shoulder for his crutch. It is a privilege to be upright and close to him and a delight to have my Coupé back in the crook of my arm.

We three could walk to St. Petersburg this way.

Mikhail surprises me. He's used his rubles to buy an old army tent and created a haven for us three at the back of the building, inside the dense trees where the park backs onto the studio's land. The little sanctuary is well hidden and perfect for our time together.

Inside it's dry, and he has lined the floor with dozens of newspapers and a thick blanket. Soon the little tent is heated by our bodies, and as we three nestle into each other, he asks about my day. I tell him how odd it is that the other understudies, not familiar with my background since they are from other cities, are warm and wonderful. There is no animosity between us.

Mikhail's love is unconditional and his joy at having Coupé as his co-conspirator all day are two generous gifts he gives me. In my whole life, I have never been happier. I want nothing more of my life.

"I've been thinking about the story of *Swan Lake*. It's so sad. Perhaps one day Tchaikovsky will write a score for us and Vaclav will create a ballet from our ill-fated love." Mikhail smiles sadly.

"Why should it be ill-fated?" A shard of invisible glass sticks into my heart.

"My Polina, how can it be anything else? You are a ballerina and I, a lowly beggar."

"You will never be lowly. What you are on the outside makes no difference to me. Why should it to you?"

"It may not now, but what about all the men with two legs who will pursue you after opening night? Oh, the privilege of being seen with an understudy to the prima ballerina for the most anticipated event on the Bolshoi calendar! You will have your pick of princes and sheiks, lords and kings."

"They are nothing to me. I want you."

"But how, my love, how?"

I am struck by him calling me his "love." It is the first time our shared intensity has been verbalized, though I knew it was so since the first minute when an electric cord joined our souls.

Tears fill my eyes. "It will always only be you for me, my Mikhail." I promise, but words will not convince him, so I tilt my head up and part my lips in invitation for his mouth to cover my own. Our kiss is deep with promise, and I hope his faith in us is restored.

He hugs me and kisses the tip of my nose. His smile can melt the snow around us for three square miles. "I am so proud of my eagle, so very proud."

"Anna is as strong as a bad-tempered ox." I smile. "So I will never know the feel of the stage with a real audience, but it *is* a privilege, and the work and intense attention of such acclaimed ballet masters challenges me. And the only reason I am at the Bolshoi at all is because of your faith in me, my Mikhail."

"I believe in you with all my heart," he whispers, then kisses my forehead.

Mikhail's face softens, and he finds my wonderful Coupé, picks her up and holds her in front of me so I can watch as he scratches her ears until she shows us her long front teeth in all their glory. "You had a good day with me, right, Coupé?" Giddy joy on the face of a white rat is our confirmation, and we giggle and sigh like two proud parents.

Mikhail wears only his pants, socks and a shirt. I shrug off my father's coat. It is warm in the tent now with three of us. Suddenly, Mikhail's lack of faith in our future attacks me like the plague. My life will never exclude Mikhail.

I turn around, wrapping my legs around Mikhail's hips, and place my arms around his neck so I can get lost in his beautiful eyes and then fall deeper and mesh with his soul. "I love our new haven. Thank you. I was thinking, once the ballet opens, if the earnings of an understudy are good, when I return to Moscow after the tour, I can get us a real place together, out of the snow."

I'm unprepared for what he does next. He moves my hands to the back of his neck and, with hands on my cheeks, he pulls my face toward him slowly until he captures my mouth with a kiss so deep, my every sense heats up to boiling. I feel his eager tongue is not only stirring every fiber of my being but reaching down, down, down ... all the way to my pulsing pelvis. It's as if his deliciously demanding self has penetrated my most private parts, and the velvet feeling becomes hot molasses pulsing from my very core—thick and sweet and impossible to stop. I smile as body parts, some of which I had never been aware of before him, respond in ways I could never have imagined.

My smile in the middle of such passion causes him to pull away from me ever so slightly, but I can't let him leave me. My body won't let him. I pull his head back down to my wanting, parted mouth.

It is indeed Mikhail who cools me down by cradling my head on his shoulder and whispering words that fondle my heart and soothe my raging body until it is limp, compliant and in my control once more.

I glance down, surprised we were still clothed. My mind had us naked with every part of our bodies joined, electrified and burning our way to a glorious, shuddering physical union ... at last.

His husky voice is soothing, loving.

Tones I've long forgotten.

I'm rich with gratitude that I am the recipient of such loving murmurs.

Mikhail is my man, and I am his woman. We are equals in every way: equal feelings, equal respect, equal desires, equal connection. I shudder, not from cold but from this paltry compromise to the release my body craves. Where does Mikhail find the strength to stop before consummating our love? I am so willing, so insistent, so engorged with passion.

"You, my Polina, are the light of my existence. I love you more than I would love my own life if I had two perfectly functioning legs and could be with anyone in the whole world. If it were up to me, I would marry you today and make love to you for eternity. But, my darling, you have a career. How many Russian women can say that? I will not let you squander all the years you have tortured your body to become a ballet dancer. I will not. I dare not. Not because I don't want you—I desire you more than I have ever desired anything—but because you will never forgive me if I make love to you and make you stay with me."

I quickly pull my head back and dive headfirst into those dancing green eyes. "I want to stay with you, Mikhail. I want it more than ballet, more than a career, more than ..."

"And I am old enough to know if you gave up your ballet passion for me, you would love me less. And if, because of my seed, your body becomes distended with child and you can no longer dance, you would hate me. I will never let that happen, my love."

At last, I can say it. "I love you, my Mikhail."

He pulls my mouth to his, but this time he kisses me as if I were made of delicate porcelain.

Oddly, I feel the taste of tears.

They are not my own.

CHAPTER 28

BRIE

Hull, present day

"So help me, Brie, if after all this exquisite love and tension and passion you have not met Mikhail in this life, I think I might ..." Chantelle pulled her intense stare from me, looked around, picked up someone's half-finished mimosa, chugged it and slammed it down as she stated finally, "drink myself stupid!"

"Too late," said BJ. "You're already there!"

Chantelle gave her a dirty look before she turned back to me. "Oh–my–God. What you share is pure utopia. The height of ecstasy without having sex." She sighed and added her odd hair fluff.

"We don't want to put the cart before the horse or, in this case, the reality before the dream, but a question, Brie. Tell us in one word whether you have found that again in this life," Lucky asked me.

"Holy shit. You think one word will do it? The answer is ... I always thought so, and I want it to be."

"Then that's why you're here. Why we're all here," said Lucky. "We need to find in this life that equality and passion, that divine unity that is not just sex but loyal, true friendship with our soulmates, just like our dreams showed us. All of us deserve to have this again."

I felt myself nodding until my head buzzed, and in the silence that followed Lucky's passionate insistence, there was quiet. Complete silence as we, no doubt, contemplated our current lots.

But I wanted more. I wanted to go back.

I was missing my Mikhail already.

CHAPTER 29

POLINA

Moscow, 1877

Entering the famous Bolshoi is a privilege I never thought I'd experience, not as a paying patron, let alone a cast member. I'm heady with the feel of fame for the first time though quite aware I have little chance of ever performing on that reverent stage for an audience.

We four mirror Anna's every balletic movement. She is indeed exquisite, and emulating her enhances my own artistic finesse.

She is difficult and demanding, and I vow never, ever to be like her, no matter how wonderful a dancer I might become. Her tantrums are monumental. The pianist fairly quivers and quakes in fear of her next flurry of fury. Vaclav handles her superbly, and Stanislav Gillert, as Prince Siegfried, does everything to appease and please her.

During my days at the Bolshoi, thoughts of my Mikhail and Coupé together warm my heart, and when I'm not thinking of them or watching the prima donna in action, I am focusing on ways to not just mimic Anna but to improve on her performance.

It is Mikhail's fault.

Gone is the girl who never aspired to do or be anything remarkable.

It isn't as if I am angling for Anna's lofty status as ballerina for *Swan Lake*. I am merely analyzing that special *je ne sais quoi* that makes her worthy. Then trying to better it.

Later I discuss with my Mikhail my plans to improve on Anna's acclaimed perfection, and I dream aloud of what I would do if I was dancing the part. I confess this experience has broadened my mind, and he smiles and nods as if he always knew it would.

Sharing the drama of my days at the grand Bolshoi in our little tent made for three keeps me grounded, and watching Mikhail beam with my stories makes our tent so bright, I think the sun has come out over Moscow in February.

Precious moments in our hidden haven with the two beings I love most in the world at the end of my long day are my reward for pushing my body beyond its limits every minute of every hour of every day, seven days a week. I feel I am the luckiest girl in all the world as we spoon into each other for warmth, comfort and closeness while Coupé runs over us until she finds a place to settle between us.

One night as he cuddles into my back, he whispers, "My Polina, you have long surpassed the most daring of eagles, and you are on your way to the stars."

I sit up abruptly. "No, no, no, Mikhail, I have no aspirations to oust Anna. I am merely learning from her, understanding what makes a prima ballerina. Besides, if I ever must replace her, I will lose my life."

Leaning on his elbow, his eyes widen in concern. "Lose your life?"

"Anna constantly warns us four understudies. 'You had better hope you never have to take my place. You will find your life is no longer your own.'"

He laughs and touches my cheek kindly. "Surely a turn of phrase, my love. She means she is so adored she lives to please her audience."

"Perhaps," I say, unsure.

"But that you have a desire to learn and understand means you are pirouetting?" His brow furrows, not sure his ballet term is correct. I nod, smiling. "Pirouetting your way towards the brightest object in the sky, Venus. Yes!" He hits his head with his hand. "Of course, you are not just a star. No! Not my Polina. You are Venus! You can't burn out because you're a substantial planet shining brighter than all the stars."

I rise up and give a deep curtsy, head bent to fit inside the tent. "Venus at your beck and call, my Mikhail." And he pulls at my hand until I am down and we face each other once more.

"'Venus' is a perfect name for you. You have become less like a wisp of exquisite air and more like a churning, twirling, fireball orbiting because of its passion to expel heat. I love you, my Venus." He leans in and captures my always-ready lips in his.

I could have lived the rest of my life seeing my love but-not-yet-my-lover in his little tent, sharing the events of my day with him, him sharing his with me, having Coupé almost doing somersaults because she has us both at the same time. I could have gone on forever, learning from a prima ballerina and enjoying the camaraderie of other dancers for the first time in my dancing career.

But life teaches us that on this earth, nothing is forever.

CHAPTER 30

POLINA

Moscow, 1877

"Do you still have tavolga?" I ask as I check under the blankets and a few layers of newspaper.

He takes my fingers and kisses the tips and smiles that beautiful smile. "My love, how could sickness or disease ever impair a body that houses a soul which loves as much as I love you? Being in a state of love is so good for my body, I think my handsome leg is growing back." He chuckles.

I refuse to laugh to illustrate my genuine concern. Strong arms encircle me and hold me tight as he whispers in my ear, "My pallor can only mean I will miss you today, as I missed you yesterday, as I will miss you every moment you are away from me. And yet knowing that you are soaring higher and higher makes me happier than you will ever know."

On my way to the Bolshoi, a newspaper page, caught by the wind, lands close enough for the front-page photograph to catch my eye. I pick up the soggy paper and glance at the date:

16 February 1877. My eyes move quickly down to the ballerina in full swan costume, dominating the page.

The headline shouts: "Prima Ballerina called 'Thief.'"

My eyes travel faster than my brain as I read the article. "Anna Sobeshchanskaya, prima ballerina of the much-anticipated ballet to Tchaikovsky's score, *Swan Lake*, was accused of thievery by a government official in Moscow last night. He made the following statement: 'Yes, it's true Anna Sobeshchanskaya was my mistress. And it's also true that I lavished her body with a fortune in jewels and trinkets. All the while, and unbeknown to me, she fraternized with a fellow danseur who she married just yesterday.'"

The reporter must have asked the question buzzing in my head because the article continued thus: "'No, not her male principal from *Swan Lake* but another soloist from the Bolshoi. She was caught selling my family jewels for cash last night. No doubt my family's heirloom cash was intended to feather her new love nest. She has not only disgraced herself by her wrongdoing, she has tarnished her art. I insist she be removed from the cast of *Swan Lake* immediately.'"

My blood runs Moscow-cold, and suddenly the icy air constricts my breathing. I take a deep breath, concentrating on forcing air down my tight throat. At last, air hits my lungs, and I cough as I exhale.

I have a vision of bad-tempered, irrepressible Anna murdering the meek pianist by stuffing music notes into his mouth and down his throat. She's threatened him thus more than once.

I stand outside our rehearsal studio with thick trepidation, not knowing what to expect. Oh, how I wish I could talk to Mikhail. He would know what I should expect, how I should act, but I am halfway to the Bolshoi and already late when the newspaper delivered its shocking message.

I'd lingered too long saying goodbye to Mikhail and Coupé. It would have been so easy to lie down in our tent, to curl up and feel Mikhail move his body to fit perfectly into mine. Two warm spoons in a small drawer, we'd lie there quite still, sharing our heat, letting our breaths catch up to each other so hearts could beat in unison as the universe intended.

But no ... my love reminded me the Bolshoi was equivalent to reaching something better than the stars—Venus—and not only reaching but *becoming* the light planet, and for his sake, I had to hurry.

So here I am. Alone. Without even Coupé to give me moral support. But then I hear Mikhail's voice in my ear. "Be brave, my Venus." And, head held high, I walk into the studio like a ballet dancer.

The atmosphere is heavy, as if a thick, chilly, miserable fog has swirled into the room and, finding itself trapped there, it's in a bubbling rage.

Vaclav's bulk is heaving with stress, like a laden goods train finding it impossible to leave the station. His hair stands on end from the number of times he's run his hands through it.

Siegfried—Stanislav Gillert—looks dazed and confused.

Three other Odette/Odiles stand, feet fidgeting, because they have no clue what ballet position such a catastrophe calls for.

My uncertainty and I join them.

The calmest person in the room is the pianist, who wears a small smile. I feel relieved he's alive.

Vaclav pulls himself up to his maximum height and breathes out, a steam engine's huffing release. With his distended middle and his wild hair, he's the epitome of a mad baker who's cooked a batch of pies ordered by the king but has eaten them all.

"Anna is no longer our principal dancer. A most unfortunate event so close to opening. As you know, my superstitious nature would not allow me to name any of you four understudies as secondary soloist. It would have been bad luck." He snorts, but instead of the sound of contempt or disgust he's been aiming for, out comes a donkey's bray.

I want to laugh. I have to tighten my core with all my might to stop my giggles from multiplying and spewing from my lips. I will be thrown out of *Swan Lake,* perhaps out of ballet itself, for life.

The only thought that quells my giggles is a vision of Mikhail's unusual pallidity lately, and I quickly sober.

"So, there will be no second soloist. There will only be a new principal dancer. A new ballerina." Vaclav eyes each of us, and I reckon he looks at the others much longer than me. I relax. The pressure is off.

"Polina Karpakova."

In a daze, I feel all eyes on me. Still my mind is blank because the possibility is so ridiculously *im*possible.

"Yes, you, Polina, are the new ballerina for *Swan Lake.*"

My muscular legs conk in at the knees. Wha ...?

I see my three counterparts swarm forward to embrace me, and I feel fleetingly sad that I am still too wary not to question their sincerity. Stanislav beams and moves forward, offering his hand in gentlemanly welcome.

Vaclav's face changes not a twitch, but the pianist smiles for all his worth.

CHAPTER 31

BRIE

Hull, present day

My stomach was knotted like a Jamaican braid when Moxie's loud exclamation brought me back to my friends sitting on the red and aqua suite in Hull.

"You've done it! You're the principal ballerina! And all because of Mikhail!" Moxie gleefully attempted to cartwheel, but furniture got in the way.

Chantelle and Lucky wiped their eyes. I smiled. They were proud of Polina.

BJ nodded like she knew it was coming.

Chantelle, my fairy godmother, said: "With Mikhail's help, yes. But it was Brie ... Polina who did it. She studied Anna and made what she did better. She took an opportunity and made the most of it."

"But it was Mikhail who gave her the confidence to do so," said BJ, and she was right. Mikhail, my beloved, was the hero of my story.

Lucky watched this debate with a wry grin. She was proud

as punch. I had the feeling this reunion was going better than she'd imagined.

"How do you feel, Brie?" Lucky's hazel eyes bored into my soul.

"Like I am about to dance *Swan Lake* as the principal ballerina and I am shit scared!"

"Don't be," Lucky said softly. "You know what to do. You've been trained. Mikhail believes in you. Vaclav believes in you. We believe in you. You believe in you. Nothing else matters."

And her soothing tone took me back to Moscow, 1877.

CHAPTER 32

POLINA

Moscow, 1877

So close to opening, long, long hours are spent rehearsing at the Bolshoi.

The Bolshoi has a bedroom with an indoor bathroom close by that is mine to use as I please. But at the end of an exhausting day, if I have an iota of strength, I walk the six blocks to be with my little family. The comfy bedroom cannot replace my Mikhail's touch and my Coupé's sweetness, and I don't sleep there because I am so lonely. But if I know in advance that a particularly bruising rehearsal is coming up, I pick enough tavolga to keep my Mikhail healthy in my absence.

As we get closer to opening night, I manage only every second night in our tent haven. We make the most of our time together. Mikhail understands. Coupé does not.

Rehearsals are grueling, and I have never danced with Stanislav before. We understudies rehearsed with Stanislav's understudies. Melding with anyone other than Mikhail makes me feel guilty. Like I'm being unfaithful.

I try because I know trusting someone else with my body will make my performance believable.

Vaclav screams at me to relax, to look at this man with love and tenderness, and I realize if I can't let go of my ridiculous guilt, I will lose the chance of a lifetime and disappoint my Mikhail.

Eight disastrous hours into our second rehearsal, I find the solution. During a fifteen-minute break, I run like the devil is chasing me to the botanical garden and I grab some tavolga.

Before we start our pas de deux, I corner and thrust some flowers into his hand. "What do you want me to do with this?" he asks, perplexed.

"Chew it," I command and prepare for my entrance from stage left.

As he picks me up, I smell honey, I smell tavolga, and voilà! Stanislav Gillert becomes my Mikhail.

As soon as I see the face I love so dearly instead of Gillert's perfectly pleasant one, we become a unit.

Instead of dread, I look forward to Mikhail's hands being there to catch me, lift me, turn me and balance me. If I half-close my eyes when we are entwined and tavolga's gentle scent engulfs me, I can convince myself, even close-up, that I am dancing with Mikhail.

The days shorten as opening night draws closer. I use the ache of longing for Mikhail and Coupé to portray Odette's tortured soul. It is indeed they who propel me as I turn flawless pirouettes and fouettés.

It is Mikhail who turns me from ballet dancer to ballerina in that rehearsal hall.

A whirlwind of dress rehearsals and photography sessions

ensue, and my time with my beloved man and my rodent best friend becomes shorter still.

I am sustained only by the make-believe world I've created, one where Stanislav wears not only Mikhail's face but his lithe body, strong arms and, of course, his breath. This illusion is fueled by my Mikhail having two legs so that we may meld together and spin and twirl and pull apart and back together as the music goads us, unencumbered by a wooden crutch.

Dancing with Mikhail keeps my feet off the floor and my heart etched on my face, and I know no Odette could ever love a Siegfried more than the one I've conjured up.

At rehearsals, after our duet, "my Mikhail" and I bring the company, orchestra and crew to tears. Vaclav and his cronies, sitting in the plush Bolshoi seats, never fail to give us a standing ovation. I hear it whispered that Anna would be green with envy if she saw my Odette "because it is so much more ethereal, more captivating than hers." Newspaper headlines confirm.

But the minute I can sneak out of the Bolshoi with only four hours between late-night rehearsal and early morning call, I do, by way of the botanical gardens, which are too far away for my Mikhail to walk to on one leg.

My heart pounds faster than it did after twenty pirouettes and a grueling allegro, and I run the many streets in sleet to the little tent hidden in the brush behind Madame's studio, where the two who matter most wait for me, no matter the hour.

And then it is opening night.

CHAPTER 33

POLINA

Bolshoi Theater, Moscow, April 26, 1887

Resin crunches under my toe shoes, one satin-tipped toe, then another, as the orchestra warms up. Butterflies in my stomach turn into hairy squirming caterpillars and back to butterflies.

The heavy velvet and brocade curtains hang in folds from three stories up, dropping in a dramatic waterfall that pools on Siberian larch floors. Even those weighted curtains swish now and then when bustling backstage crew, led by famous designer Karl Valts, follow Tchaikovsky's demand for realistic scenic effects.

Painted trees with real branches have been crafted for the storm scene. When the lake "floods" the stage, the boughs and branches break off and fall into the water and are swept away by the "waves."

Even in my wildest dreams I never imagined such lavish scenery and attention to detail for the backdrop: Synchronized swans are the backdrops for Odette and Siegfried. The realization that I—"Poor Polina"—am now Odette causes another bout of caterpillars to inhabit my flat, empty, abdominal cavity.

The six legs on my caterpillars become sixty and they weigh me down ... until Mikhail's words from last night tickle my ear.

"My love, you have indeed become Venus. And as I take in the night sky, even on a stormy night, I will see you blazing through. I will be watching you soar and shine from your divine energy and the sun's reflected rays, and my pride will lift you even higher off the stage than you can lift yourself."

How I wish he could see me perform. The least expensive Bolshoi theater tickets for opening night are equivalent to two years of a skilled artisan's salary.

Although I have tried to convince Mikhail to allow me to pay for his ticket, he will not hear of it, even though I explained I can take an advance on my soloist salary to do so. I have stopped offering because it seems to offend him.

And now it is opening night.

I sneak a peek between the heavy curtains. It's a full house. The six-tier auditorium has boxes with anterooms or small drawing rooms where patrons can entertain visitors from the stalls or neighboring boxes. The lettered boxes closest to the stage on both sides of the auditorium are reserved for the tsar and his entourage. Altogether the theater accommodates nearly two thousand, three hundred patrons.

The orchestra warms up below the stage. I limber up in the wings with the swans and my understudies. *My* understudies? The caterpillars and the butterflies are staging war games behind my ribs.

When the lilting happy note that introduces me to the audience sounds, I become Odette, and I think of the joy Mikhail brings me as I leap onto the stage from the wings. Filled with *joie de vivre* and desire, I dance with the peasants around the fountain in the square.

By Act II, when Odette meets Siegfried, I have each of those twenty-three hundred shoulders proudly sporting the head of my Mikhail wearing a friendly, well-trained white rat on his shoulder. And only then am I able to set those bewildered butterflies free.

For the duration of the first *Swan Lake* performance ever, it is I, Polina, and my Mikhail who love, lose, and then love forever as we move from this worldly plane to the next.

I see Stanislav only during our first curtsy and gasp in surprise. Then I take in the smell of sweat, feathers and face powder, of resin and wood, the sight of the elaborate set around me still echoing with the sounds of cascading water; the velvet curtains—thick as my thigh—pooling on the floor in front of the wings; the sea of now faceless heads below me and the *whoosh* of love, appreciation and awe coming from them ... directly to me.

I quickly discover euphoria is a heady game.

I am no longer a ballet dancer.

I am a ballerina.

I feel audience adoration like a quilt of the finest silk wrap around me, luxuriant and encompassing.

I did it, Papa. Your dreams and Mikhail's have come true.

A flaming torch ignites in my mind.

Becoming a ballerina must have been my dream too.

I pushed myself for sixteen years to be the best I can be.

And now I am.

I allow myself a long wallow in this surreal self-congratulation as the entire audience in the Bolshoi stands, shouts, claps, and beats the seats in front of them. They warned me to expect nothing more than dainty applause from this elegant, spoiled audience. But here we are, connected by raucous admiration and my greedy and unconditional acceptance of it.

When I come to, I'm shocked to realize I have been thinking only about myself and in doing so, the heads of twenty-three hundred Mikhails have been erased. I chastise myself for my lapse into such self-importance.

Panic sets in.

Blind, unyielding panic.

I want to flee, to run off that stage through the Bolshoi and on through the bone-chilling Moscow cold in my costume until I can burrow into my safe haven—a tiny, body-warmed tent beneath the park's trees.

I am surprised to feel a firm tug on my hand and look up to see Stanislav. He smiles at me and holds my hand tighter, then moves back to present me, his arm extended to the wild audience. I manage to stay with my right leg bent, foot pointed behind me, and hope my stilted smile remains plastered on my face before I drop my head in humble thanks.

Stripped of the veneer of vanity that had boosted me above all else, I am naked and vulnerable.

Vaclav joins us on stage to uproarious applause, and he pushes a bouquet bigger than Mikhail's living quarters into my arms. I kiss him on both cheeks, then bow my head graciously because the audience expects a modestly confident ballerina and Vaclav says nothing is more important than what the audience wants. Not what you want or need or desire. Only the audience decides how long you remain a ballerina.

When I lift my head, I see him.

I nearly drop the garden of flowers.

In the flesh, my Mikhail.

He wears a stately caftan, his hair combed back off his clean-shaven, beautiful face. He is more handsome than the handsomest man in all of great Russia. How did he manage it? He sits two rows behind the tsar's entourage, which take up half the gallery. He fits in easily amongst the opulence in this, the finest theater in all the land. I am so proud of him. He doesn't have a rat on his shoulder—Coupé is likely in his pocket—because Coupé has as much cause to be there as the tsar.

It is no illusion. My two beloveds sit in a coveted seat in the Bolshoi. They are as real as the roses in my arms.

I smile with my soul, and our eyes connect. I feel again that electric cord between us, sizzling, binding.

I am a hair away from dropping the rose garden and fleeing off stage, past the wings, down the steps so I might immerse myself into the masses with the unflinching assurance that Mikhail's cord will find me and his familiar, loving arms will hold me tight ...

And when Stanislav pulls me back by the hand so the great curtain can fall, I panic.

Gone. My Mikhail has been taken away.

Stanislav holds tight to my hand, as if he knows I long to run away.

Each time the curtain rises, I search for them—my family of two—but the audience is a blur of movement as ushers bustle people, at least the plebeians, out of the theater. The tsar and his party may stay as long as they like.

The last time the heavy velvet curtain rises in a whoosh in front of me, I see my Mikhail standing at the end of his aisle. His smile lights up the auditorium, and I want to shout, "All this is because of you, my love," but alas, he'd never hear me. And then an usher pushes him toward the exit.

Stanislav's hand is now a vice on my wrist as I watch, help-less, as my love, who must feel as reluctant as I to lose our visual connection, now has three burly ushers forcing him farther and farther from me. My heart aches and breaks as I watch him laboring on his crutch, trying to fight them off and stay turned to the stage so that our eyes might connect.

Oh, God.

He gets smaller and smaller as my heart is pulled from its cage of ribs. His now tiny head keeps trying to turn to look at me, but the bullies won't let him. And we are still forced to stand on stage, mostly for the pleasure of the tsar and his guests, who continue standing and clapping.

Though he is far away, I see Mikhail grasping the exit's frame with his strong hands, and for a second, he leans on it for support and smiles his dazzling smile for me and our cord vibrates, jostling every fiber of my being. We stay like that as long as we dare and at his own peril, until more burly ushers crowd around to force his exit into the cold.

I feel the cord being pulled as if Mikhail and I are in a tug-of-war.

Oh, God. How I want Mikhail to win. To pull me to his side, where I will stay forever. One night of being a ballerina is all we needed, he and I, to see how much our love was capable of.

The orchestra plays a last bar, and Vaclav, standing next to me, extends his arm toward the musicians. They bow. Then we on stage, Vaclav, Karl Valts, Stanislav and I, bow one last time, then remain a stoic tableau for the tsar and his party, porcelain dolls on a pedestal, until the whoosh of the heavy curtains cuts us off from the audience for the last time.

I toss my roses in a heap and run through the wings and out

the side stage door, letting it slam behind me. I am risking becoming an understudy once more, but I don't care a fig as I strain my neck to seek out my love. I believe I am still shocked that I have come to think myself so remarkable. In one single performance I degraded myself to the level of all the wolves in Madame's studio. Self-serving. Opinionated.

How I have shamed my papa. No matter how proud I just made him, thinking myself so important would make him growl from his grave. He was a gentleman by nature if not by breeding.

I don't care if I am ever on stage again.

I pray to the dance gods for another look at my handsome Mikhail.

I believe I no longer need an audience of twenty-three hundred; an audience of one will suit me just fine. I am too shattered to ponder how, without my earnings, we will survive. Not on his cup of coins. Not indefinitely in the little tent. But practicality is not the pressing issue, and love is a powerful driving force.

I use my elevated position on the landing to scan the faces behind the arches, making their way through the exit door.

I see him. My heart flutters and bursts. Just before he's tossed into the cold, Mikhail finds a gap, turns and smiles at me, crutch under his arm, hand over his heart.

I feel the tears then, pouring down my painted cheeks, and warm air behind me warns the door from the side stage has been opened. Vaclav pulls me back through the door and out of public view.

I try to pull away from him while he's turning the knob of the door so I might run after my love, my life ... but Vaclav grabs my arm roughly.

"Where do you think you're going?" It is not a question. It is a threat.

I glare at him, confused.

"You did well, Polina. I am very proud of you. But your life as you know it is over. Tonight, you became the property of Russia. Your accommodations are ready. They are superior, fit for a prima ballerina. You will be granted whatever you wish, except independence. We cannot stand the chance of losing another ballerina to scandal. Cossacks will guard you day and night. Call on them if you need anything."

"But what about my family?" I ask, hysterical now and making no reference to my mother but rather to my love and my best friend.

"As long as you are Bolshoi's prima ballerina, Polina, they will have to see you from the audience or in their dreams. And after ten days in the Bolshoi, we tour Russia, Europe, Asia."

I wonder if he can see my heart lying broken and bleeding in the wings, forever staining the Siberian larch floors.

CHAPTER 34

BRIE

Hull, present day

I was shaking so hard, it looked like I was having a fit.

Or so the hosties standing around me said.

On the inside, my body convulsed and heaved with the memory of Mikhail exiting from the theater. From my life.

Moxie, a roll of toilet paper under her arm, was oddly still as a statue. No sarcasm or Shakespearean insult out of BJ. Chantelle blasted her nose noisily into the middle of a long piece of toilet paper, the ends of which hung down her torso in equal parts, like a white flowy scarf. Her intention, it seemed, was to weep as long as I wept, and boy, did she come prepared. Lucky gazed with her intense stare through my eyes and into my soul.

I realized they were all waiting expectantly.

There could be no chickening out. Sharing was expected. It was why we were here.

I cleared my throat and remembered how it felt when I

woke up lying on the bottom middle bunk in the crew rest of ZS216 so long ago.

"I felt the world go black. I must have fainted in my dream, but in real life, I bolted upright on the middle bunk of that 747, breathing hard, sweating, heart pounding in my throat.

"Ballet lessons weren't a top priority in the caravan park in which I grew up. I knew no French ballet terms, and Russian was a mystery. Yet I knew I was Polina the Ballerina as surely as I knew I was 36,000 feet in the air."

All four retreated to their seats and sat dead still, sober as unbiased judges. Tula stood in front of me, his head resting on my knees. With beautiful blue eyes clouded with concern, he looked up at me. My heart softened, and I placed both hands lovingly on each side of his face. I whispered what I'd heard Lucky say to him when she thought no one was watching. "Thank you, Tula." And he lay down, his head on my foot.

"Oh, my God." Chantelle's eyes were as big as twin ostrich eggs. "So, what happened then?" She growled, fluffed her dark curls from back to front and gave her odd little head shake.

"Well, it was most peculiar," I said, recalling that flight. "I had three-*D* pounding in my head. It was repeating like a stutter. Three-*D*-three-*D*-three-*D*. I had not the vaguest clue what it was all about, but it pushed through Polina's sadness, which was still hovering over me.

"I went to the loo and remember looking at myself in the mirror to the left of the tiny stainless-steel toilet. It was Polina's face I saw in the mirror, but she faded as quickly as she'd appeared, and it was a lemon-meringue-pie-short-of-plump-Brie who stared back.

"I sat on the closed steel lid for a minute." I let myself gather my thoughts as I had then. I looked up and asked in a dull voice,

"Do you remember that feeling after a crew rest sleep? Your skin felt like sandpaper, your mouth tasted foul, and you had to unclump your eyelashes, brush your teeth till they hurt, then plaster on more mascara in an attempt to look fresh before serving breakfast?"

They nodded sagely. Overseas flights killed normal sleep. Killed regular bowel movements. Killed the fresh glow of youth, even at twenty-three and a half.

I continued, "With every cup of tea and coffee I served, three-*D* pounded in my head. A mantra I didn't understand after my Russian immersion ..."

"Oh! and those scrambled eggs that'd been prepared two days before and stored in a trolley in the cooler." Moxie shuddered. "I can still smell them."

"Oh, you girls are such wimps." BJ smiled sardonically.

"And what exactly were *you* serving in first class, Queen BJ?" Chantelle asked in her old smoker's tone.

BJ studied her fingernails, which was an act because hers were a no-fuss short and colorless. "Smoked, hand-caught salmon, avocado fresh from Mauritius, freshly baked baguettes, French champagne ..."

"Oh, shut up, Queen!" Moxie said with feigned annoyance, and we all laughed. "You were the only one of us five who was a senior hostie."

"And don't you forget it." BJ's pointy chin lifted to assume a mighty air. "When you've got it, you've got IT!"

"Go on, Brie," Lucky urged, fearful I'd lose momentum, but there was little chance of that. It was as if I had just stepped out of Polina's skin. That feeling was going to live with me for quite some time.

"Remember how many people used to ask for liquor for

breakfast? I think that's what started my loving but respectful relationship with booze," Moxie reminisced.

"Doesn't look all that respectful to me." BJ raised her eyebrow.

"I am on holiday! Translated for you pseudo-Yanks, that's 'vacation.'" Moxie's sarcasm was ignored.

"Drinks were free on board in our day and available twenty-four seven," Chantelle said. "No time wasn't a good time for free booze."

"Especially if they were dreading what they were arriving into," I chimed in.

"Or they were piss-cats," Lucky said, matter-of-factly.

"Or they had to drink so as not to remember what they did with the strangers beside them the night before," BJ drawled.

Lucky urged again, trying desperately to herd us cats. "Let Brie do her thing here, ladies. Let's get back to the real life on the 747 after the dream."

She had a knack, did our hostess, of being able to take me wherever she wanted me to go. I was back on that 747 in a millisecond. "A little boy in my section had been nagging and nagging to see the cockpit, so after breakfast, I called the captain from my jump seat and asked permission to take the boy up to them. I took the six-year-old's hand, and we dodged the people standing in the aisles waiting to do their morning ablutions."

We all groaned. Except BJ. Of course. When you were a senior hostie working first class, your memory of the plebes in economy was quickly obliterated by all the elegance, class and celebrities you rubbed shoulders with.

"We wove to the cockpit, where I delivered the excited boy to the bored cockpit crew. I watched for a minute as they made an effort to entertain the little guy, then started back to my station. The first officer would call me at my jump seat when they were done entertaining him. But five steps up the aisle, the heels of my cabin shoes seemed to have super-glued themselves to the carpet. I couldn't move. It was so odd. I looked up for no particular reason and saw the seat number '3D.'

"My face flushed as my brain picked up the three-*D*-three-*D*-three-*D* beats where they had left off, and through the haze I heard, 'Are you okay, miss?'

"The voice. I knew that voice. I knew it as well as I knew the sound of my pet white rat who squealed with glee when I got home from a trip."

"Wait!" It was Chantelle's gravelly shout. "You had a pet white rat outside of your dream?"

"Yes, loved her. Got Elvis from the pet shop, and two weeks later 'he' had babies and hid them all over my tiny flat—in my pillowcase, under the couch cushions, everywhere. I managed to find them all before I squashed them, and when they were old enough, I donated them back to the pet shop and made them sign a promissory note not to sell them as snake food. Elvis was my friend."

"Oh lordy lord ... she has a rat," Chantelle growled, almost angrily, maybe because it negated the uniqueness of Polina.

I was about to defend my pet choice when Moxie chimed in. "Perhaps she remembered Coupé so fondly, she had to get a white rat in this life."

BJ clapped her hands slowly. "My, my. Aren't we showing a much deeper soul, Moxie."

"I am not a naive new soul," whined Moxie. "I've been around."

"You have," BJ said, "but not many times. And right now, you have to wait. It's not your turn."

"Girls!" Lucky admonished. "Then what, Brie? What happened after a voice asked you if you were okay?"

"I knew the voice. More than that, my soul knew it."

That did it! They were all schtum. Not a breath was heard. All eyes were on me. Even Tula had lifted his head to hear more.

"I gazed down at the man looking up at me. His eyes were the kind of green you only see once in your life or maybe once in *each* life. Wait! Did I actually say that?"

Nobody found a smart-ass retort.

"Then?" Lucky asked softly.

"I honestly don't know how long I did that thing ... you know, when both eyes gaze into one eye then the other, back and forth? Seriously, one dive into those divine green orbs and I wasn't going anywhere. I felt like I'd found my home. And that's something I had no clue about, because my young life was a dysfunctional disaster, never a home. But those fathomless eyes made me feel peaceful. Protected. Protective. Loved. In love. It was all so crazy.

"I felt my apron being pulled, and the little boy was standing just behind me, having been released from the cockpit. I felt enormous disappointment. The spell was broken. But before I walked him back to his seat, I had the guts to ask green-eyes, 'Is your name perhaps Mikhail?'

"He laughed, a beautiful, resonant sound, and said, 'No. I'm Ryan Sekula.' He shoved out his hand, I took it, and we shook. I remember thinking my hand fitted perfectly into his. Lost pieces of a centuries-old jigsaw puzzle. I never wanted to let it go. But the little boy was anxious to tell his mom about his best day ever."

"Oh my gosh, please, please don't tell me you never saw him

again," Chantelle groaned, lifting her long, dangly piece of toilet paper up as a buffer in case of bad news.

Lovely Chantelle was referring to my meeting with 3D Ryan on ZS216 immediately after the dream, not thirty years later, having just dropped me off at the airport.

But unbeknownst to her, I was thinking about *just* that. What if Ryan had thought it over and concluded he *could* live without me? The shock of that possibility slapped me silly. I was so vain, it seemed, the thought never entered my mind. Now it did, and the prospect of never seeing Ryan again heralded a wave of emotions so raw, I likened it to watching Mikhail being forced to leave the Bolshoi theater. My heart shattered afresh.

I couldn't help myself. I hadn't cried like that since ... well, not for the longest time. I felt so empty without my Mikhail. And what if I had to live the rest of my life without Ryan?

I knew, beyond a shadow of a doubt, these two amazing men were one and the same. And it would indeed be a tit for tat if fate chose to give me a taste of my own medicine and this time Ryan would leave me.

Chants handed me reams of toilet paper, which I used liberally.

I announced between sobs, as shame pulsed off my cheeks, "Oh, God. I was so full of myself the last time I saw my husband. So confident was I that I had the upper hand because for once, I had a mission. I was the one who was leaving, and it was he who was left behind. Lonely and aching. I berated the man I love similarly to the way I had berated Mikhail. Neither of them deserved my disappointment."

The girls were gathered around me. Lucky had a hand on

my head; Moxie had her arm around me; Chants held my hand, and BJ bent down so she could look me in the eye.

"Brie, you are not perfect. Thank God! I was beginning to believe ..." BJ's mild sarcasm softened like butter in a microwave when she smiled at me. "You screwed up. May I say I am quite relieved you're human. Because, by George, you're too good to be true. Inside and out!"

I hiccupped as I looked at her, then grinned, simultaneously wiping my nose.

Hearing I was okay, it was literally hands off, and I took that as a sign my friends knew I was going to be all right.

"I think this revelation calls for a drink," Lucky announced. I wanted to say that it didn't take much to call for a drink in this house, but I held back. Seems I was finally learning from my own mistakes.

CHAPTER 35

BRIE

Hull, present day

Having pulled myself together, I helped Moxie fix more drinks. I had my usual coffee, and I brought some of the South African delights to the living room so we could snack. By the looks of the size of them, I was the chief snacker at this shindig.

Dusk was threatening to turn into night, and every massive window or sliding glass door had a different hue. To the east, the sky was ink-black, to the west an ombre starting with mauve and purple and ending in a velvet violet. A veritable smorgasbord of color.

No sooner had we nestled into our places when BJ chided, "Okay, young lady." She glared at me. "I can't wait much longer for the next installment. Besides, you never told us who you berated at the airport just a couple of days ago. We have no idea if it was that dish in 3D you landed up with."

Chantelle prompted, "He said, 'I'm Ryan Sekula,' and you were shaking hands."

"Well, I managed to get out 'I'm Brie Lenz' before the eager little boy tugged hard enough on my apron to loosen the glue under my soles. I delivered the little tyke back to his mother, my heart racing, and then the seat belt lights went on. You know how that went. Our chores began in earnest.

"When we landed in Madrid and we crew were picked up on the tarmac by a bus and fast-tracked through customs, my eyes were darting around frantically, but I never saw him at the airport.

"I hoped against hope he'd find out which downtown hotel we Air B crew stayed in, but not a single note was delivered to the Euro Building in the ten days we were there. I felt ridiculously alone after the fleeting encounter. I turned down all the crew's invitations for nights on the town. I felt so lost. Feelings I had thought the airline had quelled. All I wanted was to go home to Elvis."

Now, I saw my desperation, desolation and disappointment reflected on the faces of those around me. They were living my life with me, so many years later.

Profound gratitude for them infused my being, and my heart swelled with the feeling of inclusion as I continued: "It had been nearly a month since we'd locked eyes ... souls ... whatever it was, and just when all expectations were lost, I checked my mailbox at cabin services. A letter."

Moxie sat bolt upright, then leaned so far forward on the chair, I thought she would flip into a headstand. Instead, she said, "Praise the Lord!"

"'Brie,' it read. 'I hope you remember me. I was in 3D on the flight to Madrid on the fourth November. My name is Ryan

Sekula. I know girls like you don't ever call guys—it should be the other way round—but I am at a loss as to how to reach you. Cabin services are understandably protective of their crew. Silly as it sounds, I feel we have centuries in common, and I would love to see if we can explore a new century together, maybe one day at a time? Here's my number, in case."

"Oh, my lordy, lordy." BJ had a wicked smile curling up the edges of her lips. "If nothing else, an outstanding pickup line ... 'centuries in common.'"

"You got that right." A hint of her ever-present laughter edged Chantelle's rumble.

Moxie jumped up and down like an impatient three-year-old. It was astounding, but on Moxie, "impish" worked. "What then? What happened then? Don't stop, Brie, I beg you." She pouted and bounced, causing Tula to leave his protective spot next to me. He hunkered down, ready to pounce playfully on this strange Energizer bunny who'd invaded his house.

"Pour the woman a drink, for God's sake," BJ said, handing her own glass to Chantelle, who poured a hefty shot of tequila and passed the glass to Moxie. The little sprite knocked back the spirits and settled on the couch, feet under her body like an alert Pomeranian.

"Not her," BJ chided and pointed at me. "Her."

Moxie was unfazed and unfolded her legs from under her body and did the honors. I put the shot glass to my lips to much applause, then wondered if they noticed I swallowed nary a drop.

Pretending I had sustained liquid courage, I carried on. In truth, it was an absolute joy to share *anything* with these excited participants.

"So, I called him. Who couldn't? Who wouldn't? I felt so

comfortable, I let him pick me up at my flat. One look into his green eyes and I was done for, and, if that wasn't enough, when I went to fetch my jacket in the bedroom, I came out and Elvis was out of her cage. He held her tenderly in both hands at eye level, talking to her under his breath. Swear my dream came back to me, and instead of Ryan and Elvis, there stood Mikhail balancing on his crutch and holding Coupé up so they could look each other in the eyes.

"He and Elvis were both smiling so wide, their mutual admiration enveloped me. Love my rat, love me. I think that was the moment I fell in love."

"Please, please, please tell me you, Elvis and Ryan Sekula lived happily ever after," Chantelle and Moxie begged, each adding pieces of the sentence and ending in uproarious laughter.

"Yes, yes, happy we were; we still are, really. Except, of course, when Elvis died. I was devastated. I loved Elvis first and much, much more than those who others call 'family.' Those who I'd run away from as fast as my short legs could carry me. Ryan and Elvis were my only family, and then one of them was gone." I continued quickly, "And then our beautiful Maggie was born." I consciously refrained from touching my locket because I felt Lucky's eyes burning into the suprasternal notch at the base of my throat where my gold heart nestled. She was waiting for it and I couldn't ... I just couldn't.

"Even though you tell us you're happy, why is it I don't feel you're living your best life?" BJ asked quietly.

In the silence, I felt a lifetime of a long-suppressed self-pity thwack me in the chest. "Ryan has an important career. When I met him, he was director of PACT."

"I remember PACT ... Performing Arts of Cape Town, right?" Lucky asked, and I nodded.

"Is he a lot older than you?" Chantelle asked.

"Ten years. He wanted children, and honestly, I'd spent years trying to erase my own childhood. I didn't want to be responsible for messing up someone else's. But I did want to make Ryan happy, so we endured a great deal before Maggie was conceived quite naturally." I think I may have grinned right then.

"How bad was your childhood, Brie?" Lucky's voice was so soft, I guessed it was in case I chose to ignore her question. But I was done with secrets. Done with suppression. Done.

"We were dirt-poor. You remember the really lousy area of Kempton Park, next to the train tracks, that had a run-down caravan park where all the 'white trash' lived?"

Two out of four heads nodded.

"Well, that's what I called home. My mother was unwed, which would have been the kiss of social death had she lived two miles away, but in that park, it was the norm. I was a nuisance to her. A noose around her neck. I was passed around the park from earliest memory. Kind of a nobody's child. A librarian became my mentor, and she organized a uniform and shoes. I was nine when I started school, but thanks to Miss Palmadesso, I knew how to read and write. She urged me to become a voracious reader. Reading was my only happy place. Real life sucked big. I couldn't have any friends in case they'd see where I lived. I was lonely in the park and out of it.

"The thing I could do really well was numbers. I was a whiz with figures. My angel, Miss Palmadesso, organized a job, a room close to campus and a bookkeeping scholarship for me.

"After college, I worked for United Building Society in

Benoni, and a pilot from Air Baobab came in to open an account for his baby boy. He said, 'You're too pretty to crunch numbers all day. Don't you want to see the world?' I laughed at him. What a preposterous thought. I had never even seen the ocean four hundred miles away. The world?

"He was charming but had no designs on me. He loved his airline. And he was a decent, dapper man in a blue uniform with wings pinned to his chest who thought I was worthy of the most glamorous job in the world. Oh, to fly on an airplane ... to be an ambassador for South Africa? He was delusional. I would never qualify.

"He came back every month to try and convince me to apply. He dropped the air hostess application form in the third month. In the sixth month, I applied.

"Then the strict medical tests and the IQ tests. After that, the grueling four-person-at-one-long-table interview with all of them asking political and religious questions to see how we could sidestep them. They were officious and unsmiling as they asked us to point out geographic locations of major cities world-wide on the huge map they had under the glass. All so they could see if we were geographically astute, but more important, we were close enough for them to inspect our nails and our pores. Their eyes bored into mine so deeply, I thought they could see my background. I never thought I'd make it."

My new-old friends all nodded, clucked or both. They'd all been there, done that.

"The wait for that official letter to let you know if you were accepted was grueling, wasn't it? And when the telling envelope arrived carrying incredible news, there was no one to celebrate with. Wait! I lie! Miss Palmadesso could not have been happier for me. How I loved her.

"Miraculously, I didn't feel alone when I joined the other recruits for *ab initio* training. I thought I had died and gone to heaven or at least a very, very expensive finishing school. I was not brought up with niceties or good manners, but I'd learned by watching others outside the park. Miss Palmadesso taught me well too. So when our instruction included how to apply makeup, to execute deportment, what wines paired with what food, I felt I was watching myself in a movie. Life had never been so exciting. And for the first time, I belonged. I was equal to everyone else. It was a wonderful feeling. We were all jumping out of emergency exits and sliding down chutes. We were all fighting fires; we were all giving mouth-to-mouth to flesh-colored dummies in gingham dresses to earn our first aid badges and studying midwifery in case of an on-board delivery. We were all nailing how to converse in a third language. I was in heaven."

I glanced at the girls around me, each one lost in a dreamy haze of those initial months, where we were submerged in the intoxicating world of airline life and the tantalizing promise of exotic adventures.

I continued. I couldn't help it. I needed to talk. To relive those amazing early months that became my real life in the glamorous world that was Air Baobab.

"And all the crews were seldom anything but super-nice and stayed nice because we were all in this together, spending a few crazy, fun-filled days in each new city. Every trip was different, and mostly the crew were too. There were so many of us in our bustling worldwide playground."

I paused to watch Lucky and Moxie make Tia Maria coffees, and Chantelle helped pass them out. Lucky made me a virgin coffee with cream in the same fancy glass so I didn't feel left out.

The cream tickled my nose as I sipped, and then there was silence. I felt all eyes on me as the girls waited with bated breath for the rest of my story.

"Permanence was the last thing I needed. I felt I'd been caged by circumstance all my life. The only constant I craved was finding Elvis alive and well after a flight. Thanks to the girl next door, who fed her and played with her while I was away, she was cared for and happy. I treasured the feeling of someone waiting longingly for my return. When I was home, I spent all my time with her. No non-airline friends. Certainly no boyfriend. Everyone else was just passing through. We were nomads in uniform. Nomads with strict rules. Nomads with fabulous places to stay and money to spend. It was utopia.

"We were bused to gorgeous accommodations and a room all to ourselves in a magnificent hotel. We had a generous meal allowance, and food was never on the menu. We'd share a Carnegie Reuben sandwich between four of us and see two Broadway shows; feast on tapas and visit the Prada or tour Toledo; pig out on shrimp from an outdoor barbie and spend the day cycling on Rottnest Island, nineteen kilometers off Perth. We'd dine on peri-peri chicken and visit the gate of Lisbon; munch croquettes as we toured the waterways of Amsterdam. Skate on the lake in Frankfurt before we drank glühwein and bought knickknacks from vendors at the outdoor, snow-covered Christmas market. Nosh on baby food we smuggled off the plane so we could have portraits sketched in Montmartre and see Bob Dylan in concert. I had never been so rich in experiences and in cash. I'd never been so popular. So included. Nobody cared about my past. Life was gloriously uncomplicated."

Quiet blanketed the room, warm, comforting and surreal.

Lucky said, "It was the best and only time of my life when I could live in the moment. New crew, new city, new adventures. No regrets. No worries about tomorrow."

We could all have basked in the bliss of those days of minimal commitment and obligation, but Lucky brought the conversation back to me.

"Brie. Tell us about you and Ryan."

Chapter 36

Brie

Hull, present day

"Where do you live now?" Lucky asked me.

"Ryan works for the S.A. Broadcasting Corporation, and we live in Rosebank on the golf course. It's a long, long way from the caravan park in Kempton." I smiled, hoping they felt my sincere gratitude.

"What do you do?" Lucky asked.

"Me?" I asked ridiculously. Could I say "Nothing?" It sure was better than anything else I had to offer. I got out: "I do the books for Ryan's sister, who owns an exotic pet shop." I glanced around. Everyone was looking at me, heads cocked, as if waiting for another pearl to drop. I took an unladylike glug of the virgin coffee, and Chantelle pushed the bottle of Tia Maria toward me. In a rush, I poured the dark molasses-like liqueur through the fluffy cream, took a long sip and continued, "Frankly, I don't do much but worry that Ryan will leave me."

Silence.

"Why?" Lucky asked, incredulous. "Fine, we've all gained a few pounds since those ridiculously skinny airline requirements, but you, girl, are as sweet as a lamb, and your beauty even at fiftysomething is nothing short of spectacular."

I took another long sip. "I wake up every morning worrying he won't come home."

"What makes you feel that way?" BJ asked.

"I honestly don't know. He is attentive and loving. And we have a satisfying intimate relationship, not as often as I'd like, but ..."

"Spill," insisted our little Moxie, wiggling away. She tickled me pink. I wanted to pat her. But this pert, adorable Pomeranian was likely to bite.

"There's nothing sordid or unusual," I said, glancing pointedly at Moxie, who was clearly disappointed. "I know he really loves me, and I love him more than anything. He's surrounded by beautiful, interesting women all day. I have visions of long legs, flat abs and witty retorts, none of which I can give him. I am so scared he will find I'm not enough for him"—I felt my hands running down either side of my body—"or I'm too much for him."

Tears spilled suddenly from my eyes. Holy shit! I was making a habit of this crying thing.

Chantelle leaned over and handed me a wad of Charmin. I took it gratefully and blew my nose. I was surprised to look up and see our tough little nut Moxie's eyes pooling with tears. Yes! I knew it. Her bark was definitely worse than her bite. I took pleasure in pushing the loo roll across the coffee table toward her.

Lucky said, "Girls, the weather is going to get wicked and angry in a day or so. Let's make the most of this relative calm before the storm. I'll switch on the hot tub, so grab your costumes." BJ darted one arched eyebrow at our hostess. I remembered her legend included that she'd been born in the USA and her father was a US ambassador. The family lived in South Africa for years. Americans thought "costumes" were only worn on Halloween or the stage.

Lucky read my mind. "Grab your *swimsuits*, for those of us who no longer speak South African."

"Can I submerge myself naked?" asked the Pom innocently. "I never brought a suit."

"Hell, no, Moxie." Chantelle's bark made the little pixie jump, but it was soon followed by the country-crooner-crackled cackle I'd come to look forward to.

"Wear your bra and pants, for God's sake," BJ said matter-of-factly, and Moxie was about to go into how she loved to go commando when I felt I should save the day.

"I've got spares," I said, but a vision of Moxie in one of my suits made me giggle.

"Of *course* you do," BJ said, referring of course to my way-bigger-than-anyone-else's suitcase.

CHAPTER 37

BRIE

Hull, present day

Moxie and I attacked Lucky's wardrobe by her invitation and settled on a couple of her knee-length winter dressing gowns that fitted us two shorties like full-length coats. Chantelle had on a pair of gym shorts and a bra, and BJ and Lucky wore suits. Under the gown, Moxie sported sexy underwear and looked holy-shit-sensational.

"When you packed for six days with four women, who the hell did you think you would impress with all that frilly lace?" BJ scowled.

"You *never* know." Moxie batted her lashes coquettishly as BJ lifted an eyebrow.

We found our spots on the built-in seats and let the water lift our limbs sans resistance, so a tangle of feet and a flotation of arms bobbed between luminescent bubbles. Tula sat behind Lucky on the expansive wooden deck that spanned the full front of the house. The only male in the house was on high alert, sniffing the air and looking hither and thither for any unwelcome intrusions.

The view was stupendous.

"This is pure bliss," Chantelle started. Mine and the rest of the raves followed.

Any body part north of the warm, aqua-colored bubbles could have been downright chilly, but our veins were quickly warmed by fresh mugs of steaming Tia Maria coffee, topped with cream, in easy reach on small tables dotted outside the tub. Even I indulged. Surely, these coffees didn't qualify as liquor? They were way too delicious. Oh, what the hell. I couldn't do any harm floating amongst friends.

But this was my last. I would never again succumb to alcohol's anesthesia. I wanted to feel every single feel—shattering or uplifting. That was real life. The real life I'd missed under Ryan's cushy protection and my pledge to keep from exposing my true self to Ryan. Even to myself.

"Your bar skills impress the hell out of me," BJ said to Moxie, emerging from her cream-topped cup with a white nose. She lost no time before her tongue snaked out to snag it. I smiled to mask my keen observations of our de-crowned queen. For her own reasons, BJ was afraid of alcohol too. There it was, quietly taking down her guard. Good or bad. It was hard to tell. But she was a big girl and knew what she was doing. I vowed to stop worrying about BJ, who'd now become vulnerable under my watchful eye.

Vulnerability, I'd discovered firsthand, could be a healer.

"She is exactly what the doctor ordered, I agree. Thank goodness we don't have to rely on the lazy owner of this sky-pad to deliver much of anything. Moxie's got it!" Lucky made liking her easy. She was comfortable in her self-deprecating skin. I thought it made her all the more alluring. "Where the hell are *your* lumps and bumps, Moxie? Don't you know we're middle-aged and our flesh is tired?" Lucky blurted.

"Bitch hasn't even had plastic surgery," BJ noted.

"How'd you know?" asked Chantelle.

"I asked," BJ said.

"Well, talk about me like I'm not sharing this hot tub, why don't you." Moxie laughed as did we all, giving our bodies up freely to the bubbling buoyancy of the water.

I watched Moxie and realized it was impossible to despise her cuteness and tight body. She owned her taut self, just as she owned her constant movement, and there was nothing stronger than a woman who knew herself and made no apologies. I surprised myself by really liking the woman who used me decades before.

The night was starry, but the wind had picked up and occasionally howled like a lonely wolf. The lights of Boston diminished the stars to the west of where we languished, but to the east, light was gifted by the moon and night sky, and the vast ocean was dotted with dimly lit fishing trawlers swaying in Atlantic swells.

"We're in paradise." BJ lifted her steaming mug to Lucky in thanks. She was so interesting.

"Stile waters, dieper grond." I quoted an Afrikaans expression. Still waters run deep. It occurred to me that not much had been shared by anybody except me. But I guessed that was Lucky's plan. One at a time.

"Haven't heard that for years," said Chantelle. "Not since school days."

I glanced at BJ, who wore her Mona Lisa smile.

Lucky said officiously, "Okay, girls. I am going to ask you to do something when it's your turn. Something you might think is entirely off the wall. But it's the first step in finding out more about our 747 crew rest experiences."

"I'm in!" spunky Moxie declared, lifting her steaming mug in salute.

"Not so fast," Chantelle's voice crackled, and I could feel trepidation rumble behind her lovely laughter.

"Tell us more," I said, excited that it was still my turn.

"Whatever it is you're intending, what kind of experience ... expertise do you have to conduct this, whatever it is?" Chantelle prodded, not unkindly.

"I'm a certified hypnotherapist, and I intend to hypnotize each of you so you can see your past lives much more clearly. When you're under, you're simply in a higher state of consciousness. Your deep subconscious won't allow you to harm yourself, and nor will I. That is not my intention." Lucky looked at me. "My goal is to take you back to find the rest of the story of Polina and Mikhail, beyond what the dream allowed you to see, so we can find out what became of these star-crossed lovers. Your protective subconscious only lets you dream about the parts your psyche can handle. It's the rest of the story that's laden with parts that are so damaging they may break us irreparably. That's why we unconsciously suppress them. Those kinds of memories are too powerful to dissipate through centuries and our many lives. They linger in the recesses of our subconscious, making us feel desperately afraid or inadequate or insecure in this life, and we don't know why. Those feelings must be brought to the surface and dealt with. We must dig and unearth them like gnarly old potatoes. Once we've dug them up, we'll hold them in our hands and turn them over, one way, then the other. And in the clear light of day or Boston night, where we hostie sisters are gathered, we will see they are not as scary as we imagined."

Lucky let her words sink in before she continued. "We'll boil those potatoes and eat them with loads of butter, salt and pepper, proverbially speaking. As we do, we'll thank them for their sustenance and the chance they've given us to advance our understanding of the fears and inadequacies they epitomize. Then we'll re-till and replenish the soil they once occupied and sprinkle it with good intentions, nourishing it to freshness so it will be untainted for beautiful things to come. It is only then our plantings in *this* life may grow unimpeded and glorious in the sun's rays.

"In a hypnotic state, it's easier to unearth that tough emotional baggage because you know you're safe and you're simply following your hypnotist's—my—directive. It's you looking at you from a distance. And it's an easier perspective than confronting the baggage head-on and unprotected. Or, heaven forbid, on your own. We are here to protect you.

"Brie, only by unearthing the hard past you've long suppressed can we find out what subconsciously triggers yours and Ryan's fears and insecurities; we'll understand the cause of your angst and reservations, then release them all, so the two of you can live your best life together without all that baggage."

"That's ambitious," BJ said with a hint of admiration.

"Look, I know you're all here—we're all here—because we have unfinished business. Business that started on the middle bunk of ZS216. And we have to understand what the unfinished business of that past life is, then deal with the baggage our souls have dragged into this life so we can all move on and make the most of this incarnation, this life we are living now."

Holy shit, Lucky was brave. She had no idea of our individual religious backgrounds or inclinations. For all she knew, there could be practicing Catholics, Buddhists, or atheists in her home. I felt like I had to stick up for her. Endorse her.

"Lucky, I reckon if we're all still puzzling over that dream like I am, then no matter what we believe or don't believe, we should give whatever it is you're proposing a chance to see if we can improve our lives. And we're all in the same boat. We can help each other." I sounded a lot more confident than I felt.

"You asked about my experience, Chantelle." Lucky looked down, then up again. "I have a 'gift,' or so my mother's young midwife, Dawn, said at my birth. I was born with a caul—a thin skein over my head. The wearer of the caul is meant to be a seer of things on the other side of the veil that separates our human world from those of our ancestors and spirit guides who are always there to help us. I had loads of experiences as a kid, then worked diligently at being 'normal' in the airline. I am trusted by law enforcement to hypnotize those who will benefit from their discoveries or for the authorities to widen their base of knowledge about a victim or a suspect under hypnosis.

"Truth is, I have never used hypnosis or my gifts in anything but a work environment, so in many ways this is new territory for me. But I know what I'm doing. It's just the application that's different. And my reasons began as purely selfish. Before I posted on the Orange Tail site to find you all, I had a message from the universe. She said to find my Roy, I had to help others. So, girls, my mission to help you is so that I might be reunited with my own soulmate. But I will confess, I've fallen in love with you all and believe with all my heart we are meant to make this journey together. So, I reluctantly admit, the universe is right again."

She glanced up at the stars as if to say, *There! I said it!*

The silence was so thick, I swear even the bubbles in the aqua warm water stopped popping as a sign of respect. And the strangest thing happened then. Like a lone wolf in the dead of night, quiet, sensitive Tula lifted his head and howled into the night. His cry sort of cemented Lucky's quiet explanation—giving it the auditory exclamation point it deserved.

"I'm in, but I am not sure what I'm in for." Moxie laughed.

"I'm in." BJ was matter-of-fact, which would have surprised me earlier, but now it was obvious she was quite otherworldly in so many ways.

"I'm scared. I'm a nonpracticing Catholic, and it sounds like voodoo, but I'm in, too," sang Chantelle. Then she added, "Thank you for allowing me to challenge your skills, your gift, whatever it is, Lucky. But I was desperate to eliminate a niggling doubt. Unfounded but there."

"Another reason you need to go under once you've shared your dream, Chants." Lucky smiled. "To eliminate *all* your niggling doubts."

Chantelle seemed contrite, but she managed a shy smile.

"Let's go inside and see how we can help our hostie sister Brie." Lucky seemed to surprise herself when she used a familial pronoun.

"Oh, I love, love, love being a hostie sister," exclaimed Chantelle, throwing her head back.

Even BJ joined in with the "Me too's!"

Lucky stood up, and steam radiated all around her like a ghostly vision. "If Brie trusts me to do this, you'll be able to evaluate whether you're comfortable letting me do this to *you*. You are not obliged in any way to see this through." She addressed us all.

"So, I'm the guinea pig," I spluttered through my smile.

"In a sense, yes. You okay with that?" Lucky asked, solemn for once.

I nodded and felt a surge of delicious anticipation. I hoped for clarity and wisdom and all the things that could heal my marriage. Though it was far from broken, it was just … chipped. But in my case the chip was as catastrophic as it would have been in that rare 16th-century Italian plate that sold for nearly $2 million a few years ago.

"Okay Brie. I'm proud of you. And remember I won't take you to places you don't want me to go. You are always in control."

I nodded, suddenly wanting to cry. Again! Lucky gave me that permission, and I realized how much I'd been denying myself. Since I'd left the Villies, no one had made me feel I was *not* in control of my own feelings, my own body, especially not Ryan. This insecurity was self-imposed. Or was it the baggage I'd brought with me from that past life Lucky talked about?

I was about to find out.

"Okay, girls," she said, "follow me."

CHAPTER 38

BRIE

Hull, present day

Once we'd all traipsed in and it was clear Lucky had finished hostessing for the day, I looked at Chantelle and wordlessly we rose together, found bread in the freezer and made toast with grated cheese and tomato under the grill. It hit the spot and diluted the liquor.

Wrapped in Lucky's big fluffy towels, or her gowns like Moxie and me, we draped ourselves over the living room furniture, back in the places we'd claimed the first time we'd gathered.

Tula found a resting place next to me again. I was quite chuffed, but he must have known I was still "in session" and he was there if I needed him. I felt myself stroking his thick, multi-colored coat as his arresting eyes watched me intently.

"Brie, do you remember anything more than the crew rest dream you shared with us?" Lucky asked.

I thought and thought and when I was sure, I looked up and shook my head apologetically. "I ... sometimes ... feel something, some sort of knowledge, right there but just out of my reach. The feeling comes in the way Ryan looks at me, in the way I feel about him that hits me for a long minute, but before I can grab at it or identify it, it blows away like a hastily blown kid's soap bubble. It floats off and soon pops! Gone. Never to be retrieved."

"Okay, I want you to take your time and allow yourself to drift into this past life so we can find some answers for you. You see, your soul is old. You and your soul have lived many, many lives together. Sometimes those lives get mixed up. It's likely the soul doesn't know when one life is over and a new one begins and you unwittingly carry soul-wounds into a new life. Like whatever is coming between you and Ryan's great and complete happiness."

"How the hell do you know all this?" Chantelle sounded quite aggressive, but Lucky didn't seem in the least offended.

"Past life regression is something I studied under psychiatrist Linda Sermon years ago. She is a graduate of renowned psychiatrist Brian Weiss. A scientist who chanced upon the concept of past life regression because of a patient he treated. Google him, Chantelle. He'll knock your socks off."

Lucky used her spooky eye-locking technique on all of us, starting with me. Her eyes penetrated through my orbs and into my soul, and only when they found my truth did she retreat with a tiny nod and go to the next pair of eyes in the room.

When Lucky was satisfied we were not just giving lip service and we were ready to rock and roll into the past, she looked back at me.

"Brie, I am only facilitating your passage to your past life so you can remember things we can fix. Talk to us when you are in your state so we can help you analyze what happened to Polina and Mikhail afterwards." Her voice was so soothing, I'd already closed my eyes when she continued: "But you have to trust me. Otherwise, it's not going to work."

I kept my eyes closed. "I trust you. Can I ask something?"

"Sure."

"What I want more than anything is to understand why I feel perpetually on the brink of unhappiness when I am the luckiest woman in the world." I began weeping copiously. Holy shit. It seemed once the geyser began, it was nigh unstoppable. I was conscious that my once insecure self would have been anxious that none of the girls came to pat me on the back nor said anything to make me feel better, but suddenly I knew this was all part of my own journey and they were giving me the space I needed to work it out myself.

I did, however, feel Tula's head on my foot again, and it was immensely comforting.

Lucky said, "There are no guarantees, Brie, but we are going to try, okay?" My head nodded up and down vigorously, but I couldn't speak. I was too choked up.

"Brie, close your eyes and think about nothing but the colors of the prism. Red, orange, yellow, green, blue, indigo, violet and again, red ...

"Now see yourself floating above those colors. You're watching the colors merge and form, then swirl and change. It's mesmerizing. As you watch them, you'll start to get weary. It's okay if you fall asleep and fine if you want to stay awake. You can even view all of the action from above, like you're watching a movie. Whatever works for you. As you float above the beautiful, colorful space that's like mist below you now, you catch a glimpse of an exquisitely carved door. You're drawn to it, and light as a feather, you swoop down through the colors to the door. Hover and take a good look. Each of the hand-carved scenes are from your many lives."

I TAKE a long look at scores of lives etched deep into the Rhodesian teak. Visions of times before recorded history; first century; ninth century. In most of them, I see him. I swallow tears of joy as I recognize Mikhail—or is it Ryan?—in so many of the tableaus. A million memories spring to mind in fleeting seconds, allowing just a quick glimpse at each of my lives, so many with my beloved man.

Lucky's voice breaks into my reverie. "Today we're only concentrating on the lives of Polina and Mikhail."

I let that sink in.

"Now the door opens a crack. Don't be afraid. Look to your right. Next to you is your spirit guide. Ask their name and tell us."

I listen and hear "Joy" and must say that out loud because Lucky's calm voice continues: "Joy won't let any harm come to you. She is your guide on this journey. Trust her. The open door is inviting you into a place you've been before. A place which will reveal all sorts of mysteries and clear up things haunting you in this life. There is no need to be afraid. I am with you. Joy is with you. Go inside that door and watch what happens like you would watch a movie. A movie of what was once your life as Polina, the ballerina, and her true love, Mikhail. A magnificent light warms you from the inside, and you feel safe as you float along, and you feel confident and brave with the gentle, wise spirit guide beside you. Joy won't leave your side. You are safe.

"You will see a scene ... a person ... and as I count down, you will reach that past life and enter that scene. You will recall that past lifetime and the lessons you learned. Five ... the door opens, and the light attracts you. There is something you need to learn or explore. Four ... keep going. Three ...Two ...nearly there. One ... and you immerse yourself fully into that life below you."

I take the plunge.

"Who are you now?" Lucky's voice.

"I am Polina." I'm completely comfortable with my thick accent.

"That's good, Polina. Now the only thing you must do is tell me exactly what you see, what you feel, what you experience. That way you will share your experience with us, your true friends. We only have your best interests at heart. Joy will be by your side. If you get scared, look for Joy. She will be there to comfort you. If you want to come back to Brie, just tell me. And so it shall be. Remember to talk to us as if you are telling a story. Polina, what are you wearing on your feet?"

"Pink satin pointe ballet shoes, with pink ribbons going up past my ankle."

"Good. Where are you, Polina?"

"I am in Madame's studio."

"Who do you see?"

"I see Madame. She has her stick. She does not favor me. I am lonely."

"Polina, you have the ability to move forwards or backwards in this life to the most significant event or events of this lifetime. In a few moments, when I count to three, you will go there. One, two, three and you are in an important part of your life. There is no pain, no discomfort. You are learning about your life from a distance. What is happening now?"

"I see Mikhail. I know him and I love him but I don't understand how ..."

"Tell us where you see Mikhail in lifetimes before this one." Lucky's voice is tentative.

"He is my husband. But he leaves me to war on the seas." I wipe my eyes.

"As you watch his ship leave safe harbor and you wave him goodbye, what does he wear?"

"He wears furs and horns on his helmet. I am crying because I fear I will never see him again ...Valhalla ...Valhalla ... but wait. Now I wear dull clothes and I am weaving wool as I watch Ryan ... Mikhail through an open window. We have never met, yet we know each other." I can feel my elation and my smile. I am so happy. Suddenly I need Joy. I look around. She is right here. I reach for and find her hand. She squeezes, and I relax.

"Joy is with me."

"Polina, take us to where Vaclav has stopped you from running off the stage to your Mikhail after your *Swan Lake* debut as prima ballerina."

After Lucky's statement, there is a loud wail, like a wild animal caught in a trap. I realize it comes from my heart. My mouth is just something through which my heart has erupted.

"Polina, it is very painful for you. So I want you to float above the scene so you can observe what happens next, like you are watching a movie. I do not want you to hurt during this process. So best you see it from a distance. Can you do that for me?"

I feel myself nod and take off upwards like a balloon. I am aloft, but I see Polina on the stage and Mikhail at the doors of the great Bolshoi, looking handsome and so very smart, like the tsar himself. I feel a pain in my heart, such is my love for him, yet I know it would be much more painful were I closer to him. I look around, and Joy is right behind me, giving me strength.

I see gruff Cossacks always there. Opulent rooms. We travel on the Tsarskoye Selo Railway to Saint Petersburg and then by carriage, sometimes even in a litter into Europe. I dance and dance and dance. There is always a standing ovation. But I feel no pride or pleasure. You see, when I stop dancing, and Siegfried ... Stanislav no longer smells like tavolga, I lose my Mikhail. It has been so long that I can only remember his face when it is conjured up by that flowery smell. My only prima donna requirement is tavolga in each dressing room. I know people from the Bolshoi have to go to great lengths to secure the flower for me where it does not grow. But without it, Stanislav won't smell like Mikhail and I cannot dance.

And afterwards ... There is Rome and Athens. Berlin. Amsterdam. Vienna. Paris. Dance. Dance. Applause. *Swan Lake.* Cossacks. Kings. Dukes. I shiver.

I am a ballerina. This is my dream. Why am I not happy? I look frantically around for Joy and relax as she squeezes my hand.

I can watch this scary movie once more.

And then I understand why I am so desperately unhappy. It's my heart.

It's broken.

"Polina, are you safe?" comes Lucky's voice.

I nod.

"Tell us what is happening in all these exotic places. Are you being treated like a queen?"

My words tumble out as I verbalize the visions before me. "I am more alone than I was with Madame and her stick. No

Coupé. No Mikhail. But I am no longer wearing my father's army coat or his tired boots. I am in fine silk gowns and furs. I am instructed to talk to kings and tsars. Dukes and prime ministers.

"I am guarded like a Fabergé egg, yet the Cossacks allow these men of power to enter my dressing room, my private quarters, at the tsar's insistence. My body is Russia's temple, and it's rented out after every performance. They come to my large dressing room bearing humongous bouquets of flowers. I come to hate the smell of flowers.

"They take me, face to the mirror. I try not to look at their reflections, but I know they are admiring themselves as they physically overpower me ... Polina, or is it Odette? Odile? Or perhaps Mother Russia herself? They insist I wear my costume in all or in part while they do with my body what they will.

"My headdress—that crown of feathers which on that first night gave me such great pride—is never removed during these humiliating procedures. Later, busy costumers will reattach feathers to my tutu and my crown before my next performance. Occasionally the makeup expert has to work her magic before my next performance to cover a particularly rough invasion of my person." I feel hot tears of sympathy for this delicate ballerina's dreadful plight flowing freely down my cheeks. Thank the Lord I am not inside Polina's body, where I truly belong. It would be simply unbearable.

"No matter how many baths I take in goat's milk or fresh coconut milk, the only time I feel clean is on stage. When Mikhail is with me. My Mikhail, my Siegfried, my love.

"My mind is dead. I learn to stare beyond the mirror—far, far back to a tent in the small park abutting Madame's studio, where I lie in the safety of my love's arms.

"It is Mikhail who holds me, turns me, catches me, loves me as Odette and even Odile. He is my reason for dancing. I cannot find him in my dreams because there are none. Sleep is merely an escape for my body. But Mikhail is the *only* reason I do not slit my wrists, because, you see, in my mind's eye, he waits for me in his tent. And I will never let him down.

"*Swan Lake*'s season is ending. I am so relieved when I curtsy for the last time in the Bolshoi, I weep and weep and pretend it is because my turn is over. It's true I am beyond relieved I will no longer be desired by the elite. I weep with pure joy. Soon I will be reunited with my Mikhail and Coupé too. Soon my love will hold me in his own arms. I need no tavolga to trick me. Soon he will kiss me and make me clean."

"Polina, where do you go next?"

"I go to my apartment in Moscow. I am amazed and surprised. It is filled with precious things. *Things* that cost me my dignity. My virginity. My sanity. Blind rage bubbles in me and then explodes. I scream and sweep my hand across the tops of cabinets and buffets, and precious crystals, Fabergé eggs, delicate China and priceless paintings shatter and splinter. They mean nothing. Because of them I have been kept from my love. I must find Mikhail. I run to Madame's studio. I peep behind the building, searching for our tent inside the tree-filled park."

Panic pounds in my chest. "There is nothing. Not even a page of the newspapers that lined the floor of our intimate tent. I rush to the soup shop and ask about the one-legged beggar. The shopkeeper says, 'The one with the rat?' I nod, and his eyes won't meet mine. 'What happened to him?' I demand.

"'They say the beggar was in love with a ballerina from that studio.' He points to Madame's, visible from his side window. 'And the ballerina became famous and toured with the Bolshoi ballet, leaving only her rat for him to care for. A preposterous story delivered by a delirious, sick man,' he says, shaking his head.

"'I am that ballerina, and he is my love. Do you not remember us?' I point to our table where we broke bread and shared soup more than once. 'He and I?'" My voice trails off as I see him staring at my fine mink coat.

"'Where is he now?' I beg him. 'Where?' I implore as tears wash my cheeks, but he shakes his head and his shoulders at the same time.

"I rip off my expensive fur hat, and my voice drops in a menacing manner. 'See? Do you remember now? He and I sat here in your shop many times. I am that ballerina, and he is my love. Where is he? Where?' The shopkeeper peers at me, unimpressed, and rubs his hands together. I throw rubles on the counter. 'Where is he?' my voice demands as he pockets the money.

"He shrugs. 'Try at the Bielygorod on the Moskva River. I heard he was living there, under a bridge.' As I run out, he shouts, 'You may have been gone too long.'

"It's a long way, but I can only search for my Mikhail on foot, because what if the shopkeeper was wrong about the where? En route to the Bielygorod, I hunt for beggars in nooks and crannies. I find too many. Searching, searching. My heart uses my throat to call out to wind: 'Why did you move from where I could find you, Mikhail? Why?'

"I see a form, and I rush to it. It's not Mikhail but a broken man. My Mikhail is no beggar and yet, he's forced to live like one. 'Have you seen Mikhail? He has one leg and a rat named Coupé?' The man shrugs apologetically. I ask another hiding from the snow underneath a bridge. He shakes his head. My body is shivering. Even my furs can't keep me warm when my heart is so very cold. On I go, one beggar to another. Then, at last ...

"'Yes,' says the man with not a tooth in his head, and he makes room for me next to him on his newspaper. I sit, fearful this is another dead end and he will forcibly take my warm coat and hat and I will freeze and die before I have found my beloved.

"The wizened, wind-whipped face assesses me for some minutes. 'You are everything he said you were.' My heart lurches before it crashes to the drain below. This beggar knows what he has to say to have an hour of company, any company. Russia's darling of yesterday is jaded, faded, finished.

"The once gullible girl is now a certified cynic.

"'What did he say his passion was?' I test him.

"The old man regards me for a while. 'You mean besides you? What did you say his rat's name was?' He too is a cynic.

"'I didn't. You tell *me* the rat's name.' It is a game of chess. Neither of us wants to make the first move. We have both been sullied by lies and misconceptions.

"'A strange name. Begins with a *C*. He said it was a French ballet term.'

"I lean over to his side of the newspaper and hug him till he dislodges my clinging arms. 'Tell me everything,' I beg, fresh tears pouring down my face."

CHAPTER 39

POLINA

Moscow, late 1877

I sit with the toothless beggar underneath the bridge, shielded mostly from the blistering snow as it slants down from angry skies. I reach again for Joy's hand to bring me solace. It may not be my Mikhail, but a being ... someone who cares ... is close to me.

"Tell me, please, tell me everything about my Mikhail."

The toothless man responds: "I met him the day he wandered into my boss's store and asked if he could use the facilities. He had met a ballerina, he told me, and he needed to look his best. After I finished laughing, I drilled him some more. To my surprise, he was an intelligent young man. His lack of leg and his pain made him seem much older, although he hid the latter well. My boss met him when he came in again and gave his blessing to use the bathroom and invited him to spend nights in the storeroom when the weather was too bad outside. Mikhail insisted that his ballerina, the love of his life, would keep him warm. My boss and I wondered if he was all there." He tapped his temple. "But he was so likable, if he had a vivid imagination, who were we to judge? Besides, he was a war survivor. But then he came to rent the suit for your premier performance at the Bolshoi. Never in all my many years have I seen a more excited man, and it was not even his wedding day. Mikhail's face was glowing, as he told me he needed a princely outfit for the opening of *Swan Lake*. It should have been hard for me to believe him—it was a ludicrous idea—but he was so earnest and seemed not even a fraction crazy. He emptied his pockets, and a white rat popped out as well as copious amounts of cash. That rat! I swear it looked equally excited and eerily human. He kissed the rat on her nose and told me the two of them needed to look spectacular so they would fit in with the other patrons of the Bolshoi.

"'Now, why would you two want to spend all your money on an outfit for a ballet?' I asked, quite honestly waiting for a good laugh, since I'd heard the ballerina story for a while. He pulled more rubles from a different pocket and placed them on my counter and said, 'The girl I love is the prima ballerina of the Bolshoi. Tonight, she is Odile and Odette from *Swan Lake*.' I laughed the laugh I knew he'd give me, with his wild imagination. 'I see you have not only lost your leg but your mind too. But you have not lost your money ... so I shall help you spend it. Come.' I fitted him with a finely spun silk caftan, rich with ornate embroidery in reds and yellows. It was almost as grand as a tsar would wear and as heavy as a Cossack's field coat. He tied it around his waist with a thickly spun silk cord, and the gold tassels on the end danced in eager anticipation. They too were going to the Bolshoi. He shaved in the back of the shop, and when I closed up, I cut his hair. We topped off his outfit by slipping one leather boot with a steel toe onto his foot. It was the perfect size. I pinned up the other trouser leg. The outfit was very expensive for one night, but he told me he was happy to spend all his money to make his love proud.

"All the while, the little white rat explored the shop, finding all sorts of nibbles of food my broom had missed. She was a sweet little thing and checked on him periodically like *she* was the one caring for *him*. He showed me where his friend would reside—in the caftan's upper pocket. And he showed me his ticket. He'd paid double for it on the black market, but he would have sold his soul to be at 'his love's' first professional performance. He told me proudly she'd skipped the corps and —let me get this right—pirouetted ..." He looks to me, and I nod. He grins and continues, "pirouetted straight to prima ballerina. Mikhail's smile of pride took away any shadow of a doubt that may have clouded my mind, even though it sounded so absurd. I have never seen a man with two legs and unlimited rubles as happy as this man with one leg, spending close to his last coin to see his beloved in her element. He was intent on doing you proud."

The elder and I wipe away our tears with the backs of our hands.

Then he says: "But when he returned the outfit the next day, I saw an entirely different man."

CHAPTER 40

BRIE & POLINA

Hull, present day, and Russia, 1877

"Polina, are you okay?" Lucky's calm voice penetrates my state of despair.

"I am so sad," I tell her, but I feel Joy's hand and her reassurance.

"What is the toothless man's name?" Lucky's voice asks from far away.

"His name is Lev, and he looks like an old, mangy lion with his mop of crazy hair and his big bushy beard."

"Can you go on?" Lucky's soft voice asks.

"I must," I say, my throat constricting.

"Brie ... Polina, go outside of your body and up, up, up. Watch your movie and hold Joy's hand. She will help you through this very tragic tale."

I feel myself float upward holding Joy's hand, and I watch the scene below. It's weird, but I can be apart and part of it at the same time. It is, though, easier up here than it is being right there, and I can continue describing this ... movie that I am watching.

"Lev continues, 'The very day Mikhail returned his fancy Bolshoi outfit was the day I was dismissed from my job. The shop owner returned from outfitting the soldiers on the front and had no more use for me. My wife had recently died, and I had no one to return to and nothing with which to pay my bills, so I left with Mikhail. He wanted to stay close to your old studio, in case you came back. And we spent months in that tent. But the summer was short and the winter arrived early, with wicked winds and violent snowstorms in August that weakened the tent until it gave up, splitting in two by month's end. Truth be told, that tent was a bit small for two burly men and a rat, even with only seven legs between us.' He chuckles. 'So we sought our refuge under bridges.'"

Lucky disappears from those present in my world, but Joy is still with me.

"'The Cossacks were told to keep the streets free of vermin, so rather than provide shelter for the homeless, they chased us out of their districts so we became the problem for the next district's Cossacks, when they found us. We were always on the move. Not so easy for Mikhail. I tried telling a pair of Cossacks that, and defending my one-legged friend and his white rat, I lost the last of my teeth ... and the fight. We finally found this bridge, and we've ... I've been here for nearly four months. Seems we were lucky to be in a district of slack Cossacks.' Lev laughs, but mirth has no place in his outburst.

"'What happened?' I ask, clearing my heart from where it is lodged in my throat. 'Please, Lev, please tell me what happened when Mikhail returned his Bolshoi outfit to your store?' The last word was barely out when I strained to reduce my hearing and steeled myself against the blistering details that would seal the coffin of my betrayal. It was as if I needed the agony of knowing and visualizing like a monk needs the repeated shredding of his flesh to pay for his sins.

"'His eyes were wild from no sleep. He had waited and waited for you a few blocks from the Bolshoi itself. He was so well dressed, nobody questioned his hanging around the theater perimeter,' the old man says almost proudly. But his tone quickly changes, becoming heavy with accusation. 'But you never came.'

"The denunciation is a hard slap across my face, and even though I am above looking down, it stings so badly, my eyes well up. 'I tried,' I cry. 'I tried with all my might. But immediately after the curtain fell on opening night, my life was over. Yes, I had every luxury at my disposal but no privacy. No freedom. Eight eyes owned by burly Cossacks bored into me every minute of every day. Even when I danced, they were invisibly in the wings, watching, watching, watching.'

"'But in eight months you couldn't slip away?' he asks, incredulous.

"'I got back from Europe eight hours ago. I would have been here sooner if you were easier to find.' My infliction rises to match his accusatory tone.

"'How did you give those burly Cossacks the slip now?' he challenges, sarcastically.

"'They have no more interest in me. *Swan Lake* season is over. There is another budding ballerina. I am yesterday's front-page news. I have my life back, and I want to share it with my Mikhail.'

"'Well, you are now sitting on the very spot where he died.' Lev's voice is flat as if to deliberately hurt me.

"'He ... Mikhail died?' My heart is ripped from behind my ribs and yanked through my flesh. It is thrown down on the hard concrete, and then the boots of ninety Cossacks stomp on it.

"Lev refuses to look at me. He stares at the curved stone supporting the opposite side of the bridge under which we sit.

"I feel I am dead. It's no wonder. When I was being abused, though I thought I had no heart, that was just to protect my mind from the abuse of my body. My heart was still Mikhail's. But Mikhail is gone, and I no longer house such an organ. Russia has seen to that.

"Somehow my anxiety has taken me back to face my pain head-on. I am there once more, in the snow beneath the bridge, as Lev takes pity on me and places his arm around my shoulders, but this makes my heartless cavity even more hollow. Joy takes my hand and whisks me back above this tragic tableau, where words are softer.

"His voice is a decibel softer from up here. He says, 'But you didn't kill him. He had been sick since he lost his leg. He said when he met you, you not only gave him hope, you healed him, mind, soul and body too ... for a time, but it's difficult if not impossible to preserve the flesh around a removed limb in the raging elements in which he lived. Nothing could have saved him. Not even you.'"

I hear my own scream of pain and see myself heaving with grief.

I hear Lucky's voice as if from above. An angel? "Polina, you are doing so well. You are finding out what happened in this life to Polina and Mikhail so you can repair Brie's current life. Stay with the old toothless man, Polina. Stay and keep speaking so we may all hear of your trauma and help you rid yourself of it in this new life. Joy will cushion your pain as she holds you safely above what you're witnessing."

Lucky's voice is so soothing, I feel a little better as I seek out Joy's hand once more.

I have a glimpse of Brie and Ryan, and then I slip back into the cloak of my Russian self and watch as I stare into the sage eyes of the toothless man and say, "Continue, please, Lev. Tell me more, I beg you."

"Lev says: 'It's likely your love coated his slowly dying body like a balm ... for a time ... until he watched you realize your dream. Perhaps that love coating would have held up if you had been able to find him after your premier performance. But I doubt that.'

"We are silent for a long time before he continues, 'In a month, when he knew he'd never see you again and concluded you no longer cared for him, he gave up and let himself succumb to the illness.'

"I am so cold, my teeth chatter, so violent are my shivers. Imagine my wracking shakes if I was down there, under the bridge. Joy squeezes my hand. 'Be brave,' she whispers.

"'What of Coupé?' I ask as softly as I dare, as a new pain tugs at the empty cavity of my heart. I am so afraid to hear the answer, but though it is gossamer-thin, I feel a faint hope.

"'Coupé died here.' Lev points inside his jacket. 'Days after I lost my friend Mikhail.'"

And that fragile glimmer of hope is whooshed away by the wind and hurtles off, leaving an even larger, gaping black hole which had once held a rhythmically beating heart.

My throat tears from the scream I hear that is my own. I am broken. Not even the pressure of Joy's hand, intended to remind me of her presence, can piece together the fragments that were once my existence.

Lucky's voice breaks through my despair. "Polina, you are safe. Safe and amongst friends. Before you leave that place under the bridge in the snow, connect the lessons you learned in your Russian lifetime to this lifetime you're in now. Is there a connection? What did you have to learn in that life? What fears did you bring with you to this new life? Allow yourself to float in this beautiful place and feel light, feel free as you contemplate this. Imagine your spirit-friend beside you, comforting you. Joy is a master, a guide, an angel, an enlightened spiritual being. Your very own, very wise, very loving being is right beside you, under this bridge. Imagine you can communicate with her via mind-to-mind contact. Are there any messages for you? Listen very closely." Lucky's voice is a whisper.

Joy steps in with her arms out, shielding me. "I hear her saying I have suffered enough and I can leave this Polina life if I wish. But I must not go before I know what became of me. Of Polina. I tell her so, and she merely steps back, still holding my hand."

Lucky's whisper again, as if from the heavens: "Is there any knowledge she will give you to help you in your current situation? What is it that you need to know or understand, Polina, to make Brie's life better? Listen carefully. Let her wisdom infuse your being. Soon it will be time to return to full waking consciousness, but you will remember everything you experienced. When you awake, the pain will disappear and you will remember only Mikhail and Polina's true love. You will also remember the wisdoms Joy has imparted, which you may share with us, your friends."

But images of what I endured as a prima ballerina shroud

my thoughts and turn sorrow into fear and pain. I want so much for Mikhail to know what happened to me while I was away so he will understand how impossible it was for me to return to him.

Lucky must sense my fear because she says, "Polina, Polina. Though Mikhail left the world you'd lived in together, he could watch you from on high. Everything is made clear when you are no longer bound by earth's restrictions. He understood your reasons. He ached for your pain and humiliation. He was likely chastising himself for pushing you to greatness. Polina. Brie. Consider this. Mikhail loved you so much, he made a contract with the universe to come back as your partner in your next life. You found each other again, Polina. Now you are Brie and Mikhail is Ryan, but your souls are the same. Fear no harm. You are safe amongst us. Joy is watching over you too. You are safe. Feel the calm as it descends on you. Remember each life is shrouded with hard lessons we have to learn. All of us. But through it all, there is love. And you are loved so very much."

I feel relief that I've been able to at least tell *somebody,* if not Mikhail, what happened, why I couldn't go to him. Lucky's assurance that Mikhail knew what had happened once he passed from this life gives me some relief.

Joy whispers, "It's not your fault your life ended like this, Polina. These excruciating lessons were those you were sent to Russia to learn. To Lucky's point, what did you learn, Polina, before we leave this Russian life?"

I look at Joy, surprised that she needs to ask this question when the answer is as clear as the nose on my face. If she is my guide, why can't she see?

Then I realize that if I unburden myself, if I share this

trauma, it might be lessened. Hers is not a question fashioned by ignorance but rather by love, to help me see my own way.

To free myself of all this self-disgust and vile anger I carry would be such a relief.

I shake my head, *no no no,* and then I say softly, "I am not yet free to go. I have another responsibility."

Joy holds my hand more tightly. "You do not have to endure one more moment of torment here, Polina. Go. Be Brie. Be in love with Ryan."

Still, I shake my head.

I begin my final confession to Joy, to Lucky, but not to Lev. "I realize one of the many seeds planted inside me in my dressing room has taken. Was it the tsar, or the king's nephew, or that son of a duke who was born misshapen? What will I do? How can I kill something God has given me? How can I not?"

I hear my own ragged pleas. I glance down and see Lev's empty vodka bottle, and I vomit. I know as the seed grows it poisons my core, and I am terrified. I cannot introduce a misshapen, unloved child into this world when I have no heart. Vodka. It will feed my oblivion. It is my only option to take away the pain. My heartache. My guilt. My unloved, perhaps misshapen baby.

"Joy, please stay close so that I may reach for you, but what I must do, I must do alone."

I rush off, this time taking a horse and buggy to my apartment. I sell all I have—that which I haven't destroyed—and use my acquired riches to pay for vodka and a warmer coat for Lev. But he dies within days of my return to the spot under the bridge, within hours of donning his new coat.

There, in my solitude, in my heartache, I drink and drink

and drink, washing away the nightmare of reality with vodka's promise of oblivion.

Joy swoops in and will not take no for an answer, so together we create a distance from most of the pain.

I watch myself with disgust and regret. Regret that I did not make Mikhail take my body willingly before others took it forcibly.

Nothing but alcohol flows through my veins. My stomach knots and jerks its objection to my murderous act. And I feel my last breath coming and I am so happy, even though it's said that I shall pay for the sin of killing my child.

But then my beloved Joy says: "A child should be conceived in love and born in a home, not under a bridge with vodka on its breath. This child was not conceived as it should have been. Only the cruelest God would ask you to keep it." Joy pats my still-flat belly, giving me permission to release the baby from my womb as she says, "Via con Dios, my darling. Come again, and in happiness."

And I let this seed go.

And in the midst of the abysmal pain, I throw my head back and drink, *glug, glug, glug,* knowing that this vodka will take me to my Mikhail.

At last.

It is my Mikhail who has come to fetch me. Mikhail who holds out his hands to me in my final earthly minute and says, "Come to me at last, my ballerina."

Lucky's gentle but firm voice stirs me. "Polina, we see you. You must return to Brie and to those of us who wait for you ... but soon you will be with Mikhail just as it was always meant to be. But his name will be different. It will be Ryan. Say thank you to your spiritual friend, Joy, who protected you all this time. Remember Joy is always close. Call on her if and when you need her. Just call her name and put out your hand. Take peace in the fact that you are never alone. Now leave your heartache and your guilt with Polina and float through the door you chose. Good. Firmly close the door on Polina's life behind you. As you do, acknowledge you are not closing the door on Mikhail because he is with you now. Mikhail is Ryan."

I feel my breathing slow, slower and slower, until it returns to a regular rhythm.

Lucky's voice: "Good, Brie. You feel light and unburdened. So light and so free you travel up, up, and follow the light. Good. And up and up with your lessons you've learned, so that you may brilliantly manage your life as Brie."

I feel sublimely peaceful. Ryan's face fills my head, and anticipation goose bumps pop up on my arm as pure love flows through me. I am ridiculously happy to know that Mikhail is Ryan in this life.

I have a second chance.

Lucky's voice inserts itself into my reverie. "Start counting down, Brie. Ten, you're excited for a do-over with Mikhail as Ryan in *this* life. Nine, eight, seven. You will recognize your glorious reunion on this earth for what it is. A gift you must never take for granted. Six ... another chance and this time for a long life with your soulmate, Ryan. Five ... relish this divine gift, Brie. Four ... a life together in which to cherish each other without fear of losing the other too soon. Three ... you have acknowledged those painful parts of your past. Now release any ugliness or misunderstandings that may linger between you from that other life. Let them go. Those old wounds no longer serve you. Two ... find your bliss with Ryan. Embrace the glorious present with him. Share your past life with him so he understands his own fears, and together, you can cast them asunder. I will count you back to full consciousness, where you will be safe and calm and confident, light and unburdened. Brie, you are sailing up toward your present life with a deep understanding of the insecurities your Polina life created for you and Ryan and the means to make up for lost time. One ... Brie, you are joining us in this life with a deep knowledge and twice the love for Ryan because you understand his fears and you feel so relieved you have answers. And now, Brie, find your friends surrounding you as you open your eyes. Feel the excitement you deserve. Make the most of your new life with your old soulmate, Mikhail, who you now call Ryan. Now awake and rejoice, Brie. Awake."

CHAPTER 41

BRIE

Hull, present day

I opened my eyes, glanced around. My cheeks were taut with so many shed tears, but my heart was buoyant. When I looked around, these eager faces were suddenly more familiar than ever. Everyone in the room seemed to be floating on air, everyone except me. I had both my feet on the ground, ready for a second chance at love.

Moxie brought me a tall glass of water and a Romany cream filled with rich chocolate filling. "See?" she said in a motherly tone. "You don't drink alcohol in this life because you died of alcoholism as Polina."

I took a long sip of water and left the cookie. Moxie was half right.

"How do you feel about your experience?" Lucky asked.

"Glorious." I felt my face glow. "You know all my life I have felt out of sorts. Incomplete. Half baked. Like I didn't belong wherever I was. Except the airline. In many ways, the airline had too many misfits for me not to feel at home. But soon after I was married, with too much time on my hands, the feeling came back."

"That was a hangover from Paulina's life. You didn't know how to fit in," BJ said.

"But now you know ... what did Lucky say? We should thank our souls for showing us that truth, then tell them they can forget that feeling and move on because you have learned from it but it no longer serves you," Chantelle said in her musical voice. Then she fluffed her hair, shivered and grinned. "Did I get that right, Lucky?"

"You were spot on, Chants! So do it, Brie. In your own time, but make it soon so there is no lingering or confusion on your soul's part."

I was suddenly worried that if I kept that in a moment longer, it would fester. So, using Chantelle's words or close to them, I said it all. Aloud. I thanked my soul for showing me the why and told her kindly that she no longer needs to be burdened with all the negativity from Polina's life. That she and I were free to find joy. Joy? Well, both literally and figuratively.

I felt bold and powerful and free. I came up from what felt like a mini trance.

Four smiles of immense pride greeted me as if I'd won the gold at the Olympics.

"Tell us," Lucky urged.

"YES," I shouted. "I understand why I am the way I am, and I now know I can choose to no longer feel that way. I CAN CHOOSE."

"Spill," Chantelle's divine voice cracked with excitement.

"That we were separated so mercilessly was a travesty, a tragedy. But in this life, I didn't know why I felt I needed to overcompensate Ryan, to downplay myself, to boost him. I had no idea I was trying to make up for deserting him, even if it was no fault of my own. And Ryan, for no reason, was afraid he would lose me. That I would leave him. But now I know why. Because of Ryan, er, Mikhail, I ... Polina found success, and he was so selfless in his wishes for me to excel.

"And when I did, he must have thought I was cutting ties with him by choice. How he must have suffered. He was the reason for my being on that opening stage in Odette's tutu. Oh, he might have imagined I was too full of myself to come back to a lowly beggar. Never. And perhaps in a way I resented him for pushing me into a life of degradation he couldn't possibly have anticipated. How my Mikhail's heart would have hurt knowing the humiliation I suffered at the hands of every tsar or king or duke. How he would have cut off his other leg if he'd known of the high price I paid for applause. Now I know I made him feel unloved because I couldn't get to him, and it makes me want to make it up to my Ryan a thousand times. And I can't wait to explain to him what happened to us *after* the dream. The dream was the reason we met in this life." I caught my breath and leaned into my new wisdom. "*After* the dream is what shaped us."

"That's deep," murmured Moxie, in a semi-trance.

Lucky looked into my very being with *that* look. "It's very possible, Brie. It's almost as if, this time, the universe is teaching you what it's like to wait for the other one, the one who is more important."

"True," said BJ.

"Karma, baby." That was Moxie, standing shockingly still.

"Consider this too. You are both beautiful people, but he is the one involved in your old world—dance, theater, the arts— and you are living in his confined world with one leg or, in your case, ungracefully, tripping on everything that isn't there and hiding from the world in your house. Punishing yourself by being a loner." BJ contributed.

"YES!" Chantelle's odd tic happened quickly before she jumped up with excitement. "And you're conscious of the beautiful, artistic women around him, but you're not threatened by them, just as Mikhail was never threatened by your professional environment. Far from it. He encouraged you to greatness."

These friends ... YES! My friends are right.

"When you tell him, perhaps his soul will calm and it will know there is no need to be wary about your relationship or to doubt the extent of your mutual adoration. Perhaps that will allow him to be confident that this time you're not going anywhere," Lucky suggested.

"It makes perfect sense," said Moxie. Chantelle and BJ nodded.

Salty tears tickled the corners of my mouth. "I feel so bad."

Chantelle rushed over and hugged me, and Moxie followed suit.

Lucky never took her eyes off me. "It's not your fault. It wasn't then. It isn't now. But you two have been given a chance to get it right and love each other unconditionally. There is no reason to feel he wants something more. He only wants you, Brie. He's just too afraid to show you, lest you leave him again. So all you have to do is think of him as Polina's Mikhail and treat him as such. Love him unconditionally, knowing how deep a wound he brought with him from his past life to your relationship. You have a chance to heal his broken soul. And yours." And then she beamed.

"Wouldn't that be wonderful?" I said, and meant it.

"Oh my God, this is soooo amazing!" crooned Chantelle.

BJ wore a small, knowing smile and nodded slowly, agreeing with everyone, everything, which I'd wager was a rare state for her. And then she blurted, "And for Shakespeare's thrasonical sake, please oh please have *deep*"—a pause that would make the Bard proud followed—"*penetrating* sex!"

Oh, how we laughed.

Moxie jumped up and down, causing laughter interruptus. "I can't believe it. This is amazing. I can't wait for my turn. Screw the straws, Chantelle, pleaaaaaaaase can I go next?"

I suddenly remembered something. "Do you know something really weird? Ryan suffers from tremendous pain in his leg. He's never had an injury. But he often wakes up, bathed in sweat, and clutches the same side that was missing on Mikhail and complains of 'deep bone pain.'"

"Fukaloolee," shouted BJ. And I high-fived myself because I'd impressed the queen.

"We've been to a slew of doctors. There is nothing there. But it gets so sore sometimes he limps for days before it eases." And then another thought struck me. I looked into the eyes of my new old friends hovering over me. "And do you know, those are the only times Ryan is short with me? Could it be that Mikhail memories came back to remind him of his hurt when he gets this fake leg pain?"

"Hell, yes!" four voices chorused.

"To coin your phrase," said Chantelle, looking at me as she fluffed and did her jazz hands, "holy shit!"

BJ said, "Well, you know what you have to do when that happens, Brie. You have to massage his leg and say, 'Thank you for reminding us that it was because of this brave, handsome leg that Polina and Mikhail met. But we are together again, and we are grateful Ryan has two legs and he can now lose the pain of losing his last leg. He is no longer Mikhail but my beloved husband, Ryan, with two legs."

Wow! We all spun around and looked at BJ.

She glared at all of us. "What? Can't a girl have a little input?"

"You're brilliant!" I said in awe.

She studied her fingernails. "So I've been told." Then she grinned for real, gifting us with her true self for what was possibly the first time in years.

I was suddenly overcome with a deep sadness. My eyes welled up, and the sobs came unbidden. I felt all eyes on me, and I didn't hesitate. "But I killed a baby. Deliberately," I said.

Lucky's voice was loud and strong. "Don't be ridiculous, Brie. Polina's seed was just the result of an invasion she had no say in. I've heard it said that oftentimes when a child dies, whether before birth or shortly after, it has no bearing on the child, but rather its divine purpose was to teach the parent or parents a lesson in *their* lives. God only knows why you had to endure that extra lesson, but if it does anything, it proves that theory. It wasn't a child; it was a growing seed that caused you to suffer less because you decided to kill yourself with alcohol to join your Mikhail. Good God, Brie. You as Polina were so damaged, you didn't have the emotional or physical ability to nurture a life. Cast out any self-blame. It has no place in your heart or your memory."

"Amen," BJ said and strummed the first few bars of the song that had the chorus using just one word. "Aaaay-a-men, Aaaay-a-men, Aaaya-a-men, Ay-men, Ay-men."

It sort of wrapped up all my uncertainties, and I was overcome by a divine peace. At least for a time.

I realized what an emotional journey it had been, not just

for me but for all of us, when BJ finished her song and accidently emphasized the end by loudly passing wind. Politeness would have been to simply ignore such a bodily indiscretion, but instead, BJ said a somber, "Excuse me," and then started to giggle and broke it with, "What an artless dirt-rotten dunghill I am!" But we barely heard her, we were laughing so hard.

This mirth caused Chantelle to fall off the couch; Moxie hugged herself as she sat cross-legged, rocking back and forth crying and laughing at the same time; BJ's shoulders rode up and down, up and down as she chortled. I giggled with alternating snorts that made me sneeze. Every giggle become a sneeze that started with a "Tsssssssssss" and ended in a belly laugh.

Lucky laughed so freely, she snorted. "Sorry!" she declared, then threw up her hands. "Oh, bugger it. Snorting 'tween friends is perfectly okay if farting is." She rose gingerly. "Unless, of course, you want to pee." She ran up the two steps to the secret loo crying, "Then by the time you get there, it's almost too late!"

How Lucky made it inside without letting it all flow with the hilarity that followed her confession, I'll never know.

When we'd sobered and she was back, I asked, "Lucky, where's Joy gone?"

And our hostess said, "She's returned to her place on high. It's where she can see you best. Now she knows what you want, she can help you better from up there than she can from here. But whenever you need her, just call. She'll hear you even if you ask in your head or in your dreams."

Now that was a comforting thought, but in that state of gratitude, I heard a name and I smelled something familiar. I was startled out of my trance and turned to Lucky. "Do you know someone ... Alan? Ala—?"

"Alana!" Lucky's face was ashen.

Tula was by her side.

Both his mistress and he had their heads in the air, sniffing like trained dope dogs at the airport. Lucky whispered, "Condensed milk."

"What the hell's going on with you?" BJ wanted to know.

Lucky looked frantic. She was our rock. I had a moment of panic. What had Joy and I unearthed here?

CHAPTER 42

BRIE

Hull, present day

Moxie brought Lucky an exotic-looking drink. She'd found an umbrella in one of the drawers, I'd guess, and had innocently added it in an effort to cheer our hostess. But though Lucky said thanks, she shook her head in refusal. She looked downright morose. For the first time since we'd gathered, there was an uncomfortable silence. Tula was squashed against Lucky's legs, and he was staring at his mistress, as we all were. A collective sigh of relief as loud as a whipping wind was released when Lucky's hands enfolded Tula's head and she kissed him on the bridge of his fine nose.

And still we women of many words remained silent. Waiting.

Lucky's face was washed with quiet tears when she looked at each of us in turn.

"Alana is"—she inhaled a jagged breath—"was my best friend in the whole world, and she loved Cadbury's Flakes

mixed into a tin of condensed milk. She saved me from mortifying embarrassment at thirteen just by being there." She tried
to laugh, but it came out as a soggy hiccup. "In the packed
school assembly hall where 'careers' were being presented, I felt
compelled to stand up and share that my lifelong dream was to
be an air hostess. My young teacher—I think she was twenty-
one—grabbed the microphone and yelled, 'You just want to be
a flying mattress.'"

Strains of "Bitch ... Miserable cow ... How *dare* she ..."
erupted. Chantelle cried so hard she said between sobs, "How
mortifying. Poor you. Thank God Alana saved you."

"I would bet the bitch applied and failed to get into the
airline, thus her bitter hatred of the vocation. Damn her for
damaging a child!" Wicked-tongued BJ was back, and this time,
we were pleased.

"Alana spent half her weekends at my house, and I spent
half in hers. When we weren't together, we were on the phone
to each other. Those big, old, heavy dial-up phones. She helped
me with my adolescent demons and I with hers. She loved me
unconditionally. She joined Air Baobab first. They snapped her
up. She was so cute and polite. I called her 'Jontue.' Do you
remember the perfume of our youth? Their slogan was 'Sexy
but not too far from innocent.' That was my Alana. She made
senior hostie in less than two years. She was the perfect hostess. I
joined when she'd been in the airline nearly three years. We flew
together as often as Oom Faan would let us. You know how
difficult the old bastard was."

We all groaned as she continued stroking Tula, who was still
standing next to her, touching her, not happy to relax until he
felt she was a hundred percent okay. What a dog!

Lucky continued. "Alana helped me through the sudden death of my beloved dad. I hope I helped her as much as she did me. She always had a boyfriend, even at school. She was gorgeous. No boys looked at me much, but that didn't stop me crushing on them." Lucky smiled.

I felt compelled to say, "Oh that can't be true, Lucky," and I meant it. Sure, she wasn't run-of-the-mill-looking, but she had *something*.

"Oh, it's quite true." She smiled openly, and I was relieved to see what she perceived her looks were or weren't hadn't stopped her. Rather, that mindset had enhanced her free spirit and her independence. *And* likely her appeal.

There was another silence as Lucky slipped inside her most difficult memories and we all watched her expressive face move silently.

When she looked up at each of us, her voice was barely a whisper. "She just disappeared. Lost to me. To all who loved her. Nobody could find her. Not even me, because I had quashed my psychic gifts to fit into the airline's paradigm. To conform."

She continued very quietly, "I think I am so driven to find people who've disappeared because I know what it's like to not know what became of a loved one."

Tula jumped up with his front legs either side of hers and nudged her chin up with his nose, as if to say, "Don't go there."

We all waited, anticipation electrifying the air.

He broke her spell. Likely for her own good. She looked at us and said, "Since I moved to the States, I haven't felt at home with anyone like I do with the four of you." She gave us a small, genuine smile. I believe we all felt the same as Lucky did.

But one thing was sure.

The subject of Alana, Lucky's best friend, was closed.

I hoped temporarily so that we might help Lucky as much as she'd already helped me.

CHAPTER 43

BRIE

Hull, present day

I think the others were all alcohol'd-out. It was late, but sleep was something we could do another time, in another place.

As if in solidarity, we all gathered around the coffeepot. When my cup was full and I'd added a dash of cream, I stood over the sugar bowl. My hand, which usually shoveled four heaped spoons of sugar into a mug, now stopped after one.

"Guys?" I said tentatively. They all turned toward me. "Something weird is happening here. Seriously, I physically cannot get my hand to pick up a second spoonful of sugar. Look!"

I moved my right hand this way and that, proving its dexterity. Fear gripped me. "Do I have a lopsided mouth when I smile?" Teeth together, I forced a grin. Just when I was looking forward to complete and uninhibited happiness with Ryan, how cruel that I should have a stroke.

"It's Joy!" they all screamed at once, and BJ said, "Joy

doesn't approve of your eating habits. If we didn't approve of her so heartily, I'd call her a bitch."

"Holy shit! I thought I was having a stroke. Maybe my subconscious just doesn't want me to be happy." In spite of all this neurosis, relief infused my being.

"I think you're right, Brie. It doesn't. You have to teach your subconscious that you will, in every waking moment, milk this life of every single drop of joy—pardon the pun—your heart can hold. That you refuse to be anything but ecstatic about your life. Forget tomorrow. It will take care of itself," Lucky said as she looked deep into my eyes. "And when in doubt, ask Joy to help you have the courage of your new convictions."

We five smiled at each other as Chantelle said, "Now that Joy knows what you want—to stay alive and have a life with Ryan and not suffer from diabetes or anything—she will do whatever it takes for you to have your full quota of the man you love this time around."

"Oh." BJ's smile was wicked. "And to have copious sex without clothes on to make up for lost time. I know I've said it before, but it 'bares'—pardon the pun—repeating."

"And dance." Moxie spun three times with her arms akimbo. "Like you two are one. No crutches. No fear of falling. No special herb or flower. Just dance, dance, dance."

"I love it," I said gleefully, feeling quite euphoric.

A bag of Simba chips lay open on the table next to my favorite chocolate treats. Three Turkish Delights and a Cadbury's Wholenut. But guess what? I felt not a single desire for any.

Thanks, Joy.

Tula was giving Chantelle a try and enjoying her stroking

his thick, multicolored coat. *How does he know she's up next?* His beautiful eyes were closed. Herding was an exhausting business.

"Brie, do you suffer from sore feet?" Lucky asked, apropos of nothing.

I'd long since kicked off my shoes, so I extended my legs and wiggled my toes. "I have endless foot trouble. I have aways thought it was because I carry a hefty BMI, so I just kept schtum about it in case someone pointed out that painful fact."

"Brie, you are so far from fat. Sure, you are not a lean dancer this time, but you have to let that big image of *this* self go. You are proportionate with great boobs and a waist and a face that could launch a thousand ships," Lucky said kindly, but I felt she meant every word, and the others chimed in with their own assurances. "But back to your toes ... do you get callouses?"

"Holy shit!" I trilled. "You *are* psychic."

Lucky was quite serious. "No, Brie, it's just that as a ballerina you would have abused your feet. They'd be hard from soaking them in vodka to take the pointe-shoe pain away, and by twenty you likely had bunions and callouses and ten out of ten untended broken toes. You can get rid of those ailments by thanking your toes for reminding you your feet were abused in one of your lives, but you promise to pamper them in this one. When you get home, have a pedi every two weeks and lavish love on your feet every day."

"She's right," said BJ, throwing her head back and glugging down her nth Diet Coke.

And we lolled in comfortable silence until Chantelle said, "The only thing I miss is music."

BJ hauled her portable guitar from next to her chair, slung the strap over her head, fixed steel picks to the fingers of her right hand and plucked three bars before we all chimed in to sing "House of The Rising Sun."

But there was an odd noise.

Goodness. Mine weren't the only eyes and ears glued on Chantelle. Hell, I think we'd all been waiting forever to hear her sing because her enchanting speaking voice, so husky with yodel-like breaks in it, promised incredible vocals. The first thing she'd announced to Tula when she arrived was that her name meant "Song." I would bet with all this hype, "Is she country or rock and roll" was the only question being brandished about in our minds.

My good ear, fairly quivering with anticipation, was tilted entirely in Chantelle's direction when the onslaught came.

Holy shit! Think Old McDonald's farm in mating season.

The girl sounded like a bad dose of cat-scratch fever.

A fire engine on a hell mission would be more musical.

BJ stopped playing to put her fingers in her ears.

The strumming had stopped, but Chantelle hadn't stopped howling about the call of the rising sun.

Lucky spoke up over the noise that was Chant's uneven screech. "Well, that's that then. I am not psychic after all. I had visions of this Mediterranean beauty singing for a living in a past life!" She clamped both hands over her hanging jaw, which must have come unhinged with the shock of the wail emitting from our gorgeous Chantelle.

Lucky had a horrified look on her face. I didn't know if it was because of her outburst or because her ears hurt.

The others' eyes were nearly popping out as their faces moved in sheer shock, watching our hostie sister. But our lovely Chantelle had her eyes closed, enjoying the sound of her own voice, which, based on her blissful look, was *very* different in her head. She was genuinely oblivious of the strangled noises she was making.

She opened her eyes. "Oh, don't look at me, sillies. Feel the music. Clearly, Lucky and BJ have no ear for a melody." She smiled to show the chastisement was mild and closed her eyes again.

Soon I joined in with BJ's really lovely voice as she strummed. Lucky followed, as did Moxie, all singing at the top of our lungs to mask Chantelle's butchering of octaves and notes.

When at last The Rising Sun had set and beautiful Chants had stopped her screeching, we all sighed with relief. BJ put down her guitar and announced, "That's as much as I can take of that for ... a goodly while."

"Oh, don't say that," said Chantelle. "I love singing."

The girl, so smart, so quick-witted, so with it, was distinctly missing some serious musical smarts. What a "gedunta," as Miss Palmadesso liked to say—pronounced *Ghha-doon-tah*!

I saw BJ lean in toward Lucky. "You did it," she said softly but not softly enough. "You fixed her. How did you know how?" I knew she was talking about me.

Lucky shrugged. "I just asked for guidance like I do when I am on a case. It wasn't really me. It was my guides who told me what to say. I am just so relieved it worked. I hope my higher powers are close by for the rest of you." Lucky smiled at BJ, and the look they shared cemented these two were both empaths.

Lucky looked around. "Okay. Whip out your straws, ladies. Let's confirm who's next, because if we just ask, we know Moxie will say it's her." There followed a wild burrowing between couch cushions and in pockets, and finally the last three held up their straws, all much worse for wear. And it was only day one.

"It's meeeeeeeeeeeeeeeeeeeeeeee," chortled Chantelle, her rasp managing to yodel the end of the squeal.

"Like we didn't know." Moxie sulked.

"Prepare yourself for a wild ride, Chants. Be sure you can let go enough to let Lucky help you lose your new self to help find your old self," I advised, now an old hand.

"Watching you kinda sorta gave me the courage. Though my ride may shock you all even worse than Brie's did."

"Can't wait," I said. And everyone else aired their two cents' worth of giddy expectation.

"It's 1:45 a.m. I guess we should really go to bed now so we can fortify ourselves to explore Chantelle's worlds in a few hours ..." Lucky stopped a second before the sound of a chime.

It was the doorbell.

CHAPTER 44

BRIE

Hull, present day

We looked at our watches and then each other, wide-eyed.

Nearly 2 a.m. Not an appropriate time for someone to pop in.

Even Tula was silent for three long beats, and then he shrieked his objection and, barking, belted down the stairs. We followed, resembling the tactical teams about to bash in a perp's door on TV. One on top of the other, inching along, not daring to lose the security of the semicircle we'd formed.

We shuffled like that to the door, which must have chimed at least three more times during our journey, managing to force its decibels past Tula's very noisy objection to the lateness of the hour.

Wordlessly we assumed our positions to protect Lucky when she cracked the door open a smidge. No doubt we were all hoping the horror of five un-made-up, tear-streaked middle-aged faces would scare the ax murderer away.

But what I saw was much more shocking.

CHAPTER 45

BRIE

Hull, present day

"RYAN?" I heard myself scream. "How ...?" but I didn't wait for his answer. I simply flung myself into his arms.

I was hanging on to him and weeping copiously, and as he clung to me to stop me from falling, I heard him say, "Hi, ladies. Sorry it's so late. I missed my wife so much I stole the company jet just to tell her so in person."

There wasn't a shy hair on the other heads in the room. "Boy! Are you a sight for sore eyes!" said BJ.

"Of course, you'd be hunky." That was Chantelle. "You've got a beautiful wife!"

Moxie crooned, "You can put your size fourteens under my bed anytime!"

Lucky's voice was firm. "Moxie, that's our friend's HUSBAND. You don't say those things to a HUSBAND!"

Moxie shrugged. "I tell it like it is."

To which Chantelle replied, "Well, stop it. You do realize the shoe size refers to the d—"

"Girls, girls," chastised Lucky, attempting to corral us to make a path so Ryan could get in the door.

I stopped my blubbing and pulled back my face to look at my husband. He smiled that ridiculously wonderful smile as the girls behind me all ooh'd and aah'd at his show of dedication.

"Please, Ryan. Come inside." Lucky gestured at the path she'd worked so hard at creating to let him in.

"No, thanks all the same. I wondered if I could steal Brie for a bit. I don't have long before somebody finds two pilots and a Gulfstream G650ER missing. I'm safe. Nobody will miss me, but that bird and those two ..."

I loved how he sounded. So self-deprecating. So strong. So brave. I was so proud of my handsome, passionate husband.

"Please, go ahead. We'll miss her, but you get first dibs," Lucky said.

I looked down at myself. I had on Lucky's big fluffy cotton gown with my swimsuit underneath.

I moved inside the door, but Ryan grabbed my hand. "Where are you off to?" he asked, smiling.

Oh, that smile. "I can't go out like this," I stammered, feeling shy he should see me so unkempt.

"You think I flew sixteen hours and fourteen minutes to check what you were wearing? I just want you, Brie. The rest doesn't matter."

There were sounds of women swooning behind me.

"Do any of you have a pair of socks for my wife? I'm damn sure she wouldn't pack any."

Lucky disappeared and came back with a pair of what looked like rugby socks.

"Great!" Ryan smiled his thanks and I sat down and pulled them on. They came above my knees.

"Happy now?" I asked Ryan, and he grinned, giving me the once-over.

"Delighted."

I turned to them. "I'll see you when I see you."

"Here." Lucky thrust a soft blanket at me.

I thanked her as I took it, then smiled at all the faces who, in such a short time, had become so dear. I was rewarded with roars of good wishes and loud applause.

Ryan bundled me up in the blanket, grabbed my hand and led the way down Lucky's long outdoor staircase. I saw a taxi sign on the car parked parallel to the house. To protect my feet feeling the sharp shale of the driveway, Ryan carried me until we got to the smooth asphalt of Spring Street.

There he bent his head into the cab window and thanked the driver, who gave him a card.

"Thank you, Ben. I can't be long, an hour or three? Can I give you a call?"

"Sure thing, man," the driver said and waved us off, as if giving us permission to do whatever we wished. We laughed at that. I felt like a teenager. Or at least what I thought a teenager should feel.

My head was reeling as we walked hand in hand down the middle of the deserted road toward the seawall.

"You did this for me?" I asked incredulously.

"I hope this proves I will do *anything* for you, my Brie."

"Will you get fired for stealing the corporate jet?" I asked. Worried.

"I'll beat them to it. I wrote my resignation letter on the way here. When my highest priority left me without any good reason I could fathom, I realized I needed to get my priorities in order. You and I will start living life to its fullest once you get home. We'll travel and picnic and sneak away for dirty weekends."

I laughed. There was nobody to escape from in our house.

Tears welled and spilled over and onto my cheeks. "Oh, Ryan," was all I could muster.

CHAPTER 46

BRIE

Hull, present day

We sat on the seawall as close as we could get, wrapped in the blanket and, as if mere words were superfluous for now, we silently watched the angry ocean. Listened to sounds of stones, grains of sand, crabs and shells holding on for dear life and then being overpowered by the sea's determination. I admired their resolve as I heard them being sucked from their resting places with a purgative swish as the sea receded. There was a moment of ocean silence as the wave grew and grew until it couldn't grow any more, then crashed angrily, furious it didn't make a tenth of an inch higher before it reached its zenith.

Perhaps, like me, Ryan was aware that pissed-off wave had just set the scene for what we needed to purge. A long buildup and then an eruption of all that we'd held inside for far too long.

"I'll start," he said.

I waited, looking at him. Why was I not fearful of what he was about to say?

"This is the first time you have not been there to greet me when I got home, and I felt the loneliness like a gaping chasm. No, worse. Like a black hole. Life is nothing without you, my Brie."

Perhaps I could delay what I *needed* to tell him by sharing not only the dream but what happened after the dream.

I told him how I found out how much I'd hurt him as Mikhail and I understood how awful it must have been for him, thinking that he'd been abandoned and that my love was not true.

I explained how I now understood why I believed, albeit subconsciously, that by dedicating myself to him, abandoning all outside interests and the chance to make friends, I was paying him back for all he'd given me. I was making up for deserting him and Coupé because the dream made it seem like I had done just that. But now I understood that it wasn't my fault. I had no control, and I was desperate he should know that.

I marveled at how Karma, though he'd waited a century, was gracious enough to allow me to right the wrong Mikhail or Ryan thought I'd committed. I was passionate about telling him we needed to reinforce our love in this life and appreciate the gift that was ours to share every day. That miraculously, we had this second chance of a lifetime together and our baggage had prevented us from giving our all.

Whether or not Ryan believed my story of Polina and Mikhail after the dream, I couldn't tell. But his relief that there were no holds barred was apparent, and he appreciated my telling him things from my heart. I knew I'd have time to convince him what I told him was real. On another day. Perhaps in the not so distant future.

But when he spoke, Ryan's beautiful timbre was edged with sadness. "I have nothing at all to hide from you. Nothing. But I know there is a disconnect from you. I realize I must be so full of myself because, after all these years, I know nothing of your life. I should have insisted long ago that you shared, even though you were reluctant."

I felt my stomach roil with apprehension.

There was so *much* Ryan didn't know about me.

Would he still love me when he knew it all?

CHAPTER 47

BRIE

Hull, present day

And my stomach only got worse when he said, "And we've never really talked about Maggie."

I gripped the gold locket around my neck.

But it was clear Ryan's need to understand forced him to hijack a corporate jet to get here.

He needed answers.

And I was scared shitless.

He put his arm around me and squeezed so tight, my tears spilled out.

He kept his arm there, very still as I nestled into him, delaying the moment he might stop loving me for my past. For Maggie.

When I felt his eyes turn away from me, terrified that he'd read my mind, I glanced at Ryan, and he was looking up into the night. I tried to allay my fears by looking at the sky through his eyes.

The fierce wind seemed confused, pushing thick clouds this way, then that. But between the gaps, the celestial bodies preened, showing off their brilliance and complexities.

"For some weird reason, every time I see Venus, the brightest object in the sky except the sun and the moon, I think of you. I should think of the sun because you are *that* important to me. You make me bloom and grow. But it's Venus ..."

"That's what he said," I blurted.

Ryan turned to me, and in all the years together, never had I seen a flicker of jealousy.

But here it was, burning between us.

"Who?" It was barely a whisper. It was clear, even in the moonlight, that color had drained from his face. I saw his lids shut, like the aperture of a camera, slowly, to shield himself from the person I was about to name.

"You," I said, grabbing his hand that had dropped from my shoulders. "You who are my Mikhail. You who are my Ryan."

He swallowed and hung his head, forcing the air trapped before my explanation to be released in relief.

"Oh my God, Ryan, I know so much more about why I love you, why you love me, about our insecurities and our yearnings, all because of the experience I've just had—"

He cut me off. "It sounds ... well, otherworldly and interesting and important."

He forced a pause, and it was laden with my misgivings.

With fingertips on my chin, he slowly tipped my face to his like heroes do in the movies, and jade eyes held mine. "But first, I need you to tell me everything about *this* life, starting at your very beginning."

And I reached up and kissed him. A desperate kiss of longing. As if this kiss was our last and I wanted to make the very most of it. He held my face like I was precious. The salt of our tears mingled in the midst of our kiss. He, too, knew what I was about to tell him could change our world forever.

CHAPTER 48

BRIE

Hull, present day

I t was the longest, most meaningful kiss we'd shared since our very first. That we could recapture all of our passion was evident in that kiss, but more than that, there was deep tenderness and care. Still kissing me, I felt his hardness, and just when I had divine visions of Mikhail and Ryan grinding me to sweet ecstasy, Ryan pulled away and held me at arm's length.

"You do this to me, Brie." He looked down at himself. "I am surrounded by lithe, often naked women during costume changes, and nothing gets to me but you. Every molecule in my body responds only to you."

I was overcome. I couldn't aptly express what his sincere words meant to me.

But he didn't know my sordid past.

Worse yet, he wouldn't let me delay telling him about it any longer.

He took my hand as if it was the first time he'd held it and pulled me back to the seawall, sat down and swung his legs over the wall. I did the same, and I snuggled into his arm as he threw the blanket over me. At least I wouldn't be looking into his eyes when I told him everything. To see those brilliant emeralds dim with disappointment would be punishment second to none.

If I had been brave, I would have begun, but fear clasped at my throat.

He knew me so well and said, "I don't care what it is or how it might hurt me. I must know all you've kept from me from your earliest memories. I always worried that breaking open your shell would be painful and make you vulnerable. Now, selfishly, I need to know everything. For my own sanity. For my own worth as far as you are concerned."

He was quiet for a long time, waiting for me to summon my courage.

I tried to start a few times, but it was as if a hand pushed the words back down my throat until I coughed and gagged a little.

Vile bile filled my mouth.

And I had not yet begun.

I shivered.

He pulled in a ragged breath. "My need to know every single thing about you supersedes my fear of how things might change because of it. But you must tell me, Brie, because I believe it's that which you keep from me that's holding you back from loving me with all your heart. And I need you to love me with all your heart. I need to understand what shaped you. I need to share *all* of you, not just the perfect parts you show me."

His sincerity squeezed my heart so hard it hurt.

I felt the tears flow. They were quiet tears. Were they tears for me? Or for Ryan. Both? I had never wanted to sully our lives together with the truth about my beginnings or what really happened to Mag.

Oh God, he would stop loving me!

I thought I was so good at pushing it all down and out of reach, where no one could find the ugliness. But I hadn't fooled Ryan, though he must have pretended I had for decades. For my sake.

I gazed out to the blackest part of the churning ocean. I was so afraid. There was so much.

I began so softly, I wondered if the sea would mercifully drown me out.

"My name was Janet Venter until I turned fifteen.

"Then I found a loaded gun. And used it. That's how I became Brie Lenz."

I took a peep at his face.

His look of utter horror was worse than I could have imagined.

I realized not even the merciless, ferocious ocean could subdue the dreadfulness I was about to share.

I climbed down from the short wall, blanket and all, and pulled Ryan's dangling legs over to the other side, so his back was to the ocean, and I sat on the pavement with my back against the seawall so he couldn't see my pain.

And I couldn't see his.

Then I let it all out—a volcano spewing not the awesome reddish-golden glow but rather a foul, poisonous black lava.

That was my early life.

CHAPTER 49

BRIE

Kempton Park, South Africa, 1959

My senses took me back.

Every smell, every taste, every disappointment. The soot. The earsplitting noise. The curses. The drunken laughter. The constant smell of body fluids, not mine, nor my mother's.

I WAS BORN and dragged up in the gutter known as The Viljoen Caravan Park, a derelict den of iniquity that spanned two acres on the wrong side of the railway tracks a mile away from Jan Smuts Airport, as it was known in my day.

Packed into the chain-link perimeter like Portuguese sardines in tomato sauce were caravans with wheels long lost, now hoisted onto stolen bricks to give them some stability.

I wished the same could be said of the inhabitants. Stability was nowhere to be found in the "Villies," so named by its inmates.

The noise was deafening, not because of the ever choof-choof-choofing trains or the cars going by as fast as they could in attempts to unsee how the other half lived, nor from the airplanes taking off so close you felt you had to duck.

No, the constant noise came from the drunk and disorderly occupants of the Villies, anointed "white trash" by the towns-folk. Those who inhabited the pizza slice of wasteland nobody wanted to buy. The land value was as negligible as the people who lived there.

No orifice or a square centimeter of skin on the inhabitants was ever free of soot. No amount of scrubbing in the tiny standup shower that mostly worked and served all of us misfits could remove every speck of black carbon from our being.

I remember wondering why people beyond our crippled fence looked so clean, even when they were splattered with mud.

I didn't recall how old I was when I found out life shouldn't be so hard, but my earliest conclusion came as a result of the lack of privacy, decency and decorum: Sometimes when naked people grunted, a baby grew. In my case, after the stork plucked me out, she surely must have delivered my resistant, squalling self to the wrong address. It was the stork's mishap that caused my mother to remind me frequently that I was a giant mistake and she'd never wanted me.

Until I was six, I believed children were only born to serve their mothers and do their bidding, so I waited on the balls of my feet for the next command: "Janet! Get me my cigarettes. Janet, pour me a brandy. Janet, go next door next time you hurt yourself. I'm busy. Janet, don't come in when my door is closed. Janet, be nice to Uncle Willie/Andy/Frikkie."

Forget kindergarten. I didn't go to grade 1 or 2 either. No one cared to tell me I should. I didn't know going to school was an option to staying put and living with the screaming and swearing and drinking around me. Even if I had known, money was spent on adults, so a uniform for me would have been out of the question. But no kid could go to school without one.

When I was old enough to have curiosity overcome fear, I ventured out of The Villies, and miles away, I saw neat girls my age all wearing the same clothes. It was a puzzlement, but I envied how neat, tidy, and sootless they looked.

One day I followed a group of four girls who wore the same hats and carried small suitcases as they went into a neat two-story building. It had an actual playground in the yard. With a swing. How I longed to go inside those big twirly gates. I sat on the grass and marveled at its soft feel. We didn't have grass where I lived.

I never took my eyes off the swing through the gaps in the two-story wrought-iron fence. A loud bell rang, and I jumped.

Chattering, laughing boys and girls streamed out of the building and spilled onto the playground. They played and played, some on the swing, the boys with little marbles, the girls holding hands and revolving in a circle, singing.

I'd never felt more alone. If only ...

When it was clear nobody missed me at The Villies, I ventured out every day to watch other children at play. I found similar buildings with similar playgrounds. Some with just boys. Some just girls. I was floored to see kids wandering from the playground to their mother's waiting car. The realization that some parents made an effort to pick up their children was as earth-shattering to me as sootless people.

One day, after their school, I followed some kids with a neat lady in stockings and high heels into a big flat building.

The smell inside was like nothing I'd ever experienced. I think I smelled knowledge.

Books. Thousands and thousands and thousands of them.

The only book I'd seen in The Villies was the one carried by old Oom Klokkie. He read from it and then shouted out words. Everyone called him a Bible thumper.

Twelve or so chairs were laid out in a half-moon shape in an open area between the neat rows of books. The family I'd followed sat down and waited. No raised voices. Another mother and two children sat down, and then another. And another until all the chairs were full. Except the chair that stood alone in the middle of the half-moon circle.

Out came the prettiest young woman I'd ever seen, a beautiful lady with thick hair, a tiny perfect body and a smile that made me feel the world was better than I had imagined. Her skin was smooth and tanned. Her eyes, dancing hazelnuts. She smelled of soft, delicate flowers that only grow in the spring and only in neighborhoods without soot. I wanted to be like her more than anything.

And she smiled. Oh, how she smiled. With warmth and kindness. Was she the angel Oom Klokkie shouted about?

Beautiful lady sat in the special chair. She opened a book and began to read. It was musical and captivating, and with eyes open or closed, an adventure played before me.

Some nights, if I sat on the roof of our caravan, I could faintly hear voices carried by the wind and I could see just a corner of a giant outdoor screen with colors and faces popping in now and then. Mom called it a drive-in.

Now I'd discovered a miracle.

Beautiful lady's words conjured up a full-size drive-in screen with characters and sounds and even feelings right in front of me. Pure magic.

I hung around that library, hiding behind one of the tall shelves, every day for a week, same time Monday through Friday. I was dying to join in, but all the other kids wore shoes. I thought shoes were a requirement to enjoy the magic close up.

One day, when there was one seat left, I plucked up courage and spit on my hands, making sure no one could see me. I rubbed my face vigorously before wiping my hands on the back of my dress. Then I took that rare empty seat, sitting on the edge with my hands tucked under me in case not all the carbon had transferred to my dress. I hid bare feet far underneath the chair, my toes curled under.

I wondered what was better, the story from up close or the feeling of being included.

From that day on, even if all the chairs were full, beautiful lady pulled in another, making the half circle bigger. She found me hovering on the perimeter and always smiled at me and dipped her head toward the chair before taking her seat.

An invitation.

She didn't seem to care I was barefoot.

In the third week, she asked why I didn't go to school. I didn't know. She asked where I lived, and I was too ashamed to tell her. Then she asked if I would like her to teach me how to read.

Miss Natalie Palmadesso changed my life.

Suddenly it didn't matter if I didn't have friends or if somebody was hollering and swearing in our caravan, the one next door or down the dirt road. I was allowed to take books back to the caravan for *free*.

And soon, I knew how to read them.

I was overcome with pleasure. Books took me far, far away. And with my new library card, I was the richest little girl in the whole world. Books shielded me from the unpleasantness around me, gave me something to take my mind off what was being done to me, and ignited my love of the written word. Miss Palmadesso had been the catalyst who spawned my imagination.

I felt very, very rich.

Miss Palmadesso somehow saw to it that I got a uniform, shoes and socks and, by grade 3, I was a bona fide student at the public school two miles from the Villies.

Books sustained me, and Miss Palmadesso nurtured my soul and my mind. How she continued to clothe me and made me look like the others, I'll never know. But she did, all the way until I was fifteen.

CHAPTER 50

BRIE

Hull, present day

"Ryan, don't cry for me. It was long ago and far, far away. But until you, I had no idea love existed."

He'd joined me on the pavement, with our backs against the seawall, looking toward Lucky's brightly lit house. She was right; in spite of the lack of window coverings, we couldn't see in. If someone was close to the window, an unidentifiable shadow appeared, nothing more.

"But what you went through ..." His voice was thick with emotion. "When did it happen ... the ... killing?"

Now began the really hard part. Gone would be any illusion of his wife once being an innocent. But I soldiered on. I'd come this far.

"I felt cursed. Being 'pretty' caused old men to be lewd and disgusting; it made young men want to feel my boobs or push me into positions I didn't want to go; it meant girls at school not liking me and boys at school becoming stupid around me. It was only in the airline I felt normal. It's where I felt I belonged."

"And I took you away from that lifestyle before you had a real chance to enjoy it."

I smiled. "I went willingly. I regret nothing as far as you are concerned, my love." I said it so softly, I was surprised when Ryan's beautiful face collapsed with tenderness. He'd heard me.

He waited patiently to hear more. That was my Ryan. Never pushy. Always respectful. Just like my Mikhail.

"I was used to being physically abused. Hit. Forced to have sex. Nobody protected me. I thought of slashing my face with the top of a can more than once. That would take away the unwanted attention." I sighed. Resigned. "I suppose *not* doing so makes me vain."

Ryan jolted upright. "Don't you dare say that, Brie. It wasn't an easy decision for a child. There was pain involved. It had nothing to do with vanity. Poor child."

Going back to that fifteen-year-old girl I was then was horrific. I closed my eyes, wanting to run away, never to think about it ever again. Ryan was the only reason I would ever, ever go back there.

"One of my mother's constant stream of paying suitors or husbands—I couldn't tell which was which—had a gun which he brandished about, showing off. Guns weren't that prevalent when I was young.

"I was reading, trying with all my might not to hear the noises coming from my mother's room, when I saw, coming up the path, an old beau of hers. He'd already had his way with me once. I knew there would be hell to pay one way or another when he realized she was 'otherwise engaged.' I snuck into my mother's tiny room and tried not to see what was going on there. I found the gun under the naked man's discarded pants and left quietly.

"Just then, this oaf came up the steps of the caravan, an evil grin marring his features. There was no mistake. It wasn't my mother he was looking for. I turned the radio on full blast. Not an unusual happenstance when mother had 'company.' It was a particularly small caravan.

"I held the gun behind my back. He didn't suspect a thing. He threw me on my bed, which doubled as the family couch. I use the term 'family' loosely. I lay shivering with my legs held tightly closed. I will never, ever forget the look on his face as he took off his belt and unzipped his fly. The former he'd used before to get me to open my legs.

"He leapt on me as 'Crimson and Clover' played on the radio. Hearing that song still makes me vomit. I grabbed for a pillow, and he looked at me, annoyed, as he reached for his belt to beat me into submission. It was the first sign that he'd actually seen me.

"I said, 'No need for the belt, but if it's like the last time, your pointy chin will poke into my rib cage and it hurts,' and placed the fat, stuffed, nylon cushion over my chest as if it would act as a buffer.

"He placed his forehead onto the pillow as he angled himself and began to force my legs apart. I pulled the gun from behind me and shot through the pillow. 'Crimson and Clover' and the cushion masked most of the noise and absorbed most of the blood.

"He went slack immediately, and I shimmied out from under him and ran, barefoot, for three or four miles. I'd grabbed my haversack and used it to wipe off any fingerprints from the gun before I dropped it inside the bag and ran like the wind. When I was far enough away from the Villies, I spied a wrought-iron grate. A public drain. Pretending I was tying a shoelace, I opened the side of the grate, checked to see nobody was around, and tipped the haversack over the rushing water. The gun disappeared after an anticlimactic plop into the rushing water.

"I hid through the night curled into a ball under a bridge. It was winter. I was freezing. Luckily, I was alone. Remember, there wasn't much homelessness back then.

"The next day was Monday, and I waited until I saw Miss Palmadesso's car arrive in the library parking lot. The minute she saw me, she motioned me over. I must have looked a sight. All covered in blood. Barefoot, just like she first found me, bar the blood.

"She took me to a friend of hers about twenty miles away, an elderly man who owned a corner grocery store. She told him I had an aptitude for figures and, in exchange for doing his books, I should get free board in the back of his shop and a small stipend. I overheard her telling Mr. Swart that I came from an abusive home and to be nothing but kind to me.

"She gave me loads of her old clothes and a couch. Those were the fanciest and only worldly goods I'd ever possessed, and the room was certainly the biggest I'd ever lived in.

"And it was all my own. Mr. Swart was a man of his word and was nothing but kind. I did his books, and he was thrilled. We had a respectful relationship though not a close one.

"Miss Palmadesso helped me change my name. We both liked Brie Lenz."

I looked at Ryan for the first time since I'd started my saga. His face was shrouded in sadness. "Ryan, isn't it amazing that I chose a last name that reflected my soulmate's profession way back in the 1870s, a man that I'd meet years later in *this* life?"

"One story at a time, Brie. Please." Ryan squeezed my hand.

"Miss Palmadesso tutored me every weekend and miraculously arranged for me sit for matric exams in a high school close by. I passed with flying colors, all thanks to her. I was sixteen when she applied for a scholarship for me, and I got it. I attended a college close to the store. By then, Mr. Swart was paying me a small salary. I was there for two years. Then I moved to Benoni because it was far enough away from the Villies and a town with families. No caravan parks for poor whites. I worked for the building society, where the pilot recruited me two years later. By that time, I had a small flat. The one you saw when I met you."

I'd run out of breath.

Ryan was gazing at me. I was afraid to read what his face expressed, but when I glanced at him, I saw something I hadn't expected.

Pride.

"You are so strong, Brie. So brave. I am so proud to know you. To know your fortitude and your ability to swim upstream in spite of those impossible odds."

"There is no reason to be proud of me. I never did anything with my life except ..."

"Except marry me?" he asked.

I threw my arms around his neck and nearly knocked him over. "Oh Ryan, you are by far the very best man that's ever happened to me."

"Well, shit." He smiled. "That's not saying much, is it?"

I started to giggle. And giggle. Soon he was giggling too, then we laughed in earnest till we were rolling around in the middle of the night on the pavement in Hull.

"Well, actually, you are the only man I ever *wanted* to sleep with."

He reached for me and held me tightly in his arms, recognizing the huge truth my words implied. I believe he took the compliment as it was intended.

We sat still, listening to the waves, feeling the bursts of wind changing direction as he held the blanket closed around us.

"Did you keep in touch with Miss Palmadesso?"

"I did. Where would I be without her?" I suddenly wanted to cry again as gratitude coursed through my veins.

"I love Miss Palmadesso. She was kind enough to help a young six- or seven-year-old; stalwart enough to support her throughout her years at school—providing for her; and brave enough to protect a teenager who'd had enough abuse. Then committed enough to see her safely to and through college." He paused, thought for a while, then said, "I want to buy her a house."

I looked at him, and he was dead serious. I smiled and shook my head. His heart was so big. "Normal people would just send her a bouquet with thanks, but that's what I love about you. You're not normal."

"Thanks very much," he said.

"My beloved Miss Palmadesso married and moved to Cape Town in my first year of college. I was so happy for her. We kept in touch for years and years. She flew in for my wings ceremony in the airline. I was so grateful. Most girls had hordes of family there; I had my Miss Palmadesso. She was worth ten of their family members. Every time I flew to Cape Town, we met for lunch or brunch. She had two beautiful kids. When I met you, I phoned and told her. She was so happy for me. But before you and I were married, her husband, a doctor, was recruited in Australia and she emigrated. We lost touch eventually. I owe her everything."

"No. I do. Where would I be without you, my Brie?"

It was a rhetorical question.

"When we met," he said, "you told me you'd had a single mother who was killed by a car when you were a teenager. I always found it strange you never wanted to go to her grave. I knew there was immense hurt lurking behind your exquisite face, but I was too afraid to push for answers, lest I lose you, and soon enough I just took you for who you were. A beautiful, smart, funny girl who loved me. I felt like ... I feel like the luckiest man alive. It's so easy to love you, Brie. It's so easy to look at you and forget there are other people also living on our planet."

A silence and a bliss descended upon us as we sat, propped up by the seawall, entangled.

Ryan gave me a squeeze. "Let's find Miss Palmadesso again so I can thank her. Better still, now I am free as a bird, let's make Aussie our first adventure."

I wanted to cry again. How did I get so lucky?

CHAPTER 51

BRIE

Hull, present day

"Now. We need to talk about our Mags." Ryan's face was somber.

I dreaded those words more than I dreaded telling him about my early life. The former he had no say in. It was easy for him to love a victim.

But what about a liar?

A neglectful mother?

A drunk just like my own mother?

Oh, dear God, when Ryan found out, he would hate me. Twenty years after the fact, he would hate me more than he would have then.

I would lose his heart.

And then mine would stop beating.

But I owed him the truth.

"My Ryan, I knew how much you wanted a child."

"I never wanted children before I fell in love with you, then I craved an extension of you."

I carried on. "Ten years we tried, IVF. That was so grueling, with constant disappointments every month, or when we made it past that, the pain in our hearts was even worse than the miscarriages we were forced to endure. And we could have bought a house at the seaside with what we spent on trying to get pregnant. And then, ten years later, a minute before my biological clock stopped ticking, together we created our Maggie. Just by loving each other.

"I never shared with you how afraid I was throughout the pregnancy. I was plagued by questions I had no answers to. Was I cut out to be a mother? Had my mother's disgusting parenting rubbed off on me? Would I let you down? Would I let our child down? Would you feel your life was complete if this child wasn't growing in my womb? From grape to grapefruit as she grew inside me, I lived only for your happiness because mine was nowhere in sight. Fear had replaced it."

"Why didn't you share this with me, my love?" Ryan's voice was forlorn, as if it was his fault I suffered alone.

"I couldn't without telling you the reason for my fears, and I was afraid to do that in case you'd run for the hills. I couldn't risk your love for my insecurities.

"And then our beautiful little girl was born and she was perfect in every way. Her bow-shaped mouth, her newborn blue eyes barely hiding the green of your gorgeous eyes that would soon emerge."

Ryan took over. "And then I went away on that trip. I begged you to come with me on the tour because I couldn't cancel. It was an important one, and I'd just been promoted to director. I begged you to have Hester come in and help you."

"Hester was your maid growing up, Ryan, not mine. I wasn't comfortable with anyone but you."

He nodded. "Now I understand even better. But even at the time, I acknowledged you wanted to take care of Maggie on your own. And I respected that. But I realized later, you had no one of your own you could call on, and I should have insisted."

"And I let you down. NO! Worse!" I cried out without intention. It was like it was spewing out of me like an apple laced with poison that my stomach could no longer hold on to.

Ryan looked at me. The fear on his face nearly made me run back to Lucky's and lock the door.

Little did he know, the worst was yet to come.

And then my stomach heaved again, ousting the long-suppressed, long-rotted piece of poisoned apple which became five toxic words: "I killed our baby girl."

CHAPTER 52

BRIE

Hull, present day

I dared not look at his beloved face in case I saw hatred there, but I had come too far to turn back now. "Please let me tell you the whole story before you judge me."

Ryan started to say something, and I held up my hand. "Please," I implored. "I saw how elated you were, and I loved you all the more for feeling that way. The nursery you painted. The crib you assembled. You were so excited. And Ryan, all I felt was ice-cold fear.

"You met me *after* I'd learned decorum and grace. I never wanted you to see the girl I once was. I couldn't risk losing you because of a past I had no part in. Where I came from, children were a nuisance. A curse. What if, when the baby was born, I felt nothing? What if I was, in essence, the same as my neglectful mother? What if I let you down because I was an unfit mother? What if I didn't deserve this child? What if God was punishing me for killing a man who was trying to rape me and running away at fifteen and never owning up, and because of what I'd done, God took her away? I couldn't bear to see the pain of loss on your face. And if we lost her, it would be all my fault because I had taken a life. It was payback.

"Oh God, how perfect our Maggie was. I loved her so. I loved her to distraction. And the way you looked at her made me love you more."

Ryan's hurt clouded his face. "What kind of a man did you think you'd married? Why would you think I would love you less if I knew of your abuse?"

"My love, all I had known before you, before the airline, was neglect and betrayal. Living in the underbelly of society makes a girl put up a very strong shield. I had killed a man with a gun, and I'd fled and changed my name. How many human beings, without being present, could justify that action? Knowing I'd never be able to share my history once I'd become a new person didn't mean I could erase all the awful things that shaped me. Yes, I was abused as a child. Yes, my mother was no mother at all. I was a pawn passed from one to another. I tried so hard to be invisible, but everyone took a piece of my body and my soul. Miss Palmadesso, who insisted when I was old enough that I call her Miss Natalie, was the only light in my life. The only pure part of my existence. She saved that part of my soul I had left, nurtured it and allowed it to grow again. I understood when that pig forced me down on the bed, only because Miss Natalie had told me I did not deserve to be treated that way, that I could do something about it."

I gathered my courage for the really hard part. "So, you see, my love, you were too important. You were only the second person in my world to love me. I wasn't giving that up for anything. I *couldn't* jeopardize your love with the truth. But when you wanted a child so badly, I was worried sick. My fears were real."

"Brie, I *had* to go on that tour. I couldn't let it float on its own. But I worried myself sick. I barely remember that success. It didn't really matter. I was too worried about you. And I was right."

"Don't think of blaming yourself. It was my choice that you go. The first two days were fabulous. I was nailing the motherhood thing. I know you knew that; you must have heard it in my voice. I hadn't slept a wink in forty-eight hours, though, because I was too afraid she would wake and I wasn't there. I didn't trust the monitor. By the third day, I was so tired I could barely lift my body to change her, feed her, rock her. But I did. Then, as the sun went down, Maggie started to cry. And cry. And cry. I panicked. I had no one I could call. I called the hospital and asked what was wrong with my child. They asked how old she was and if she was our first. The nurse laughed and said, 'Don't panic. All is well. If she's eating and pooping and burping, she's just fine. Perhaps she's airing her lungs. Don't worry. Sometimes they just like to get out any misery they might be feeling.'

"I was jolted by that. Why would Maggie be miserable at such a young age? Maybe she knew that I was not meant to have a child. Maybe she knew my fears. Maybe ... maybe ... maybe. And still Maggie cried and cried and cried. I was beside myself. I was dead tired. I changed her nappies even when they were dry, and she cried. I rocked her; she cried. I tried to feed her; she pulled her little head away. I put music on loud to drown out her cries and danced around the lounge, holding her tight, but I could hear her cries through the sound of 'Every Breath You Take.' I was at the end of my tether.

"She'd been crying for six hours straight. I have never been a drinker because I saw how drink destroyed people. I detested the smell. It was the stench of trouble. But I thought maybe I could hold my nose and down some scotch to calm my quivering nerves. I had one glass with ginger ale. I felt a bit better. And Maggie still cried. I called the hospital again. Another nurse also dismissed my fears. Too fearful to put her into her crib, I lay our beloved child on my chest. And then I must have fallen asleep, though I think ... I truly can't remember ... she may have still been crying.

"Oh, God, Ryan. I woke up to silence. I had been asleep for four hours. I thanked the Lord our child had stopped crying and I started rubbing her little back. She was so still. So very still. My heart was so full of love for her. My head pounded as I lifted her up to admire her beauty. So still. Oh, God. So stiff. I jolted up, my heart pounding, and I held her left side to my ear. Not even the slightest beat of a little heart. Nothing. I heard myself scream, and she didn't move in my arms.

"I looked down and was horrified to find her lips were blue. Oh, God, Ryan. I lovingly laid her on the carpet. I'd been trained in the airline to resuscitate all ages, so I gave her mouth-to-mouth while two fingers compressed her little heart rhythmically, lightly, so as not to break any ribs. Oh, God, Ryan. As I was doing this, I knew. Our baby was dead. And it's true I would never, ever hurt her, but I didn't cure what was causing her to cry, and worst of all, I slept through her last hours." With that, a fresh bout of gushing tears engulfed me.

His arms were around me. I hadn't sobbed that hard since we'd lost her. "The coroner had concluded SIDS was to blame. But I knew it was my fear that had killed her. My uncertainty. My ignorance. My curse. And the whisky."

"Brie, my darling. You were exhausted. You hadn't slept for three nights, maybe four. You called the hospital for help—not once but twice. And you only slept for four hours. You must have been a zombie. And terrified, not knowing what to do. You were at your wits' end. So you had a scotch. One single scotch does not make you a murderer. Or a drunk. It makes you human. Likely if that were me, I would have had three or four. When you are helpless, booze can be a much-needed numbing agent."

"It was one but a big one." I held up four fingers.

"I am not judging you."

"In my exhaustion it was all I needed to knock me out, even though our child must have still been crying."

I sobbed. "How could I tell you I had passed out from booze, Ryan? I was so deeply ashamed. I never wanted you to know that I was everything I feared most. A drunk like my mother. A neglectful mother, just like my mother. When you called and said, 'I can hear her crying. Is she okay?' and I said, 'Yes, she just needs changed; I must go'—by that time, she'd been crying for five hours. I didn't know what to do, Ryan. I didn't know what to do." Panic engulfed me all over again.

He whispered "Shhhh, shhhh" into my ear as I cried giant big wracking sobs. All these years I'd kept this secret from him.

Between great, big, wet heaves, I got out, "My track record is lousy as concerns babies. I terminated my baby and my own existence thanks to serious alcohol poisoning in the life in which I first met you, well, the first time that I know of, as of tonight. Maybe the punishment for that was the mother I was born to in this life."

He let me talk, just rocking me like he would a baby. How ironic.

"My love," he said after he'd cleared his throat. "Who the hell says you have to be punished for everything you do? Sure, I get karma and all that, but circumstances come into play with the decisions we make, and if our intentions aren't evil, well ... you've been known to give a cockroach a funeral!" He smiled, and his index finger followed the line of my chin. I laughed between tears. He was right. I hated to see anything die.

Ryan wasn't finished. "We never needed a baby to complete us. We were complete before Maggie came. It's my fault you were all alone. I knew you needed me to be there. I knew it. But work came first. It wasn't your fault. You were distraught, and who knows what other forces were at play in your psyche. Either from your youth or maybe this past life ..."

"So you DO believe in past lives?" I was part shocked and in greater part, delighted.

"I'm open to that possibility. And I want to go deeper into what you learned earlier today."

"Oh, my Ryan. You didn't seem that interested. I certainly didn't think you believed how you featured in my crew rest dream hours before we met."

"I believe in everything you share, my Brie. I wish you'd believed in me enough to share your beginnings and your fears and that you'd had a drink when our Maggie..." His voice cracked.

"I couldn't. I was so very scared. Had I not come here to Hull and experienced some weird shit that I believe to be true, and if you hadn't shown up here like a knight in shining armor, I would likely never have told you. Please, please forgive me. I never meant to hurt you, ever. Or our beloved Maggie."

Ryan held me so tight. "Please forgive me for not pushing you to share your fears and apprehensions, your past, your feelings. For letting you stay home alone while I went to work a thousand miles away."

"It wasn't you; it was me. I did it all."

"No, Brie. By my acceptance of the face value you presented, I fell in love with you, and perhaps I was too scared to dig deep because I couldn't believe my luck that such an extraordinary woman would fall for such an ordinary man."

"Ordinary man? You're any girl's dream man. You met me as an elegant air hostess. I had worked very hard, since I was fifteen, to produce a façade worthy of the society I longed to be a part of. You were conned." I hiccupped as I laughed and cried at the same time.

"I love you all the more for your suffering when you were young." He paused for breath. "How awful it must have been for you and Maggie alone."

"Keeping all that from you for so many years has been torture. I hope in doing so, I haven't burdened you with more than you can bear?" I was desperately afraid it was so.

"You love me. I can bear anything knowing that, my Brie. And it's you who should forgive me for being so neglectful. For putting my career before my girls." He wiped his eyes.

There was no need for more words.

In spite of all these tears, I could honestly say I had never felt happier. The relief of being free of secrets was an amazing gift. That Ryan understood and never blamed me was more than I could ever hope for. I was the luckiest girl in all the world. I was loved.

The sun peeped over the horizon, heralding a new day. A clean day. A day with no secrets left to share and with genuine forgiveness bequeathed.

"I suppose I should take home the jet and hand in my resignation."

"Are you sure you're ready for retirement?"

"Oh, God, Brie. Now more than ever I want to spend every hour of every day of the rest of my life with you. Work has had too much of me. Now it's our time."

He stood and offered his hand to pull me up. I nestled under his arm, and we looked out to a gentler sea. The tide was receding, and so was my aching heart.

He called his newfound cabbie friend and then the pilots who had arranged for two fresh flyboys to take him home.

"Wait," I called to him when he was off the phone and pulling my hand to go back to Lucky's. I lifted my hair and turned my back to him. "Please take off my locket. I've had some of Maggie's ashes trapped in it for twenty years."

He held my shoulders with both hands, bent and looked me in the eyes. "You told me you just fell in love with that locket, and I neglectfully never asked what you kept inside."

The pain in his voice cut me to pieces. It was ironic that through all the dreadful things I shared, it was this that seemed to cause him the most hurt. He was *that* responsible.

I realized that miraculously I had no need to harp on what I'd shared ever again. But I would never, ever keep anything from Ryan again. Good. Bad. Or ugly.

He squeezed my hand. "Are you sure you're ready?"

"I think it's time I let all of her fly free."

He stood behind me and moved my hair gently out of the way. I shivered with pleasure. His fingers lightly grazed my neck as he removed the locket. I turned to watch him. He held Maggie tight in his closed palm for a minute, his eyelashes resting on his cheek. When he opened his eyes and looked into mine, tears spilled over his bottom lids.

I took the locket from him reverently. I too held it in my hand and whispered, "My darling girl. How precious you were to us. But I think you were sent to test us over many years. And you did. And we just passed that test. I will miss having you close, Maggie, but you deserve for us to let you go."

I pulled at Ryan's hand, and we walked together along the ledge to get as close to the water as possible. The tide had passed her zenith, but the waves were still crashing and receding with enough pull to accomplish our joint mission.

The jolt of cold sea spray and the sting of salt on our faces reminded us we were still alive. I lifted my hand and threw my locket as far as I could into the churning ocean. We stood together and watched till our Maggie was claimed by the endlessly moving sea.

Away. Away. Free at last.

Ryan grabbed my hand and squeezed it tight as he shouted into the wind. "Come back to us another day, in another life, when the three of us can be together forever." We wept together, standing there, still as pillars, wishing his words would come true.

I turned in to him, and he wrapped his strong arms around me. I whispered over the crash of the waves, "How blessed we are, Ryan, to have another chance to see our lives through together this time around."

"How blessed indeed," he whispered back.

We walked back to Lucky's, me under his arm where I belonged.

I tried the door once we'd walked up the steep steps. It was open. Tula came rushing down the stairs, yipping with glee. He was so happy to see me. I was thrilled.

The cabbie pulled up to the pavement and gave a short, sharp toot. Ryan waved.

"Do you think we should get a dog?" he asked.

"But how will we travel?" I asked, smiling up at him.

He nodded and shrugged. "I'll see you in five long days, my Brie. Shit! It's six with flying time."

"I love you," I said and kissed him deeply.

"I love you much, much more," he promised before he navigated the stairs two at a time. When he stood on the shale of the driveway, he looked up at me, and I swear, even from that distance, I saw his emerald eyes shine. He looked ten years younger. My heart surged just watching him.

I couldn't bear to see him drive off. I was crying when they found me, my new friends.

I sat inside with my back to the closed door, still in my swimsuit and Lucky's gown, wrapped in her blanket, with arms around Tula, who hadn't moved. He was intent on sharing his incredible strength.

CHAPTER 53

BRIE

Hull, present day

"Oh my God, you missed so much," Chantelle exclaimed as she bounded down the stairs, doing her behind the ears and out, two-three-four with jazz hands.

The only thing I'd known about dancing growing up was that there was a pole involved. A generation before mine, someone had secured a long steel pole about ten feet high into the earth with a hefty dollop of cement next to the communal braai or barbecue area. Mothers and daughters, strays and gays practiced on it while the men charred chicken on a Sunday afternoon in the Villies.

All the while, I lay on the rooftop of the caravan in all kinds of weather—well, except for electric storms—removed from the swearing and gyrating and drinking and smoking. I usually lay under a piece of discarded canvas with a ready flashlight somebody had stolen off an usher at the movie theater. I used it for reading. Certainly, nobody missed me.

I only knew about jazz hands because my husband was in the business. Ryan educated me, and I'd seen him in action—the thousands of shows he directed, positioning cameramen, calming choreographers, appeasing sponsors. I'd come to know everything from jazz to contemporary, ballroom to hip-hop, Latin American to lyrical, and everything in between. Ryan was my teacher, my lover, my life.

I shook myself out of that past and smiled at Chantelle.

"We missed you, Brie," three more voices chorused as they spilled down the stairs to the landing, gathering around me, all touching me briefly as if to assure themselves I was really there. BJ touched my bare big toe; Moxie, my knee, as I was still sprawled on the floor with my back against the front door. Chantelle touched my cheek, and Lucky's splayed hand rested on the crown of my head.

I was elated. I was worthy of being missed. How many life-times had I waited to be included? And now, after not yet twenty-four hours, I knew I was.

Your life will change when you are in the third quarter of your life. You will open like a cherry blossom in early spring, and you will no longer be afraid to live.

"Say that again," said Lucky, looking at me closely.

"Those were the words a fortune teller in the lobby of the Hong Kong Hyatt once told me. It *just* happened, girls. I am a cherry blossom!" I was giddy and almost delirious with joy and gratitude.

"Oh, goodie. Goodie. Shall we call you Cherry Blossom now?" Moxie's face was inches from my own.

"Make that Cee Bee for short." I smiled, and suddenly I was aware of the electricity around me. "Loads to share, but you guys first."

"Well, Lucky's about to be famous, and as a result, we're all in the schtuck!" BJ lifted an eyebrow and feigned an air of nonchalance.

"Holy shit!" was as much as I could get out. "Tell! What time is it?"

"Six twenty-three," said Lucky.

"A.m.," BJ clarified.

"Will somebody tell me what happened? Please?" All tiredness was whisked away.

"You!" Moxie nudged Lucky. "It's all your fault."

"Fault? What the hell happened while I was gone?" I asked, ready for another mass gigglefest when someone retold a silliness that happened in my absence.

Lucky grabbed me by the hand and pulled me up and then up the stairs to the living area, as everyone else followed.

Back in the living room, when we were back in our claimed seats, Lucky explained, "Andy and Jim—the FBI boys—called in a panic. Apparently, some ambitious crime reporter paid a monthly stipend to a security guy at the private airport in Kansas City that is the preferred landing strip of the FBI. Security guy was to alert ambitious reporter if ever any men in suits landed in a private plane. This was the reporter's day to collect. He followed the boys to the church where Donald Cox was last seen and ... You are so dewy-eyed, Brie, do you even remember what was happening before you ..."

"Before you did the moonlight boogie-woogie or whatever the kids call it these days?" BJ finished for her.

"I've been gone for less than five hours. Of course I remember the lunatic who killed Janice!" Actually, I was surprised I remembered anything with this immense relief that flowed like sweet, delicious molasses through my veins. How long had I been afraid of being discovered for being a teenage murderer and a neglectful mother? My conscience prickled like an old dancer's muscle. It would take time to forgive myself, even though Ryan had already done so.

Lucky continued. "So, this reporter must have followed the boys to the church, then sneaked around, listening to the goings-on, rushed back, found a photo of Cox in a picture with the rest of the church choir from a news clipping, the very same one my FBI boys found and described to me. This reporter was clearly good at his job, because he must have lurked unseen long enough to hear Jim and Andy tell the priest how I'd described Cox from my foray into Janice's life and death, long before they saw this photo of him."

"Did they slip up and mention your name?" Boy, how my days spent watching crime TV paid off.

"They're ever-cautious, but if 'Lucky' had slipped out in conversation, a good reporter could dig up some manure on me. Literally. I was involved in finding a woman's body in a sewerage tank in Indiana a few years ago. The gruff old sheriff called me 'Six O'Clock' because I was straight up and down both physically—skinny with no boobs and no bum, okay, I've gained a few—and because I was a straight shooter. Reporters were swarming, and I asked the sheriff to keep my name out of the press, so he referred to me as psychic Lucky Six O'Clock, and there was a photo of us at the crime scene. My face right there!"

"Holy shit!" I looked at the others, who were all big-eyed and nodding.

"Nothing holy about that stench." Lucky smiled.

"How did the reporter work out Six O'Clock was you?"

"I was the only girl at the scene when the photograph was taken. It was a huge case that was being followed ardently and aired all over Midwest TV. He could easily have called up those associated with the lawman and asked them, innocently enough because the case has long been closed. Hell, I don't know, but he managed to find out my first name and that I was the one in the photograph taken at the crime scene.

"The boys saw all of this on the early morning news channel in Kansas City, and the Associated Press must have picked it up, so every television station in every town from the Midwest to the East Coast is airing the story."

"The teaser is: 'Mysterious psychic known as "Lucky Six O'Clock" helped identify murderer from twelve years before,'" Moxie announced.

Chantelle was scrolling through her phone and found the electronic version of the *Kansas City Star* about to hit newsstands.

"The heading is, 'Psychic Lucky Six O'clock, who nailed the Sewer Killer, is right again. Catholic church reels with her new evidence of twelve-year-old cold case. A gruesome murder and a missing suspect!'" It was dramatic enough without Chantelle's delivery in varying octaves.

"Holy shit," I said, truly astounded.

Chantelle read, "Earlier today, local and national FBI agents converged on Church of our Grace in Overland Park. They were, according to an inside source, looking for a low-level clergyman who may have committed the murder of a young woman in Springfield, Massachusetts, twelve years ago. Yesterday, a psychic often contracted by the FBI described the details of this gruesome happenstance and the place the murder was committed and gave a detailed description of the man in question from her 'vision.' Known as 'Lucky Six O'Clock,' the psychic advised the FBI to look for a clergyman. The alleged suspect is believed to be Donald Cox, now early forties, who was a seminarian in Springfield at the time. FBI agents believe Cox overheard a telephone conversation the priest had with the agents just yesterday and fled before the local FBI officers arrived at the church.

"This reporter would say the FBI got 'luckier' when they commissioned Lucky. Now let's hope Lucky Six O'Clock and the FBI find him before he kills again." Chantelle stopped, and we all looked at Lucky, who raised her eyes heavenward and shook her head. Tula wove through her legs to ease her angst. What a dog!

"Thing is, now Donald Cox knows my first name and my face." Lucky seemed angry more than anxious.

"But it's pretty vague. No last name. No location, and you are hardly advertising your psychic business online, so how would he find you?" Chantelle asked.

"Tax records," said Moxie, and I looked at her. Such sensibleness coming from our ever-revolving participant. "I'm a Realtor. You can find anybody anywhere if they own a home. It's right there in public records. You'd just have to look up all the counties and voilà. And if you have a real name like Lucky, well ... it could be as easy as doing a pirouette."

"Hey, that's my new line, being a prima ballerina and all," I objected, smiling.

"She's right," said BJ. "Lucky, it may take some doing because there are a lot of counties, but that bastard can just waltz into an Internet café or a Starbucks and search through all the counties, entering Lucky under 'owner,' and your Spring Street address will eventually pop right up."

"Holy shit. Now what?" It was all I could muster.

"Now I must give Tula his insulin shot. It was due hours

ago. I'm so sorry, my fellow." Lucky bent down and opened her arms, and he walked right into her embrace. They touched noses. I was unduly moved by this beautiful show of love between woman and dog.

All eyes were on Lucky as she administered Tula's diabetes injection and gave him a treat. I was really getting fond of that part-dog, part-human.

"How did you find out?" I asked.

"The boys called in a rage before the news was released." Lucky gave a small smile. "They're sending over a patrol car to look after us. Pretty thoughtful."

Moxie leapt up and went to look out of the window. "Man, are they quick on the trigger, those boys of yours. There's a police car outside already."

We all converged on the window to check out the cop car. Such children we turned out to be.

"Since they're on a stakeout, I think I should take them some milk and cookies," said Moxie, hands on her hips, boobs pointing sharply at all and sundry.

"Put your big hormones back inside your little body," ordered BJ. Then she grinned. "If anybody is going to entertain those lawmen, it will be me!" She stood up and stuck her boobs and hip out too.

We all hooted and hollered and rolled about.

Laughter is a great stress reliever.

"Girls. This is not a pissing competition. This is serious business," Chantelle said with flappity-flap-two-three-four jazz hands. What could possibly have caused her peculiar tic? She was twitch-less when we had our night stop in Cape Town.

"Who's tired?" Lucky asked.

There was a collective shake of heads. We were all on a high.

I was on a double high. I was loved. I was forgiven. I was the luckiest woman in all the world. And now a serial killer was after our hostess. Could life get more exciting?

Lucky looked at me in that eerie way she did sometimes. "Don't tempt fate."

"What?" I mustered.

"You just asked if life could get more exciting, Brie. That's a challenge to the universe." Damn! Six O'Clock was truly psychic AND a mind reader! I was stunned.

"Maybe going down to the bedroom level will at least remind our bodies it's time to sleep," Lucky said, leading the way downstairs.

"We tried tricking our bodies with the same reminder a few hours ago, if you recall, Lucky, and we never got as far as the steps." BJ's voice was laden with sarcasm.

"Because *you* started talking about airline shenanigans, BJ, and no one could sleep through your years of monkey business, so it's all your fault." Moxie got her dig in.

As we got to the landing, Chantelle emerged with a shower cap she must have found in Lucky's cupboard balanced at a jaunty angle on top of her curls. She was holding a toothbrush with greenish black gunk hanging off it, threating to drip on the lovely floors. When she opened her mouth, all we saw was a black hole and green teeth, and through her charcoal toothpaste, she said in a deep voice, "I am Donald Cox. And I will kill you all."

We all knew it was Chantelle, but that didn't stop us from screeching at the top of our lungs and huddling together, even BJ and Lucky. And Tula squished in too.

Then we collapsed in Lucky's bedroom, landing in a heap on the bed, laughing till we cried until—

There was a loud *RAP-RAP-RAP* on the front door.

We stopped abruptly, looked at each other, and silently formed our tactical-team line and inched down the steps to the landing and the front door.

Time Flies Book 3 is coming soon!
Chantelle's story: *Timeless Melody*

Afterword

If you enjoyed *Timeless Pirouette*, it would really mean the world to me if you went onto BookBub, Goodreads, or your favorite reading site, and left a review.

Your positivity keeps me writing.

Look for Chantelle's story, *Timeless Melody*—the third book in the Time Flies Series, which started with *Timeless Beginnings*—and start collecting all six books!

Be sure to join my newsletter for release dates, shop discounts and more. Sign up at **jillwallace.com**. I value my readers so highly, and my goal is to consistently delight you.

At my website, you can go behind the scenes and read my musings, listen to audio clips and get firsthand news of coming events. You'll also find interviews, media resources, the inside scoop on my books and my Books & Goodies Shoppe.

My Books & Goodies Shoppe has all manner of fun stuff, including South African lucky packets and signed books. I'm always adding cool things I think you might enjoy.

Join me on Facebook and together, let's contemplate, cogitate and celebrate as we strive to make life as fabulous as it can be at Facebook.com/jillwallaceauthor.

I *love* to hear from my readers, so please never be shy to email me: jillwallaceauthor@gmail.com. It would be my great joy to see your name in my inbox!

Rest assured, your reviews of my books are the ultimate gift to me. Thank you, in anticipation, for taking your precious time to write them.

If you enjoyed your soiree into my South African world, I think you'll be moved by the epic saga of love conquering all odds in the multi-award-winning *War Serenade*.

Those who love action, adventure and coming-of-age stories about the complexity of friendship will surely enjoy *Zebra,* an Amazon #1 new release.

Both *War Serenade* and *Zebra* are inspired by true stories. Read on for more details.

WAR SERENADE

When bon vivant Italian opera star-turned-pilot Pietro is shot down during World War II, he nearly loses his life. Worse, he's lost his passion for music and is close to losing his sanity in a soul-crushing prisoner-of-war camp in South Africa when he meets Iris. He has a vision of a love worth dying for-worth living for-and realizes he must find his voice if he ever hopes to find her again.

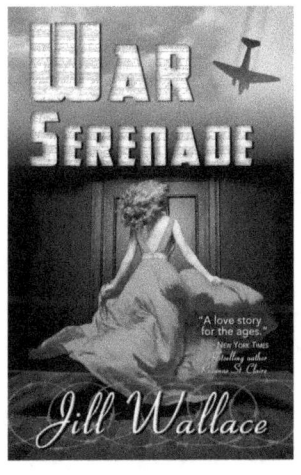

Iris's dreams are at stake when she meets Pietro. All she wants is for her brother to come home alive from the war and to fulfill her destiny as a costume designer in Hollywood. But this spirited redhead's life turns upside down as her eyes meet Pietro's through the cage of his prison. The world may be at stake, but so is her heart.

Their secretive and daring courtship raises the suspicions of the bully who runs the camp, a scarred and damaged tyrant who once dated Iris. Consummating the couple's almost mystical connection will mean crossing the barbed wire, risking the deadly charge of treason and confronting their worst fears.

Inspired by a true story, *War Serenade* is compelling, heart-wrenching, sometimes funny and always dramatic as it celebrates the endurance of the human spirit, the evolution of rich friendships, and love's triumph against impossible odds.

ZEBRA

A young white boy and a Zulu teen grow up together, building an extraordinary friendship as they explore the rugged Drakensberg mountains around a remote South African hotel during the apartheid era.

Jock and Papin forge an indelible bond while learning to love and appreciate each other's cultures. Despite whispers from intolerant guests, the boys are oblivious to the consequences of their friendship. "There goes the zebra," guests remark, claiming they can't tell where the white boy ends and the black boy begins.

But the boys' friendship is strong enough to conquer all—until society's impossible expectations wrench them apart, leaving bitter disappointment and soul-deep wounds that will not heal.

A decade later, these long-lost friends converge on opposite sides of a harrowing battlefield, one a reluctant soldier, the other a passionate freedom fighter. Their intimate knowledge of the other's way of life could be the very tools that save them...or destroy them. And an unimaginable choice will put Jock and Papin's once unbreakable bond to the ultimate test.

Jill Wallace, author of the multi-award-winning World War II novel *War Serenade,* brings together a fascinating coming-of-age story with a compelling tale of human connection in *Zebra*.

Author's Note

Time Flies, the Series, begins during a unique time in aviation history: The Golden Age of Air Travel.

This was a time shortly after Boeing 747SP aircraft were introduced to the South African fleet and immediately set a world record for their long-range capability. This was particularly helpful when air space over central and north Africa was banned to all South African aircraft due to worldwide sanctions and jumbo jets were forced to fly around the humongous bulge of Africa.

Consequently, numerous flying hours were heaped on all northbound flights. There were no unions to protect the cabin crews or limit their flying hours. But the airline compensated with generous downtime in upscale hotels and exotic locations overseas. Five-day London night stops; ten days in Perth, Australia; twelve-day Madrid trips with two nights in Paris; a seven-day Frankfurt and so on.

South Africa was literally spreading her wings and, at last, the world became smaller.

This was a time when the wealthy luxuriated in First Class;

Business Class was perfect for eager corporate representatives set on expansion abroad; and Economy Class was the first chance for South African travelers to feel part of the rest of the rest of the world and get there in a hurry!

At a time when passengers dressed up to fly, even in economy class, the service in all classes was preempted by hot towels, and magazines, kids' toys, and note pads with pens were distributed. Travel kits with personal accessories were delivered freely by friendly crew members. Passengers (known to crew as "Pax") in all cabin classes were presented with an embossed, full-color, two-page menu with a satin ribbon describing the culinary choices available during the flight. Cutlery was stainless steel, napkins were cloth, ashtrays were built into armrests, movie screens were rolled down from the ceiling of bulkheads in each section of the cabin, seats were oversize, leg room was ample, and booze was free and unlimited.

A time when being an air hostess was the most coveted of all jobs for young women, but standards were ridiculously high and obscenely superficial. Training required 80 percent pass marks in all sixteen subjects, one of which was a third language. Rigorous overseas conversion classes lasted seven weeks.

But these women never expected their dream job to morph into a career.

You see, when a girl's looks grew tired, she was forced to retire.

Male cabin crew had no such limitations.

The crew rest on a jumbo 747 was a hole in the wall in the aft of the main cabin just in front of the half-moon galley. The thick curtain that hid this necessary gem blended so well, when a passenger saw a crew member "disappear," they assumed they'd slipped into the back galley. Thick Velcro tape on the inside ensured wandering passengers never interrupted sleeping cabin crew.

This necessary sanctuary, used by each crew shift for no more than two hours per flight, measured nine by seven feet tops, and the distance from one bunk to the one above and then to the bulkhead at the top was three feet. Three narrow bunks opposite each other nested one atop the other, and there was one last resort for latecomers and junior crew: the mattress in the middle. The latter was a mere inch of foam pad dressed in airline-seat material set on the floor and squeezed between the two lower bunks. No amount of airline-issue pillows and blankets could diminish the sound of the engines throbbing through the steel floor of the fuselage.

Flying during those years, in spite of the prejudice, the long, long hours, the need to be consistently well-groomed whenever in uniform, was indeed a privilege. Air travel was excessively expensive, and there was no other career for a young woman that would pay enough to explore the world for fun. Accommodations in every destination were superior, sustenance and travel allowances were based on three meals a day in expensive hotels and paid in cash on arrival, and the layovers were like a mini vacation.

And yet, best of all was the tremendous pride every hostess felt being an ambassador for South Africa.

ACKNOWLEDGMENTS

First and foremost, I'd like to thank my husband for never nagging me about spending too much time or money on my passion: Writing! I love you forever, my Athie.

I'd love to thank my readers. Without you, who let me know by way of an email, or a Facebook post, or graciously bestowing the ultimate gift, a review, I would not be motivated to tell stories. If I thought nobody but me enjoyed them, my lust for storytelling would dry up and I would barely exist. I'd become a hollow husk. So, a million thanks to all of you for keeping my imagination alive.

Thank you, Debby Clark, my once-real-estate-partner and friend of twenty-eight years who inspired Brie in the way she talks and looks and acts, but who I mercilessly manipulated to create this heroine. It was such fun!

To my darling sister of the heart, Debbie Sekula. You may well recognize many of Lucky's words during her hypnosis. They're all yours and originate from our Sister Circle soirees, as do many of your wisdoms Lucky brandishes about so cleverly. Thank you for letting me plagiarize them. You are a constant joy and blessing, and without you and my sisters of the circle—Beautiful Sands, Stunning Audra, Foxy Karen, Sheri Amore, Angel Norah and Ravishing Renee—the seed of this "Time Flies" series would probably never have germinated.

Thank you to my amazing SSCGs. You four inspire me,

guide me, lead me and amaze me with your smarts. It's a privilege to be amongst you.

Kerry Evelyn, beautiful author, beautiful woman, beautiful soul, you spent many hours with Brie, and I thank you with all my heart!

Thank you, TJ Logan—supreme author, great friend, talented marketer and Canva magician! You're always delighting me with your creative touches for promos, ads and ideas, without me even having to ask!

Thanks to you, my talented Trescina Bell on social media, patient Crystal Wadele on newsletters and fabulous Chrissy Chicory on my website, without you all, I would be silent. Thanks to Keiti Pierce for her smooth handover.

And my GetMyBookOutThere girls led by the inimitable, brilliant, witty and wise Narelle Todd. The last years together have been a divine privilege, and I value each and every one of you. Thank you for your endless support. You prop me up when I need it most.

To amazing international author S.E. Susan Smith, I cross my open palms in front of me and bow my head. 'Tis the show of deepest respect and gratitude in the African tradition. 'Tis you, Susan, who, when I started this series, gave me your precious time and your infinite wisdom as you gently pushed me to get out of my own way and START WRITING! Thank you for gifting me the wings to fly with my new series. Your generosity of spirit is as rare as a pygmy elephant and a thing of great beauty and fascination. I am forever in awe of your kindness and patience.

To my beloved Alana McIntosh and Kitty Low, who have taught me enough about true friendship to write about it with confidence. I love you more and more each passing year. We're well past five and a half decades now! How lucky we are: Faith, Hope and Charity.

Thank you, Nat Palmadesso, for buying "Your Name in My Book Forever" on Kickstarter. I hope you're happy with your character. I sure am!

Thank you, lovely Ann McIntosh, my editor. I am deeply grateful for your insights. You consistently make me feel like my work is important. WOW! You lift me up!

Thank you to wise and wonderful Chris Kridler, who first gave me wind beneath my wings and who continues to do so. I am so grateful to you and for you.

To all my Virginia Girls: Debby Clark, Beth Barg, Brenda Morcom and Betsy Galbraith. THANK YOU for allowing me to put words into your mouths while you're wearing your pseudonyms. Love you all!

BOOKS BY JILL WALLACE

War Serenade

Zebra

Sunshine's War in
Festive Fates: 11 Spirited Holiday Tales

Timeless Beginnings

Timeless Pirouette

ABOUT THE AUTHOR

Jill Wallace is a storyteller. Born and bred in South Africa, she's lived half her life in America. Just as it's hard to tell the roots from the branches of a baobab tree, Jill no longer knows where the South African ends and the American begins. Her stories will always be rooted in her birth country but may have branches elsewhere in the world. Her wish is that readers will remember her characters long after 'The End.' She married her soulmate, helped raise two heart-children and lives too far from her granddaughters. Jill writes happily from home in the Space Coast of Florida, which she shares with her husband and two fiercely opinionated Aussie Shepherds.

What makes Jill tick? Well, buckle up! Long-lasting friendships, unwavering loyalty, the unconditional love of dogs, the power of kindness, and the magic of chocolate and imagination, served in any order you please. And let's not forget her affinity for creatures great and small—they all find a place in Jill's world of wonder and whimsy. So, grab a bar of chocolate, cuddle up with a furry friend, and as Lucky told the old air hostesses who've just become her new friends, "Clear the skies for us to fly in. I have your wings."

Learn more and sign up for Jill's newsletter at JillWallace.com.